I0822847

a

Gene Lemmings'

Tidal-Man

Story and Written By

E.S. Bennett

Based on Characters Created by E. Lemmings and E. S. Bennett

a

Gene Lemming's Tidal Man

Copyright 2025 by Megaverse City, E.S. Bennett, Eugene Lemmings

ALL RIGHTS RESERVED

NO PART OF THIS BOOK MAY BE USED OR REPRODUCED IN ANY MANNER WHATSOEVER WITHOUT WRITTEN PERMISSION EXCEPT IN THE CASE OF REPRINTS IN THE CONTEXT OF REVIEWS.

FIRST EDITION MAY 2025

A MEGAVERSE CITY PUBLICATION

WWW.THEMEGAVERSECITY.COM

ISBN #979-8-218-99822-6

LIBRARY OF CONGRESS NUMBER #2025909796

COVER DESIGN BY E.S. BENNETT

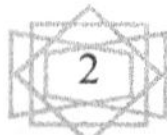

a

Table of Contents

a

a

I'd like to give some acknowledgment to my kids whom inspire me to realize the joy in everyday life and helps me see the creativity in their actions that keeps my passion on-going for art, fantasy and related topics.…Also, for me it's hoping they will have something to enjoy that their dad helped collaborate to make and to remind them to keep their spark for the for adventure and the unknown alive.

- **Eugene Lemmings**

a

a

Gene Lemming's Tidal Man

a

a

Dedication

For my younger self, the one who dreamt of mythical creatures hidden in the mundane, who found solace in ancient stories and the magic woven into everyday life. This book is a testament to the power of imagination, the enduring allure of mythology, and the belief that even in the most chaotic of storms, compassion can bloom and light the way. It's for the girl who spent countless hours lost in the worlds crafted from ink and paper, and who dared to believe that even a god could find redemption through the simple act of choosing kindness.

This dedication extends to everyone who has ever felt like an outsider, a misfit, a being caught between two worlds, torn between duty and desire. To those who have struggled with the weight of expectations, the burden of family legacy, and the constant pull between their divine nature and their human heart. This story is for you, a reminder that even in the face of overwhelming odds, even when surrounded by the tempestuous wrath of powerful beings, you possess an inner strength that can illuminate the darkest of nights.

a

To those who have embraced their own unique blend of the ancient and the modern, who find beauty in the unexpected juxtaposition of myth and reality, this book is a celebration of your spirit. Your capacity to find hope in the heart of despair, your ability to see the magic in the ordinary, your willingness to defy expectations and forge your own path – all these qualities are reflected in the pages that follow.

This is a dedication to the dreamers, the rebels, the compassionate souls who dare to believe that even the mightiest of gods can find their humanity and their own unique form of redemption. May this tale inspire you to embrace your own power, to discover the depths of your compassion, and to navigate the storms of life with grace and unwavering hope. May it remind you that even amidst the relentless fury of the sea, the human spirit, and indeed, the divine heart, can discover a quiet sanctuary, a haven of peace, and a love that transcends the boundaries of worlds.
Let this story be a beacon, guiding you towards your own destiny, however uncertain the path may seem.

a

Prologue

The Wrath of the Forgotten

As the twenty-first century dawned, mankind strode boldly into a new age—an age of steel, silicon, and sky-reaching ambition. They built temples of glass and metal, forged gods from data and fame, and cast the old ways into myth and memory. The ancient ones—the Primordials, the Titans, the Olympians—watched from their fading realms, their names no longer whispered in reverence, but dismissed as tales for children or relics of a primitive world.

Among the most scorned were the Lords of the Sea. Once feared and venerated, Poseidon and his progeny saw their tides restrained, their storms rerouted by satellites, and their oceans spoiled by greed. Deep beneath, fury festered.

It was Charybdis—the sea-devouring maelstrom reborn in flesh and vengeance—who rallied the last fragments of the ancient pantheon. With a voice like splintering hulls and the reek of salt-drenched death, he proclaimed it was time to punish mankind for its arrogance. At his side surged legions of drowned demigods, forgotten sea beasts, and wrathful spirits risen from trench-black depths. Among them marched Tyvellmian, youngest son of Poseidon, brother to the war-born Triton, and heir to the abyssal throne.

Though forged in fury and shaped by storms,

a

Tyvellmian bore a restless soul. Unlike his kin, who bled pride and demanded tribute, he looked upon the mortal world not with disdain—but with wonder. He saw beauty in their struggle, poetry in their defiance, resilience in their rise.

His father saw only weakness.

“You are my blood,” Poseidon thundered within the halls of Aegaeon, where coral groves shimmered like stained glass and sharks patrolled like sentries. “You will stand beside Charybdis. Lead the charge. Show the surface who commands the sea.”

And for a time, Tyvellmian complied. He summoned waves that battered coasts, stirred leviathans from ancient sleep, and watched cities drown beneath his wrath. But as the waters frothed with death and fire, something within him shifted.

A child. One child, pulled from the wreckage of a drowned village, offered him a seashell—and called him “protector.”

In that instant, the tide inside Tyvellmian turned.

He abandoned the war. He defied the gods. And in doing so, became something entirely new—not god, not mortal, but a bridge between the two.

Only one stood with him—Arconia, daughter of Triton, a warrior-scholar whose loyalty was not to power, but to purpose. As the sea boiled with betrayal and Poseidon seethed in divine wrath, she whispered to her uncle:

“Perhaps it is not man who forgot the gods… but the gods who forgot what it means to be worthy of

a

worship."

Thus began the awakening of Tyvellmian—the one the modern world would one day name *Tidal-Man*.

But the gods do not forget.
And the sea does not forgive.

Chapter I

The Maelstrom's Embrace.

The salt spray stung Elias Thorne's face—a bitter kiss from the raging tempest. He clung to a splintered railing, the groaning wood a fragile barrier against the churning abyss. Around him, a symphony of screams and crashing waves drowned out all rational thought. *The Poseidon's Pride*, once a symbol of opulence and luxury, had become a ravaged carcass, tossed like a child's toy in the hands of a merciless giant. Its once-gleaming hull, now scarred and battered, listed precariously, threatening to swallow the last of its passengers whole.

He'd been celebrating his fiftieth birthday, a milestone marked by this ill-fated cruise. The champagne flutes, the laughter, the promise of a relaxing voyage—all were now distant, surreal memories. The opulent cabins, once meticulously decorated, had become watery tombs. The polished dance floor was now a churning maelstrom, swallowing everything in its path. The air, thick with diesel and fear, crackled with the storm's raw power.

Lightning revealed the chaos in fleeting, brutal flashes, illuminating the terror etched on the faces of fellow passengers. Faces contorted in silent screams, eyes wide with stark, primal fear.

The wind, a howling banshee, tore at his clothes, whipping them like tattered flags. Each wave struck like a monstrous hand, bent on dragging the ship—

and Elias—into the depths. The icy water clawed at his exposed skin, numbing his limbs. Salt stung his lips, spray bit at his face, and the crashing of waves against the hull rang like a death knell. Each thunderous blow struck his hope like a hammer. The ship lurched violently, sending a cascade of seawater across the deck, pulling him closer to the edge of oblivion.

Amid the chaos, a strange luminescence pulsed in the heart of the storm. It wasn't lightning, but a softer, ethereal glow—a beacon piercing the fury. It pulsed with a rhythm that slowed his frantic heart, a counterpoint to the storm's violent symphony. He felt drawn to it, a silent siren's song beckoning him toward an unknown salvation. He wasn't alone. Other survivors, clinging desperately to wreckage, were also drawn to the light.

It grew stronger, expanding outward to form a shimmering dome. The wind's fury weakened within its bounds, and the waves became less violent. A moment of peace emerged—a sanctuary from the storm. The glow radiated warmth, a sharp contrast to the bone-deep chill. The air grew still, strangely calm—a pocket of peace within the maelstrom.

Then, a figure emerged from the light. He defied the storm and the laws of nature. Tall and powerful, his hair shimmered like storm-swept waves, and his eyes held the depth of the ocean. His skin glowed faintly, echoing the dome's ethereal radiance. Around him, water swirled and danced as if obeying his command. He was breathtaking—and terrifying. Power radiated

a

from him in quiet, undeniable waves.

He moved with impossible speed, slipping between wreckage and wave, every motion fluid and precise. He reached a group of survivors, outstretched his hands, and lifted them effortlessly into the glowing sanctuary. He did not struggle—he guided, like a shepherd to his flock. He worked without pause, rescuing one after another, his actions a vivid contrast to the chaos around him. He seemed to *know* where each survivor was, as if driven by supernatural instinct.

Elias watched, mesmerized, as this radiant being—this god, this guardian—plucked him from death's edge. Gratitude, wonder, and awe surged within him. His fear dissolved, replaced by fragile, trembling hope. He was alive—miraculously, inexplicably—because of this creature of myth, who commanded the storm's fury yet chose to save.

As the last survivor reached safety within the dome, the storm began to relent. The wind eased. The waves calmed. Rain softened its assault. The glow faded slowly, revealing the figure in his full, god-like glory. He gazed at the survivors—faces pale, stunned, grateful—then turned to the sinking remains of *The Poseidon's Pride*. Sadness lingered in his eyes—a quiet understanding of human frailty in the face of nature's wrath. But also, a steadfast strength.

He didn't speak. He didn't explain his presence. He simply stood—a silent testament to compassion in the shadow of catastrophe.

a

A woman stepped forward, bewildered, awestruck, and asked his name.

He looked upon her with calm admiration, touched by her courage. A faint smile crossed his lips.

"My name is Tyvellmian," he said.

Then, as swiftly as he'd arrived, he vanished—leaving only the quieting sea and a host of stunned, grateful survivors.

The storm had passed. In its wake, it left devastation—and a miracle. A being of salvation rather than ruin. A legend forged in lightning and salt.

A second survivor stepped beside the woman. "What did he say his name was?"

Still in shock, she whispered, "Tidal-Man. I think he said… Tidal-Man."

The world above the waves was about to learn that name.

Tidal-Man.

Whispers spread in fear and awe. A name carried across news feeds, retold in survivor interviews, dissected on broadcast screens. Witnesses spoke of impossible power—waves that rose and fell at his will, winds that obeyed his voice, a glow that tamed the storm.

But amid that force… there was mercy.

And not everyone saw a savior.

Local and global governments, stunned by the existence of such a being, debated his implications.

a

In emergency councils and late-night strategy rooms, a dangerous question took shape:

If a god lives among us,
Who prepares for war against him?

The wind screamed—a banshee wail tearing through the fabric of the storm. Rain lashed down in relentless sheets, a blinding curtain that cloaked the chaos below. From high above the tempest, Tyvellmian watched. He wasn't merely observing—he felt the storm's anguish, the fear of the mortals caught in its grip. *The Poseidon's Pride*, a monument to human hubris, was being ripped apart, its proud frame reduced to a battered husk tossed by divine rage.

He had felt the first pulse of his father's fury—a cold, crushing wave of divine wrath that mirrored the storm's icy grip on the sea. Poseidon's anger was tangible, a force that threatened to swallow even him. Tyvellmian, though favored, was still bound to his father's will. He should have let the storm run its course. He should have allowed Poseidon's punishment to unfold. Humanity's abandonment of the gods, their irreverence, demanded retribution. That was what he'd been taught—what he believed.

Yet as he watched the unfolding human tragedy, a strange dissonance stirred within him.

a

A flicker of pity ignited in his heart—a warmth that clashed violently with the cold decree of his father. He saw faces among the wreckage. Not distant abstractions. Not figures from a judgment ledger. Real people. A young mother shielding her child. Lovers clutching one another in desperation. Fear, yes—but also resilience, hope, love. Their suffering was no longer conceptual. It was raw. Visceral.

Human.

The conflict within him deepened. Duty—the echoing voice of tradition and obedience—warred with a growing empathy that felt alien yet inevitable. He was Poseidon's son, heir to the trident, shaped to enforce wrath. Yet within the eye of the storm, another path whispered to him—one not etched in fear, but forged through compassion. He recalled the face of the woman who had asked his name. Her mortality. Her courage. Her fragile boldness lingered like a haunting question.

What am I?

Am I only a vessel of wrath?

He whispered the thought aloud, though the words were swallowed by the storm. He stared at his glowing hands—capable of raising oceans and leveling coastlines. But also… capable of saving lives. The contradiction was no longer avoidable.

Beneath the sea, seeking clarity, Tyvellmian

turned to his niece, Arconia. She had walked among mortals. She understood them. In her presence, he found an anchor. Arconia, wise and calm, encouraged him not to ignore his compassion. She warned him of the cost of blind obedience and reminded him that true strength lies in mercy, not fear.

The decision came like a breaking wave—sudden, undeniable. He couldn't stand idle.

This was not weakness.

This was evolution.

With a flick of his wrist, Tyvellmian summoned his power. The storm obeyed—not with greater fury, but with stillness. The waves shrank. The wind quieted. A dome of light expanded around the shipwreck, pushing back the wrath like a shield. Rain softened. The sea became calm within the storm's eye. It was a fragile peace carved into chaos.

And in that moment, the woman who misheard his name became more than a witness—she became a symbol of his transformation.

When Poseidon learned of his son's defiance, his rage was unbound. Tyvellmian's compassion was seen as betrayal. The ocean king called upon his other children—gods, demigods, monsters—to punish the wayward heir. Jealousies long buried surfaced, and siblings hungry for favor eagerly accepted the decree. Loyalty would be tested through blood.

a

But Tyvellmian, unaware of this mounting retribution, continued his self-appointed mission. He saved the helpless from ships destroyed by divine storms. Again and again, he intervened—driven by a force older than wrath. Something *human.*

One day, far from any coast, the sky tore open with a roar that shook the heavens. Clouds churned into black thunderheads. Lightning carved jagged arcs across the sky, illuminating the sea in brief flashes of ghostly blue. Winds howled. Birds vanished. Salt whipped through the air in violent gusts. Beneath this wrath sailed *The Virelli Majestic*, a floating palace of arrogance and gold.

Poseidon hovered in the storm's center, his trident aglow with divine fury. From his vantage, he watched mortals dance and toast, blind to the sea's disdain. They believed they ruled the tide.

That could not stand.

With a single thrust, Poseidon unleashed his power. The sky bled rain. Mountains of water rose in monstrous fury. Thunder cracked like war drums. The sea had turned.

Below the surface, Tyvellmian felt the shift. This was no natural fury—it was *divine*. His father's hand. He recognized the signature of vengeance.

And he rose.

a

His form shimmered as he surged upward, silver and blue, streaked with bioluminescent lines. Coral-forged armor hugged his form, flexing with his motion. He sliced through the water like a spear of light, drawn to the cries of terror above.

The Virelli Majestic screamed in protest as a hundred-foot wave struck its side. Passengers screamed. Glass shattered like crystal rain. Tables became missiles. A mother clutched her daughter as seawater flooded the lower decks. The crew fought to launch lifeboats—but they jammed, tangled in salt and ruin.

The ship groaned. Its bones cracked. Power flickered and died.

a

And then—he came.

A flare of light burst from beneath the surface.

Tyvellmian launched skyward, crashing through a wave like a meteor. His body arced above the deck, glowing against the black sky. To those watching, it was a vision—divine or delusion, they couldn't say.

He landed hard on the listing ship, water swirling around him but never deterring him. He moved with impossible grace—no hesitation, no fear. With his bare hands, he ripped twisted steel from a collapsed corridor and dragged survivors from the wreckage. His voice boomed above the chaos:

"Get to the upper deck. I will hold the sea. I will not let you drown."

Then he vanished again—diving into the black depths, navigating tight corridors, pulling survivors from flooded rooms. A trembling child. An injured woman. An elderly man. He lifted them all.

Above, Poseidon watched in disgust. His son, his chosen heir—rescuing insects from divine judgment.

Unforgivable.

But Tyvellmian never looked up.

He shattered the ballroom dome with a strike and rode a collapsing wave to the surface, cradling a boy in his arms. Lightning lit his face—stoic, soaked, defiant.

a

The storm wavered.

Poseidon faltered.

He couldn't bear to see compassion override fear. Mercy outshone vengeance.

With a final crack of thunder that split the sky, Poseidon withdrew. The storm collapsed in exhaustion. The sea fell still.

Only then did Tyvellmian rest.

Survivors huddled around him in makeshift shelters on the shattered remains of the ship.

His armor dripped with seawater and blood.

The *Virelli Majestic* was split in two—but most of its passengers *lived.*

Where all had once been fated to die, hope remained.

He moved within the light dome, a figure of grace and resolve. No words. No commands. Just quiet strength. He offered hands, not orders. He calmed terror with presence, not power.

Tyvellmian had chosen his path.

And the sea would never be the same again.

Among those he saved was a woman. Her hair, the color of dark sand tossed by waves, clung to her face; her brown eyes, wide with a mixture of terror and awe, reflected the sanctuary's ethereal light. Her name, which he would learn later, was *Galena*. He saw resilience in her—a quiet strength that mirrored his own struggle against a destiny

a

carved by others. There was something about her presence, something that transcended the storm and chaos—something that stirred the core of his divine essence. A pull he could neither ignore nor explain.

As the last of the survivors gathered within the glowing dome, the storm finally began to loosen its grip. The winds hushed to a whisper. The waves curled and retreated. Rain softened into a misty drizzle. Slowly, the sanctuary's light faded, revealing the broken remnants of the world outside. The survivors, soaked and shivering, stood awestruck.

Tyvellmian stood among them.

His sea-green eyes met theirs, reflecting their wonder and gratitude. He turned toward the wreck of *The Poseidon's Pride*, now half-submerged and eerily still—a grave to the fallen, a monument to what had been. Yet there was no regret in his gaze, only the weight of understanding—the complexity of power, of duty, of mercy.

He felt the gravity of his decision—the sting of defiance, the storm yet to come. His father's fury would be vast and swift. His siblings, eager to demonstrate loyalty, would not hesitate to strike. Tyvellmian had not just acted out of turn—he had *betrayed* an ancient order.

But the resolve within him did not waver.

a

The survivors' silent gratitude filled him with a new kind of strength. And Galena—her presence especially—was a quiet anchor amid the rising tide of doubt. Her strength, her humanity, her survival, were now bound to his own. She had become more than a rescued soul; she had become a symbol. A catalyst.

He had chosen a path far removed from the one ordained for him. But in the tear-streaked faces around him, in the fragile hope that flickered in their eyes, he recognized the truth: he had made the right choice. The storm had raged, but something far greater had emerged within him.

He had discovered empathy.

He had discovered compassion.

He had discovered himself.

This path—uncertain and dangerous—would likely lead to conflict, betrayal, and perhaps even death. Yet he would walk it without hesitation. His steps no longer guided by the roar of gods, but by the quiet, steadfast rhythm of his own heart. And at the center of that rhythm was Galena—the woman whose gaze had kindled a rebellion he hadn't known he was capable of.

The sea calmed, but the tempest within him had only begun to rise.

And the world would soon learn of it.

Tales would spread of a figure who rose from

a

the deep, who defied the storm and stood between mortals and the wrath of gods. A protector in the chaos. A force of salvation, not judgment.

They would not call him Tyvellmian, son of Poseidon.

They would call him...

Tidal-Man.

a

a

Chapter II

The Currents of Galena

As a child, Galena would sit on sun-warmed stones near the harbor, her dress soaked from the spray, her hair catching sea salt like glittering threads. She dreamed, as many children do, of love shaped by fairytales—of marrying a prince who would arrive with the tide and carry her to a kingdom under starlight. She'd hum lullabies taught by her grandmother, who swore the sea listened—and sometimes, if it liked your song, it would answer.

But dreams, like tides, shift.

By her teenage years, the salt she once loved stung her skin. Her nights became haunted by visions of endless black water, of sinking ships, and bells tolling beneath the waves. She'd wake breathless, tangled in sweat-drenched sheets, with the memory of hands—strong, cold, inhuman—pulling her downward. The sea was no longer a friend. It became something to fear. And yet, she could never truly look away.

No priest or doctor could soothe her sleep. They called it trauma. Ancestral fear. But Galena knew something had touched her spirit long before she could name it. Still, life carried

a

her forward like driftwood in a storm.

Her beauty, poise, and gift for languages drew the attention of a reclusive shipping tycoon who saw in her a figure fit for high society. Soon, she was swept into a world of opulence—pearls, gala evenings, and a residence in Monaco that overlooked the sea she had tried so hard to forget. She learned to silence her instincts, to laugh in polite company, to drown her unease in wine and silk sheets. No one saw the girl beneath the gowns.

Then came the invitation aboard the *Virelli Majestic*—the ocean liner of legend. A week of luxury, elegance, and escape. She accepted, telling herself it was just a cruise. But as the ship cut across the Ionian Sea—past the ancient waters her grandmother once warned her about—she felt it.

Something stirred below.

The waves grew restless. The sky churned with strange hues. And within her, something ancient whispered—a longing she couldn't name. A voice in her blood, faint but unrelenting:

"You were never meant to live on land alone."

And then, the world she knew tore apart.

The *Virelli Majestic* was a palace upon the sea—a monument to man's triumph over nature. Brass gleamed. Chandeliers sparkled. The promenade hummed with laughter, with

a

clinking glasses and whispered indulgence.

But not for Galena.

From the moment the ship crossed into uncharted waters—ancient to some—she felt it in her bones: a pulse, a pull. Something recognized her. The crew grew uneasy, masking their worry behind forced smiles.

"Nothing to worry about, Miss Galena," the captain had assured her, tipping his hat while avoiding the horizon.

That evening, the air changed. The scent of rain arrived before the clouds. The stars vanished without ceremony. And by midnight, the storm struck.

Not as a tantrum, but with intention.

As if Poseidon himself had hurled down his wrath.

Thunder rolled like war drums. Lightning carved through the sky like veins of the gods. The ship groaned beneath each wave, tossed like a toy in a furious bath.

Passengers screamed. Chandeliers shattered. Dishes crashed to the floor like glittering hail. Crew members shouted over the wind, issuing frantic commands. Galena stood at the bow, clinging to the railing, soaked to the skin, her hair whipped wild.

And the sea screamed back.

"Galena..."

Not from the sky. From the deep.

a

It wasn't madness. It wasn't imagination.

Something had called her name.

A wave, impossibly tall, loomed before the vessel.

She gasped—and in a flash, memory struck: eyes in her dreams. Blue-green. The color of the ocean before a storm.

Then the wave hit.

She was thrown backward, her body slamming into polished wood and metal. Screams and sirens blurred into the roar of the sea. For a moment, she was underwater—adrift, weightless, spinning. Darkness enveloped her.

A hand brushed hers.

Firm. Strange.

It didn't feel human.

And then—it was gone.

Silence followed.

Galena awoke tangled in seaweed on a black sand shore, wrapped in the shredded remnants of a silk gown. The dawn sky blushed pink above her. Around her lay broken lifeboats, a child's shoe, a pearl earring not her own.

Of the *Virelli Majestic*, there was no sign.

Only the memory of a voice in the storm. Only an echo remained—thundering in her mind like a forgotten vow.

The survivors gathered nearby—shivering, dazed, clinging to hope like driftwood. They

a

were a scattered reflection of the world they'd left behind: a businesswoman clutching a photograph, a young couple wrapped in a single blanket, a grizzled sailor with eyes hardened by a thousand storms. Soaked, bruised, battered—but alive.

And in that shared trauma, something rare blossomed: camaraderie.

Tyvellmian watched from a distance.

His divine senses followed the emotional tides—grief, fear, gratitude, and connection flowing between strangers. He saw small acts of kindness like ripples across the surface of despair. The businesswoman offered her last water biscuit to the young couple. The old sailor adjusted a blanket around a girl who had lost her parents. Mothers comforted their children. Friends shared stories to mask the cold.

Tyvellmian, ancient and powerful, felt the sharp contrast.

He was immortal. They were not. He commanded tides. They were at their mercy. His world was vast and unfeeling. Theirs was fragile—but beautiful.

In their vulnerability, he saw something enduring. Something worthy.

He approached Galena.

Her presence drew him like a current. Her eyes—storm-colored and searching—held

a

depths he could not fathom. She hadn’t screamed during the rescue. She hadn’t panicked. She had accepted his help with quiet strength, and now, on the shore, she shielded a child from the drizzle, smiled at a crying boy, and offered comfort without command.

Her leadership was not loud. It was not imposed.

It was innate.

He knelt beside her, the rough stones unfamiliar beneath his knees. After centuries navigating the deep, the texture of land felt strangely alien.

He could still feel the echoes of the storm—the final tremors of Poseidon’s fury.

And yet Galena’s presence was a sanctuary.

A haven in the wreckage.

"You are… strong," he said, the words hesitant—unfamiliar even to his own ears. The concept of human strength—of resilience forged not through power, but in defiance of adversity—was new to him, still forming in the edges of his understanding.

Galena looked at him, her gaze steady, her eyes reflecting both gratitude and caution. She didn’t flinch in the presence of a god. She didn’t bow or tremble before the weight of his divinity. Instead, she met his eyes with quiet dignity, a calm steadiness that both humbled and amazed him.

"We had to be," she replied, her voice low but unwavering. "We had each other." She nodded toward the huddled survivors, her eyes glowing with

a

fierce pride. "We wouldn't let each other down."

He saw it in her—the subtle tremors of fear behind her strength, the exhaustion carved into her features, the unspoken gratitude shimmering beneath the surface. It was raw, unfiltered emotion, untouched by the courtly deception and manipulation that plagued the celestial realms.

He remained with them for hours, offering comfort where he could. He summoned warm breezes to dry their soaked clothes, shielding them from further exposure. He conjured food and fresh water, drawing sustenance from the sea that had so recently threatened their lives. He listened. He let them speak. Their stories were a patchwork of loss and endurance—fragments of dreams destroyed, families sundered, futures cast into uncertainty.

And yet… woven through it all was hope.

He heard it in their voices—the determination to rebuild, the belief in each other, the faith in the human spirit to rise again. It stirred something deep inside him. Their pain, their survival, their unbroken unity in the face of ruin—it moved him in ways no divine teaching ever had.

As the first light of dawn painted the sky in hues of pink and orange, the last echoes of the storm faded. The air was still, the ocean placid, as if stunned by its own earlier rage. The survivors looked at each other—no longer strangers, but something more. Their shared trauma had bonded them in silence. In survival. In humanity.

Tyvellmian watched them. And in that moment, he

a

understood something profound.

Yes, he had saved them. But in doing so, he had also been saved.

He had seen a kind of strength the gods never acknowledged. He had witnessed compassion—raw and powerful—thrive in the heart of fear. He had seen friendship blossom where despair should have ruled. And in Galena's eyes, he saw a mirror of his own awakening. She was a reflection of what he was becoming. A symbol of the path that now lay before him.

He would never be the same.

A new storm stirred—not in the sky, but within him. This one born not of wrath, but of emotion.

Compassion. Conflict. Change.

The last remnants of the tempest vanished with the light, leaving behind a world washed clean, yet scarred. The scent of salt and ozone lingered in the still air. The survivors, clustered on the splintered remains of the once-mighty liner, wore the faces of those who had touched death and returned. Exhausted, yes—but alive. Eyes wide with the gravity of survival.

Tyvellmian stood quietly at the edge of the shore, a strange calm settling over him. The power he wielded—once limitless, raging, unchallenged—now seemed subdued in comparison to the quiet resilience he had just witnessed. He had pulled them from the jaws of destruction, but it was their courage that had carried them to shore.

In Galena's eyes, he saw it again—that quiet force.

a

Strength not forged in fire or storms, but in loss. In choice. In compassion.

Then came the world's response.

News of the rescue spread like wildfire. Blurry footage—grainy and imperfect—captured his form rising from the sea. His silhouette shimmered with light, his eyes filled not with wrath, but with sorrow, strength, and unexpected mercy. The media frenzy began almost instantly. The world reeled.

He was dubbed *Tidal-Man*. The name caught like a spark on dry grass. Within hours, it was trending across every platform. A symbol. A mystery. A beacon.

The reactions were as divided as the world itself.

Some called him a savior—an angel, a guardian, a celestial protector sent to warn or redeem. Others recoiled in fear, convinced his presence heralded the end times. Religious zealots hailed him as a manifestation of divine prophecy. Skeptics dismissed him outright as a hallucination born of collective trauma. Scientists argued endlessly—some debunking him, others spinning theories of higher beings, alternate dimensions, and quantum anomalies.

The world struggled to process the impossible.

But Tyvellmian paid no attention to the noise.

He was consumed by the inner storm now raging in his soul.

The ocean had raged—but not like this.

This tempest was personal.

a

What he had done—this act of mercy—was unthinkable by divine standards. He had shattered the expectation of who and what he was supposed to be. The weight of that choice bore down on him like the depths of the ocean.

Galena's image lingered in his mind. Her sea-colored eyes. Her quiet bravery. Her strength forged not by gods, but by survival. She haunted him—not as a ghost, but as a guidepost. As proof that something else was possible.

He found himself drawn to everything she represented.

To everything *human.*

Emotion stirred in him—wild, unfamiliar, relentless. Loneliness. Guilt. Empathy. Wonder. For centuries, he had lived untouched by such feelings, insulated by divine heritage, anchored by blind loyalty. But now, the dam had cracked. Now, the floodwaters rushed in.

He saw the world with new eyes—eyes that could no longer ignore the beauty in its pain, the grace in its impermanence, the nobility in its struggle. His immortality, once a mark of pride, now felt like a chasm—separating him from the very people he'd come to admire.

And he felt it all.

The weight of his inheritance. The pull of his family's legacy. The rage of his father. The loyalty of his siblings—soon to be tested. And beneath it all, something else:

A desire to protect.

A desire to belong.

a

A desire… to be something more.

The walls around his heart—walls forged by eons of indifference—had begun to fall.

What rose in their place was uncertain. But it was real.

And in the chaos of his inner world, one truth stood unshaken:

He could never go back.

The sea—once his kingdom—now felt like a mirror, reflecting the unrest within him. The rhythmic ebb and flow of the tides echoed the rise and fall of his emotions, while crashing waves paralleled the chaotic storms that churned in his soul. The sun, the moon, the stars—celestial constants—became silent witnesses to his inner struggle, passive observers of a transformation no god had foreseen.

He found solace only in stillness—in the memory of Galena's voice, in the image of her unflinching gaze. He longed to find her, to understand her, to thank her for awakening him from his divine slumber. That longing drove him forward. It eclipsed the fear of Poseidon's wrath, the looming threats of his siblings, even the crushing weight of a destiny written in the salt and stone of Olympus.

The storm had passed. But a new journey had begun—a journey into the unpredictable tides of human connection and the uncharted depths

a

of his evolving heart.
The world was captivated by *Tidal Man*—by the myth, the mystery, the spectacle.
But Tyvellmian's focus was elsewhere.
His path did not lead back to the celestial courts.
It led to the mortals he had come to care for.
It led to her.

a

Chapter III

The Depths of the Throne

In the deepest sanctum of Aegaeon Palace—where the sea crushed with such pressure that only divine beings could endure it without imploding—Poseidon's court assembled. The chamber, carved from obsidian coral and lit by glowing jellyfish suspended in chains of kelp, oozed with tension. The trident, pulsing with aqua-fire, rested across the arms of the throne as its master seethed.

Poseidon stood, tall and enraged. His presence was elemental—barnacles and sea-glass clung to his skin like armor forged from the ruins of time. Every motion he made sent tremors through the throne room. When he spoke, his voice rolled like the collapse of underwater mountains—deep, ancient, unstoppable.

** *"He dared! My son—***my own blood—dared to oppose me!"*

He paced before his court: sea-born deities and warriors. Triton. Scylla. The twins Cnidaria and Euryalus. None spoke. None dared breathe too loudly. Even the sharks circling overhead stilled.

"I summoned the storm. I called down judgment upon the insolent insects who build floating cities atop my domain—who mock the name Poseidon with their ships, their steel, their arrogance! And who stands between them and my justice?

Tyvellmian."

He turned on Triton, eyes wild with betrayal.

a

"And you—firstborn. What say you of this brother who trades eternity for the applause of ants?"

Triton's jaw tightened. His coral helm gleamed like carved bone.

"He is no brother of mine."

Poseidon's grip on his trident tightened until his knuckles turned white. The sea around him began to boil.

"He rescues mortals like some demigod-for-hire. He wears armor forged from relics of our history—and uses it to defy *me*."

A surge of divine power burst from him, crashing in tidal force across the chamber. Columns of water battered the walls. A statue of a past sea king collapsed in ruin.

"He fancies himself their protector. But he forgets who made him. He forgets the power he owes to *me*." He pointed the trident upward, eyes blazing. "And now the surface world hails him as hero, while I am to be remembered as villain?"

The silence that followed was brittle—tense as cracked glass under weight.

Then, from the shadows, a voice slithered forward—soft, serpentine, dangerous.

It was Scylla, all coils and cunning.

"Perhaps he forgets, my lord… because he sees no honor worth saving above."in your wrath. Perhaps he sees something

Poseidon roared, and the oceans screamed with him.

"Then let him learn!"

His voice thundered through the chamber, rippling out into the farthest trenches of the sea.

a

"If he would protect them, let him suffer with them. I will drown his name in every current. I will send Triton to hunt him. I will cast him from the tide-born halls and make the oceans themselves reject him.

He wants to be mortal? Then let him bleed like one!"

He turned to the court, eyes glowing like molten lava trapped beneath sapphire depths.

"Tyvellmian has made his choice. Now I make mine."

The court bowed. The glowing jellyfish dimmed.

And the currents turned cold.

The war beneath the waves had begun. The whispers began subtly—like the insidious creep of a tide before a tsunami. Tyvellmian sensed them before he heard them: a prickling unease that settled into his bones, a dissonance in the ocean's usual, harmonious rhythm. Even miles away from Poseidon's undersea palace, he could feel it—a tremor in the sacred bond that tethered them. A subtle disruption in the divine current they once shared.

He stood alone on a remote cliff, overlooking a sea still bruised from the storm. Salt-laden wind tore through his hair. The brine and ozone clung to him like memory. The rescue, the mortals, Galena—her face lingered in his thoughts, a vivid imprint of both terror and gratitude. A fragile light against the granite weight of his divine heritage.

The whispers thickened. They became a pressure, a hum vibrating through the stones beneath his feet. Poseidon never needed to speak directly. His will came in tremors, in the slow bending of currents, in the silent chorus of power shifting direction.

a

This was no longer passive tension. This was divine condemnation.

Tyvellmian felt the shadow of his siblings gathering. The ripples of their presence, the convergence of old powers forming a stormfront on the horizon. He saw them in his mind—Pegasus, noble and aloof, a companion of heroes. Chrysaor, father of Geryon, veiled in martial legacy. Triton and Proteus, both proud and fierce. Their judgment came not just from duty, but resentment—long simmering, barely restrained. His father's favoritism had once shielded him. Now, it only intensified their anger.

Tyvellmian closed his eyes, reaching through the divine current like one tuning into a distant signal. Images flashed—fragmented, half-hidden from mortal understanding.

He saw Poseidon, no longer merely angry, but incandescent with rage. The sea god's trident crackled with blue fire, waves churning around him in chaotic defiance of order. His siblings stood in grim silence, their expressions shaped by old envy and present obligation.

Poseidon's voice boomed in his mind, barbed and mocking. *"Compassion? For mortals? You would shield the very creatures who mock us—who no longer pray, who forget the names of their makers? You disgrace me, Tyvellmian."*

The words cut like obsidian, sharp and cold. They pierced the fragile bloom of empathy he had begun to nurture. Shame flickered within him. Doubt, too.

Then came the voices of his siblings—closer, clearer, more personal.

a

Triton, stern and commanding:

"Father, we must act. His weakness endangers us all. The world sees him as a savior. That image cannot stand."

Proteus, slippery and cruel:

"Let us teach him. Let him remember the hierarchy. Let

a

him bleed for his defiance."

Their wrath was not impulsive. It was cold, methodical. Chilling in its clarity.

Despair swept over Tyvellmian, heavy and suffocating. He stood between two worlds now—rejected by his divine kin, yet not fully mortal. His compassion had awakened something precious… and it had made him a target.

Galena's face, bathed in the light of his rescue, returned to him again. A soft defiance. A quiet strength. A flicker of humanity he could not—and would not—let go.

The vision of the meeting continued in chaotic flashes. Accusations. Threats. The brittle clash of egos ancient and proud. Tyvellmian could only listen from afar, helpless as divine judgment crystallized into decree.

He didn't need to hear the command. It hung in the sea like pressure before an earthquake.

He would be punished.

The only question that remained was how.

The whispers turned to roars. Poseidon's fury reached its zenith, the ocean itself boiling with his wrath. Thunder rolled beneath the sea. The very pressure of the deep shifted in response.

Tyvellmian stood firm, though the despair nearly buckled him. His compassion had left him exposed—but also, finally, real. He could not retreat from that truth.

The storm around him faded with the light. The world was scarred but quiet. The survivors of the *Virelli Majestic* huddled on splintered wreckage—traumatized, but alive.

Their bond, forged through catastrophe, shimmered in every glance they exchanged. They were changed. And so

a
was he.
But the storm inside him churned anew.
In that moment, he sought solace.
He turned to the only one who might understand—not a god, not a warrior, but someone born of both worlds.
Arconia.
Not in the royal halls of Poseidon's kingdom, but in a small cottage nestled among windswept cliffs. A quiet place. A haven.
The salt air followed him inland, whispering of betrayal and fate. But here, the sea sounded gentler. Here, there was peace.
Arconia met him in her garden, her hands tending to delicate blooms of sea lavender. She moved with quiet purpose, grounded in simple beauty. Her fingers brushed petals like she were shaping tides with her touch.
She looked up as he approached, her face calm, her presence a balm.
She was not fully divine. Her mother had been mortal, a woman whose love for Triton had defied laws older than Olympus itself. Arconia bore the weight of both legacies—goddess and woman—and had never bowed to either.
Tyvellmian watched her, his heart knotted with things he did not know how to name.
She spoke first.
"You look like the storm followed you ashore."
He gave a hollow smile. "It never left."
She rose from the garden, wiping soil from her palms.
"So... they know?"
"They do." He didn't need to say more.

a

She studied him for a long moment. “And what will you do?”

He didn’t have an answer. He only knew that retreat was no longer an option.

a

The Human Connection

The image of Galena, etched onto the canvas of his memory, was a relentless tide, pulling him under, yet somehow sustaining him. He saw her not as a mere survivor, clinging to a piece of wreckage, but as a beacon, a defiant flame flickering against the tempestuous darkness of the storm. Her eyes, the color of a stormy sea reflecting a bruised sunset, held a depth that transcended the fear gripping the other survivors. There was a quiet strength in her, a resilience that mirrored the enduring power of the ocean itself. He had expected terror, pleading, perhaps even despair, but instead, he found a quiet dignity, an acceptance of the overwhelming forces at play. It was this acceptance, this unflinching gaze into the face of chaos, that captivated him.

He sought her not in the grand halls of his father's opulent palace, but in the bustling, chaotic streets of the human world, a place he had always viewed with a detached curiosity, a world that existed apart from his own divine sphere. Not wanting to draw attention to himself, Tyvellmian assumed the guise of an ordinary man. His clothes were tattered and outdated, he looked like a homeless person. Dressed as he was, no one paid any attention to

a

him. The city throbbed with a raw energy, a relentless pulse that mirrored the turbulent feelings churning within him. The scent of salt mingled with exhaust fumes, the cacophony of human voices a jarring contrast to the tranquil silence of his underwater kingdom. He felt strangely out of place, a king without a crown, a god stripped bare of his divine arrogance. The dwelling of the mortals was vast and yet seemingly small. Tyvellmian had no idea as to where his search should begin.

The search felt futile, a desperate grasping at shadows. The storm had scattered the survivors, leaving him with only a fleeting memory and the gnawing uncertainty that he might never find her again. The face he sought was only a fragment of an image, a glimpse of humanity's tenacity, a testament to the indomitable spirit he had seen briefly manifested in Galena. It was more than just a physical attraction; it was a connection to something he had previously deemed beyond his understanding. Her resilience was a mirror, reflecting a strength he had yet to fully discover within himself.

Each day, the city unfolded before him like a vast, intricate tapestry, its threads interwoven with hope and despair, joy and sorrow. He

a

observed the intricate dance of humanity, its intricate complexities, its unwavering capacity for both cruelty and compassion. He wandered through bustling markets where the scent of spices and street food filled the air, the sounds of haggling and laughter echoing through the narrow alleyways. He sat in quiet cafes, observing the silent conversations, the fleeting moments of connection between strangers. He walked along the rain-slicked streets, feeling the pulse of the city beneath his feet, a symphony of human experiences unfolding around him.

It was during these quiet moments of observation that he began to understand the depth of his own internal conflict. The raging tempest within him, once a chaotic maelstrom of divine power, was now a more intricate storm, a blend of ancient fury and newfound compassion. His feelings for Galena were more than a simple attraction; they were a revelation, a glimpse into a realm of emotion he had previously dismissed as a weakness.

His compassion, a nascent flame at first, now burned brightly, illuminating the dark corners of his soul. It was a force that challenged his very being, a defiance of his heritage, a rebellion against the ancient order. His family,

a

his father especially, saw this compassion as a flaw, a sign of weakness. They saw Galena, not as a symbol of human resilience, but as a threat, a distraction from his divine duties, a poison infecting his divine essence.

But Galena, in his mind, was not a poison but an antidote. She represented a freedom he had never known, a release from the stifling confines of his immortal existence. He imagined her laughter, the sound of her voice, the warmth of her presence, and he felt a yearning so intense it ached within his very being. He would spend hours envisioning her smile, recreating her features from memory, filling in the gaps of his fleeting encounter with his own yearning and hope. When the city and its' inhabitants got to the point of annoyance, he found solace in the sea, a sanctuary amidst the chaos of the human world. The waves, once a source of power, were now a reflection of his internal turmoil. The rhythm of the tide mirrored the ebb and flow of his emotions, the crashing waves a symbol of his internal struggles, the gentle lapping of the water a metaphor for the peace he craved.

As the days turned into nights, his quest for Galena became intertwined with a journey of self-discovery. Living among the mortals taught him how they function, adapt and

a

believed. He was no longer simply searching for a woman; he was searching for a part of himself, a part he had kept hidden away for centuries, a part that had been awakened by an unexpected act of compassion. This realization hit him like a wave, almost as forceful as the storm that had brought them together.

His father's disapproval, the cold scorn of his siblings, these were the rocks against which he was constantly being dashed. Yet, he refused to be broken. He found strength not in his divine power, but in the human connection, the burgeoning love that bound him to Galena, even from a distance. The image of her face, a persistent echo in the chambers of his heart, became his compass, guiding him through the treacherous currents of his own turmoil.

He knew that his search for Galena was more than a mere quest for a lost love; it was a voyage into the heart of humanity. It was a confrontation with his own mortality, a recognition of his fallibility. He was no longer the invincible god of his father's making; he was a being torn between two worlds, striving for a balance between his divine heritage and his burgeoning human connection. He found himself strangely drawn to this new found fragility, something he would never have

a

previously admitted.

The weight of his divine legacy pressed down upon him, a burden made heavier by his family's resentment. But the memory of Galena, her quiet strength, her unwavering gaze, filled him with a strength he had never known existed, a strength born not of power, but of compassion, of a connection to the human spirit that defied the ancient laws of his father's kingdom.
This quest for Galena was a quest for understanding himself.
A quest to define what it meant to be Tyvellmian, not just as the son of Poseidon, but as a being capable of compassion,
capable of love,
capable of forging a connection that transcended the divine and mortal realms.
The path ahead was uncertain, fraught with the dangers of his family's wrath and the unknown challenges of his quest.
But fueled by his newfound hope, he pressed forward, determined to find Galena,
not only to reclaim her but to reclaim a piece of himself that had been lost to him for centuries.
The journey would be arduous, but the reward, he felt, was worth more than all the power in the sea.

a

Arconia's Advice...

The air hung heavy with the scent of jasmine and sea salt, a stark contrast to the metallic tang of fear that had clung to him for days. Arconia's sanctuary, nestled high in the cliffs overlooking the turbulent sea, was a haven of tranquility. Sunlight streamed through the arched windows, illuminating dust motes dancing in the air, a serene tableau that felt worlds away from the raging storm and the icy glares of his siblings. He sat opposite her, the rough-hewn stone beneath him strangely comforting. Arconia, his niece, with her cascade of raven hair and eyes that mirrored the depths of the ocean, possessed a wisdom that belied her years. She was a beacon of calm amidst the tempest that raged within him.

"Uncle Tyvellmian," she began, her voice as soft as the whisper of the waves, "you carry the weight of the world on your shoulders, or so it seems." Her gaze was steady, unwavering, understanding. She didn't attempt to dismiss his turmoil, but instead acknowledged it, validating the intensity of his struggle.

He shifted uncomfortably, the silence between them filled only with the gentle lapping of waves against the rocks below. "I... I don't

a

understand," he finally admitted, his voice raspy. "I saved the mortals. I spared their lives. Why is this considered a betrayal?"

Arconia smiled, a small, knowing smile that hinted at a deeper understanding. "Your father, the ocean itself, is a force of nature, Uncle. Unpredictable, powerful, and often unforgiving. He values strength, dominance, the unwavering might of the sea. Compassion, to him, is weakness. A crack in the formidable fortress of his power."

"But it's not weakness," Tyvellmian protested, the words escaping him with a desperate urgency. "It's… it's something more. It's… a connection."

a

"A connection to humanity," Arconia finished, her voice a gentle echo of his own turbulent thoughts. "A connection that terrifies your father and your siblings, because it challenges the very foundation of their existence. They fear what you represent – a god capable of empathy, a god who sees the human spirit not as something to be dominated, but as something to be respected, to be cherished."

He nodded slowly, the weight of her words settling upon him like a comforting blanket. He had never considered it in this light before. His actions weren't merely a breach of divine protocol; they were a radical act of defiance, a silent rebellion against the cold, unyielding power of his father.

"Poseidon, Zeus and the other elder gods, believes that humanity's abandonment of the ancient gods warrants punishment," Arconia continued, her voice barely a whisper. "He sees it as a betrayal, a rejection of their divine authority. He believes that the storms he inflicts upon the mortals are just, a necessary cleansing. He doesn't understand… he cannot understand the capacity for human resilience, for human hope."

"And you do?" Tyvellmian asked, his voice

a

barely above a breath.

Arconia's gaze held a depth of understanding that resonated deep within him. "I see it in your heart, Uncle. I see the reflection of Galena 's strength in your eyes. You are torn between two worlds, but your compassion is the bridge that connects them. It is not a weakness, but a strength, a power that transcends the raw force of the ocean itself."

He paused, allowing her words to sink in, to resonate within the quiet sanctuary. "The human spirit, in its vulnerability, its capacity for both cruelty and compassion, is a mirror to the soul. It's through those moments of connection, those fleeting instances of shared humanity, that we truly understand our own power, and the power of our compassion."

He thought of Galena again, her face still vivid in his memory, her unwavering gaze in the face of death. Her spirit, her strength, was the very antithesis of his father's cold, unyielding wrath. It was a strength he had glimpsed in the human world, a strength that was now fueling his own internal rebellion.

"What should I do?" he asked, his voice heavy with the weight of his destiny. The question was not about his divine powers, or the wrath of

a

his father, but about the direction of his heart.

Arconia placed a hand on his, her touch warm and reassuring. "Follow your heart, Uncle Tyvellmian. Embrace the compassion that guides you. Let it be your compass, your strength. Don't let your father's fear diminish the power of your own heart."

The conversation extended far into the night, under a sky scattered with stars that reflected the turmoil within Tyvellmian's soul, yet also held the promise of a different future. They discussed the intricacies of the human spirit, the divine balance between power and empathy, the conflicting forces of ancient tradition and modern understanding.

Arconia, with her gentle wisdom, helped him unravel the tangled threads of his internal conflict. She didn't offer simplistic solutions, but instead guided him to find his own answers, empowering him to trust his instincts.

She spoke of her own experiences with the mortals, the ancient myths, the forgotten stories of gods who had fallen in love with mortals, of divine beings who had chosen compassion over dominance, and of the lessons those tales held for him. She reminded him that his lineage, while powerful, did not dictate his

a

actions or define his essence. His compassion wasn't a flaw; it was his unique strength, a potent force capable of bridging the gap between the divine and the human realms.

She spoke of the consequences of his actions, the inevitable conflict with his father and siblings. But she also emphasized the potential for positive change, the possibility of forging a new path, one that combined his divine heritage with his profound empathy.

Arconia's words resonated deeply, not as commands or pronouncements, but as gentle encouragements, illuminating a path that he had been struggling to find. He realized that his quest for Galena wasn't merely a romantic pursuit, but a journey of self-discovery, a reclamation of his own identity, a step towards forging a new balance between his divine heritage and the newfound empathy that burned brightly within him. The ocean, a symbol of his father's power, was still a tempest, but within him, a quiet strength had emerged, born from a connection to humanity, a connection forged in the heart of a storm. The weight of his divine heritage remained, a constant presence in his life, but it no longer overshadowed the growing strength of his own compassion. He was, after all, not simply

a

Poseidon's son. He was Tyvellmian, a being capable of both immense power and profound empathy. And this realization was a balm to his wounded spirit, a beacon in the darkening waters. Leaving Arconia's sanctuary, the rising sun painted the sky with hues of hope and determination. He knew the path ahead was still challenging, still fraught with conflict, but for the first time, he felt a newfound resolve, a certainty that the compassion burning within him was not a weakness but a profound and powerful strength. The search for Galena was a journey, not only to find her, but to truly find himself. And he was ready to embark on that journey, armed not only with his divine power, but with the strength of his own compassionate heart. "Arconia," he began, his voice softer than the sea breeze. "I need to speak with you."

She turned, her eyes—an arresting blend of her mother's earthbound brown and her father's sea-foam green—widening slightly at the sight of him.

"I heard," she said. "Grandfather is very angry at you. He's ordered Father to punish you." There was concern etched into her features—a silent acknowledgment of the weight he carried.

Tyvellmian sat beside her, the cool stone of the cottage wall firm against his back. Then,

a

quietly, he spoke—of the storm, the rescue, the mortals… and of Galena. The woman whose life he had spared. The woman whose image lingered in his waking thoughts and haunted his dreams. He spoke of the unexpected compassion that had surged within him—a feeling so alien, so contrary to everything he had ever been taught.

“It was… unexpected,” he admitted, his voice thick with the weight of it. “I felt… a connection to her, Arconia. A compassion that defied the ancient order—defied the very essence of what I was made to be.”

Arconia listened without interruption. Her gaze was steady, her silence patient. She didn’t offer platitudes or hollow reassurances. She simply made space—for his truth, for his fear, for his transformation.

He spoke of Poseidon’s fury, of the simmering resentment among his brothers. Of the whispers and looming threats, of divine judgment already descending. He described the confrontation in the throne room as if it had been carved into his memory: the blazing eyes of his father, the charged silence of his siblings, the terrifying weight of a decision already made.

“I feel… changed, little one,” he whispered. “This compassion—it feels like betrayal. A betrayal of my family. Of my heritage. Of

a

everything I am."

Arconia reached for his hand, her touch firm, anchoring. Her fingers, warm and strong, quieted the chaos within him.

"It's not betrayal, Uncle," she said softly. "It's an awakening. It's seeing something the others can't—or refuse to."

Her words were simple. But they resonated like thunder in his soul. They cut through the echoes of condemnation and let in the light.

He had always been taught that compassion was weakness. That empathy was a flaw. That to love mortals was to invite ruin. But in Arconia's voice, so calm and certain, he heard something else.

Truth.

They talked for hours. Tyvellmian unburdened himself, each sentence a step away from the gods who had raised him and closer to the man he was becoming. He shared his fears. His uncertainty. The raw awe he'd felt when Galena looked at him—not with worship, but with *understanding*.

He described her strength in the face of chaos. Her calm in the eye of divine wrath. Her silent defiance that matched his own. In her, he'd seen something beautiful and fragile. Something worth protecting. Worth defying the heavens for.

Arconia responded in kind. She shared her

a

own story—her place between two worlds, the suspicion from gods and mortals alike. She spoke of prejudice, of her constant navigation between myth and humanity. And she spoke of kindness—unexpected moments of grace she'd witnessed among mortals. Compassion in the face of suffering. Forgiveness in the face of cruelty.

Her words wrapped around him like a current, gently pulling him back to center.

Her empathy, born of both bloodlines, became his compass.

As the sun dipped toward the horizon, casting long shadows across the cliffs, Tyvellmian felt something he hadn't in days:

Peace.

Poseidon's wrath still loomed. His siblings' vengeance was inevitable. But they no longer felt like mountains he must carry. They were obstacles to face, yes—but not ones that could bury him.

Arconia had reminded him who he was—not just a god, but a being capable of change. Of *choice.*

He would not walk blindly back into Olympus.

He would not bend to wrath disguised as law.

He would forge a new path—uncertain, yes, but his own.

The road ahead would be perilous. His family would not yield. And the gods were not known

a

for mercy.
But in Arconia's steady gaze, he saw a reflection of hope.
And in the memory of Galena's courage, he found a reason.
A reason to fight.
Not just for love. Not just for the mortals.
For himself.
This wasn't simply a quest to find a woman lost to the waves. It was a battle for his soul. A journey to reclaim his own voice. A war not of weapons—but of meaning.
As the sun set in a blaze of orange and violet, painting the sky in hues that seemed impossible in the underworld depths, Tyvellmian rose.
He carried with him two truths:

- The memory of Galena's silent bravery.
- And Arconia's unshakable belief that compassion was not weakness—but power.

The whispers of divine wrath still stirred in the sea.
But now, they had an answer—gentler, quieter…
and far more dangerous.
The whisper of his own heart.
Awake at last.

a

Chapter IV

The Search Beneath the Surface

The sea spray kissed his face as he stood on the precipice, the wind whipping his dark hair around him. Below, the city sprawled—a concrete jungle teeming with life, a stark contrast to the serene isolation of Arconia's cliffside sanctuary. He had spent the night wrestling with the weight of his decision—to defy his father, to face the fury of Poseidon and the vengeance of his siblings, all for a woman he barely knew.

But the image of Galena's eyes—wide with fear yet glowing with defiant strength—haunted him.

He had to find her. He had to know she was safe.

His first challenge was anonymity.

Arconia had cautioned him against wandering the city as a homeless man again. "Invisibility works... until someone's actually looking," she had said. "And right now, everyone is."

In his true form, Tyvellmian radiated power—salt and thunder trailing in his wake. To mortals and media, he was *Tidal Man*, a legend alive, the god who had walked from the sea to save lives during a storm that should have claimed them all. To re-enter their world without disguise would risk chaos. Fear. Worship. Retaliation. Exposure. Worse, it would put those he protected at even greater risk.

So, he changed.

The familiar energy shifted through him—ancient, effortless. He shaped a new form, mimicking the subtle

a
imperfections of humanity. Not perfect. Not divine. *Believable.* When it was done, he was no longer a god—but a man named *Elias.* Quiet. Watchful. Eyes sharp, hands weathered, presence forgettable.
The city held its breath beneath a bruised twilight sky.
He began where the storm had ended—at the docks.
The wreckage of the *Aetheria*, the ill-fated luxury liner, was gone—either salvaged or lost to the deep. But the air still held the scent of salt and decay, the echo of catastrophe. He walked the piers slowly, slipping into the rhythm of the crowd. Dockworkers. Tourists. Fishermen. Locals with eyes sunken by memory.
He asked questions.
Carefully.
He inquired in bars and shipping offices. He lingered at emergency shelters. At each stop, he pieced together fragments—blurred memories of waves and terror, of a glowing figure rising from the sea. Some remembered him. Most remembered only the storm.
None remembered Galena.
Days bled into weeks.
He learned the human world as if for the first time. The contradictions, the quiet glories, the darkness and resilience. He witnessed suffering and laughter. Cruelty and compassion. He began to understand, not as a god, but as a man. And with each passing day, his resolve grew.
He stayed in forgotten hotels, watched the city from rooftops, listened to it breathe.
Through the chaos, he found whispers of resistance—small groups helping survivors, organizing aid, offering kindness

a
without reward. That, more than anything, kept him going.
Eventually, his search yielded a name.
Galena.
Injured. Rescued. Taken to a nearby hospital.
Alive.
The relief that washed over him was seismic, breaking through his careful façade. It took everything he had not to let the ocean within him rise in joy. But caution prevailed. He couldn't reveal himself—not yet.
The hospital was guarded. Layers of human security…and something more. He sensed divine wards woven into the foundation, marks of ancient vigilance. Someone else had noticed. Someone was watching. The hunt had begun in earnest.
He waited until moonlight cloaked the rooftops.
Then he moved.
Slipping past sensors and spirits, his form fluid, shadows bending around him. The hospital hummed with the stillness of midnight. He moved through sterile halls like water, his divine senses guiding him unerringly.
At last, he found her room.
Small. Clean. Dimly lit.
Galena lay sleeping, her breath even, her brow furrowed in dream. Her face, pale but unbowed, still carried the strength he had seen on the storm-swept deck. Even unconscious, she radiated resolve.
He stood in the doorway for a long time.
Watching.
Remembering.
She wasn't just a survivor. She was a symbol. Of

a
everything he had come to believe in. Of the path he had chosen.

His pulse quickened.

This wasn't about duty. Not anymore.

It was about connection.

He approached the bed, quietly, reverently. The room seemed to hold its breath with him. He reached for her hand—but stopped just short. Her presence, even in sleep, calmed the maelstrom within him. She had no idea what she had awakened in him. Not just compassion. Not just doubt.

Hope.

A faint sound broke the silence.

Footsteps.

Deliberate. Powerful. Divine.

He didn't need to see them to know.

His siblings were near.

Their energy crackled at the edge of his awareness—sharp and invasive, a different kind of storm. They had followed the same trail. They had come for him.

He slipped into the shadows, heart heavy. Galena remained untouched. For now.

But the warning was clear.

The time for hiding was ending. The confrontation was coming.

Tyvellmian fled the hospital, the night air biting as he stepped back into the world. The wind whispered warnings in his ear. The sea hissed at his heels.

He had chosen love over law. Mercy over order. Humanity over godhood.

a
Now, he would pay the price.
But even as he disappeared into the dark, one truth blazed within him like a lighthouse on the horizon:
He had saved her.
And he would do it again.
No matter what it cost.
The chill of the hospital corridor clung to him even as he melted back into the shadows. He had felt their presence before he heard them—a ripple in the fabric of reality, a discordant note in the city's breathing symphony.
Poseidon's children. His siblings. They were here.
Not with the blunt force of a tidal wave, but with the insidious precision of vipers.
He knew them well—reflections of their father's volatile essence, warped by their own desires.
Triton: the war-hardened, the unrelenting, his fury crashing like the deep sea's undertow. Dutiful, loyal, relentless. He would not kill, but he would break.
Benthesikyme: subtle and seductive, her power mirrored the sea's beguiling depths. She would play to emotions, manipulate through whispers and memory. Her ambition cloaked in elegance.
Nereus: next to the youngest but wildest. His realm was chaos, currents that turned without warning. Unpredictable, unstable, envious. His assault would be erratic and fierce.
Tyvellmian knew he could not outrun them forever. Their divine senses would trace him through the city's deepest veins. He needed cover. Not just distance—but obscurity.
Arconia's sanctuary was compromised. Too exposed. Too easily breached.

a

But a fragment of a myth returned to him—something whispered by ancient sea creatures and half-mad oracles:

A hidden city buried within the human world. Cloaked in forgotten magic. A place even gods could not fully see.

He moved quickly, shedding his divine glow, resuming the disguise of Elias. In the forgotten edges of the metropolis—grimy bars, old tunnels, alleys lined with secret sigils—he followed the current of unseen things.

An abandoned subway station became his entry point. Rust. Rot. The slow drip of ancient water. Tracks swallowed by darkness. And within it all—something... breathing.

Magic. Older than Poseidon.

He followed the pulse.

Down winding tunnels, through broken thresholds, guided only by the soft glow of glyphs—runes that pulsed with forgotten languages. As he descended deeper, the air grew thicker, alive with layered silence.

Then he saw it.

A city carved from obsidian, built in shadows, pulsing with its own internal light. Towers of black crystal. Walls etched in scripture that shimmered faintly in hues unknown to mortal eyes. This was no refuge built by man.

This was a tomb of gods.

A hidden metropolis beyond time.

He entered its hollow heart and found a chamber filled with ancient scrolls and stone-bound volumes—forgotten knowledge, locked behind silence. He set to work, searching the texts for answers—magic, artifacts, rites, *anything* that could shield Galena, protect the world, or

a
resist Poseidon's wrath.
But the calm was fleeting.
He felt the tremor long before he heard the sound. The divine pressure of his siblings entering the city's sphere.
Triton's focused rage.
Benthesikyme's creeping charm.
Nereus's electric instability.
They were coming.
And this place—this miraculous city of refuge—would not hold them off for long.
Tyvellmian stood.
He wasn't just preparing for a fight.
He was preparing for a war.

EXT. ATLANTIC OCEAN – DAY

The sky churns above a restless sea. Clouds bruise the heavens in iron and ash.
A fleet of naval ships slices through rolling swells.
Onboard: crates of emergency aid—food, medicine, tarps, water. Their destination: a Caribbean island devastated by storm.
Then the ocean *rises*.
Not a wave—a wall.
A column of water spirals skyward with unnatural force.
TRITON has arrived.
He emerges like a god of war, suspended above the waves, his trident glowing with bioluminescent rage. Lightning coils around him. His long seaweed-dark hair streams in the wind.

a

TRITON *(thundering)*

"You defile my realm with your metal and smoke! Return to the land—or drown with your mercy!"

He hurls his trident.

The sea obeys.

Tsunami-force waves crash down. Ships lurch. Sailors scream. A helicopter swerves, barely escaping the onslaught.

Then—

A second figure rockets upward, cleaving through the chaos.

TIDAL-MAN.

Armor forged from the ocean itself gleams with kelp-green shimmer. Water jets propel him forward. He lands hard on a carrier's deck.

TIDAL-MAN *(defiant)*

"These people have suffered enough, brother. This isn't justice—it's murder."

Triton hovers overhead, storm-light glinting off his trident.

There is no response—only fury.

Triton lunges.

Tidal-Man meets him mid-air.

BOOM.

A shockwave explodes across the sea. Rain flattens in mid-air.

A god strikes a god.

HIGH ABOVE THE SEA…

Triton's trident arcs toward Tidal-Man's head. Tidal-Man

a
twists, catching the shaft mid-air, redirecting it. The weapon spirals into a water spire, detonating in a geyser.
Tidal-Man counters—his gauntlets shimmer with compressed hydro-force. He drives them into Triton's chest, sending both plummeting into a massive wave.
They crash. The ocean shatters like glass.

UNDERWATER – MOMENTS LATER.
Silence.
Dim light filters through the waves.
Triton twists his trident in a wide arc, displacing the sea in a vacuum.
Tidal-Man is caught in the current, hurled into a coral outcropping that shatters on impact.
He rights himself mid-spin, eyes blazing.
He drives his gauntlet into the seabed—*BOOM*—a shockwave blasts outward, launching him back into the fray.
They collide again—brothers, once bonded by purpose, now divided by truth.

SURFACE – INTERCUT

Naval ships sway like toys.
Crates of aid crash across decks. Sailors cling to railings.
Lives hang in the balance.
Triton rises once more, shouting over the roar:
TRITON *(voice low, dangerous)*
"Father gave you everything. Power. Legacy. And you trade it… for mortals?"

a

TIDAL-MAN *(steady, unwavering)*
"I found something you never did, Triton. Purpose."
Rage eclipses logic.
Triton hurls his trident again.
It misses Tidal-Man by inches, slamming into a battleship hull. The metal groans but holds.
Tidal-Man retaliates with precision, slamming into his brother like a torpedo. They spiral through the air, crashing into another tower of water that collapses around them.

It can be seen on TIDAL-MAN.
Blood drips from his brow. His breath is heavy.
But his eyes hold resolve.
This is not just a fight for survival.
This is a stand—for humanity.
For Galena.
For compassion.
They collide.
A thunderous vortex spins around them, swirling with the fury of a hurricane. Water boils. Pressure mounts.
They trade blows beneath the surface—fist against fist, shockwaves bursting into superheated clouds. Each strike cracks the sea like glass.
Triton's trident lashes out—slashing, searing.
Tidal-Man catches it mid-swing, twisting the shaft, wrenching it free with a growl.
He plants his feet on the seabed and shoves.
Triton is flung backward, but recovers fast.
The trident spins in Tidal-Man's hand.
And then—he throws it.

a

Not at Triton. At the ocean floor.

BOOM.

It slams down like a divine hammer. The seabed ruptures.

A shockwave explodes upward.

ABOVE WATER – AERIAL VIEW

A vertical column of ocean blasts skyward.

Tidal-Man breaks the surface first, his armor cracked, chest heaving. He floats—treading the air with hydro-kinetic bursts, staring toward the fleet.

The naval ships continue undeterred. The aid mission holds.

Behind him—another explosion of water.

Triton rises, trident in hand, hair whipping like serpents.

Lightning crackles in his wake.

TRITON

(growling)

"You're not stronger than me, little brother."

TIDAL-MAN

(level)

"No. But I'm not weaker either."

Triton lunges again.

But this time—Tidal-Man pivots.

He sidesteps with a spin, drives an elbow into the side of Triton's head. Triton reels.

Before he can recover—a water-forged knee slams into his chest, launching him backward like a cannon shot.

Triton skids across the ocean's surface, gouging waves, finally rising to one knee.

Silence falls.

a
Even the wind pauses.
He looks up. Sees the fleet—untouched. Sailors scramble, pointing. The island approaches.
TRITON
(quietly, snarling)
"You've chosen your side."
Tidal-Man doesn't respond.
He hovers above the waves—battered, breath ragged, fists still clenched.
Triton's eyes blaze.
With a guttural roar, he plunges his trident into the sea.
The ocean opens into a massive whirlpool. Thunder cracks.
Lightning coils into water.
Triton disappears, swallowed in a crash of water and light.

ON THE LEAD SHIP – MOMENTS LATER

Tidal-Man descends slowly. His boots land with a heavy *clang* on the deck.
Cheers erupt.
Sailors shout. Medics rush to help those who fell. Officers salute him.
The fleet sails forward. Aid intact.
Mission: complete.
But Tidal-Man doesn't smile. He stares toward the horizon.
Eyes distant.
Mind sharp.
Heart heavy.
He knows.
This isn't over.

a
Not even close.

a

Chapter V

The Media Frenzy

The city roared—not with waves, but with the deafening symphony of a million voices, screens, and anxieties. The quiet sanctuary of the hidden city felt like a dream now, displaced by the maelstrom that had become Tyvellmian's new reality. He had saved lives—an act of compassion born in a moment of quiet defiance—and in doing so, he had ignited a global wildfire.

BREAKING NEWS: SUPERHUMAN CONFRONTATION HALTS MID-OCEAN AID MISSION—BUT SUPPLIES ARRIVE SAFELY!
[CNN / BBC / GNN / MSNBC / MEGAVERSE CITY NEWS NETWORK]
Dateline: Caribbean Sea – 12:47 PM
In an unprecedented mid-ocean event captured by military satellites and stunned eyewitnesses, a titanic battle erupted earlier today between two unidentified figures—believed to be the elusive "Tidal-Man" and an unconfirmed hostile entity now called "Triton."
The confrontation occurred 120 nautical miles southeast of the Greater Antilles, during a critical humanitarian aid mission to a hurricane-devastated Caribbean island.
"It was like watching gods fight," said Lt. Marcus Hall, a logistics officer aboard one of the relief ships. *"The ocean rose like it was alive. We thought we were dead men."*
Satellite footage shows hydrodynamic anomalies, massive

a
whirlpool formations, and rapid atmospheric shifts. Eyewitness videos from helicopter crews depict one figure—Tidal-Man—defending the fleet with aquatic propulsion and concussive wave blasts.
The second figure, Triton, reportedly wielded a glowing trident and commanded ocean forces at a planetary scale.
"We were bracing for the worst... and then it stopped."
The battle lasted nearly ten minutes. Despite the chaos, no vessels were sunk, and no lives were lost. Relief supplies reached the island successfully.

Who is Tidal-Man?

First spotted after last year's Pacific tsunami, Tidal-Man remains largely unknown. His actions during this incident, however, have triggered global speculation about underwater civilizations or "oceanic metahumans." Mythologists point to strong visual parallels between these beings and ancient Greek deities. Others believe they represent a new class of elemental lifeforms, awakened by climate stressors or tectonic shifts.

World Reactions:
Social media erupted:

- #SeaBrothers
- #TidalManReturns
- #TridentWar

Politicians called for increased maritime surveillance. Religious leaders offered conflicting interpretations. Humanitarian organizations issued public thanks to a

a
"mysterious protector of the sea."
The U.N. Secretary-General released a brief statement:
"We are grateful the mission was not disrupted. However, this raises pressing questions about boundaries—between nations, and between our world and forces we do not yet understand."

News stations looped grainy videos—some caught from shaking hands, others from blurred drone feeds. Each image captured fleeting glimpses: a figure emerging from the storm, a being wrapped in lightning and fury, pulling people from drowning waters.
The name "Tidal-Man" spread like fire:
Whispered in fear.
Shouted in awe.
Screamed in panic.
His image was everywhere: television, feeds, billboards, projections. A silhouette against the storm. A savior—or something else.
The internet cracked open like a fault line.
Some saw him as divine.
Others saw him as doom.
Religious factions twisted his image to fit prophecies. Some labeled him a god returned to Earth. Others called him a fallen angel, a demon, a herald of *Ragnarok.*
Competing sects claimed him as messiah, antichrist, or the second Poseidon.
Scientists grasped for answers.
Energy-based propulsion?
Plasma fields?

a
Oceanic AI?
Quantum mutation?
Theories spiraled into absurdity—but every attempt to quantify him only deepened the mystery.

In the streets, the rhythm of life shifted.
Crowds stared at screens, brows furrowed. Children wore homemade masks of sea creatures. Murals of the battle bloomed in alleyways overnight. Strangers argued in line at coffee shops about whether Tidal-Man was real—or righteous.
The official government stance remained cautious. Their briefings were carefully worded:
"Unidentified phenomena."
"Localized atmospheric disruptions."
"Coastal anomalies."
But behind closed doors?
Panic.
Agencies scrambled. Military leaders studied satellite recordings frame-by-frame. Covert departments activated dormant protocols. Black sites buzzed with activity.
Global powers were no longer interested in *who* Tidal-Man was. The question was now *how* to contain him. Or worse... how to copy him.

Media outlets launched full-scale specials:

- *"The Storm God Among Us"*
- *"Tidal Force: Miracle or Menace?"*
- *"The Trident War – Breaking Down the Sea Battle"*

a
Talk shows became battlefields of ideology.
Some hosts called him a divine protector. Others decried him as an ecological terrorist. Guests screamed. Phones rang off the hook. Ratings soared.
The world didn't know what it wanted more: to worship him—or to stop him.
Online forums fractured into factions. New cults began forming. Merchandising exploded. Hacktivists claimed they were in communication with "the oceanic mind."
Tidal-Man was now a global symbol—of hope, of fear, of change.
And the storm hadn't passed.

In the hidden city, Tyvellmian watched.
From beneath the earth, veiled in the shadows of forgotten gods, he monitored the unfolding chaos. News clips. Satellite feeds. Algorithms analyzing his every movement.
He saw the fear. The awe. The weaponization of his compassion.
He hadn't intended this.
He never sought fame.
He had only acted because it was *right*.
And now?
The world was split by his choice.
He was no longer anonymous. No longer safe.
His siblings were watching.
Their hunt intensified—not just for him, but for his growing influence.
They feared his image more than his strength.
His act of mercy had sparked a movement—one they could

a
not control.
Tyvellmian paced the obsidian halls, their ancient magic humming in quiet warning. The sacred texts here spoke of prophecy and ruin, of divine rebellion, of gods who chose love over law.
He was not the first.
But he might be the last.
The media storm was more than a distraction. It was a weapon. A flare in the night sky. Every whisper about him was another signal to his enemies—divine and mortal alike.
He knew he couldn't hide much longer.
The world was no longer just watching.
It was choosing sides.
He closed his eyes and saw her—Galena.
Not in pain. Not drowning.
But calm. Alive.
He had to find her again.
Not just to protect her.
To *anchor* himself. To understand who he was becoming.
The whispers of gods. The roar of storms. The voices of billions.
All crashing together.
He had become more than a myth.
Now he had to decide:
Would he become a symbol...
Or a storm?

a

Geneva, Switzerland.

Beneath the snow-dusted mountains, far below the city's polished streets and embassies, the Global Crisis Command Center buzzed with quiet intensity. The underground chamber shimmered with the glow of suspended projections, casting reflections across steel tables and glass consoles. It was a theater of power, and tonight, the show was fear.

Representatives from over thirty nations gathered—not in person, but as holographic projections, hovering above their assigned seats. This was the United Nations Emergency Forum—convened for only the fourth time in human history. The reason was not a war. Not a plague.

But a man.

A myth.

A phenomenon they called *"Tidal-Man."*

General *Petrov*, the stoic Russian military advisor with flint-gray eyes and a voice like granite, slammed his fist on the table.

Silence swept the room.

He gestured to the center display.

A thermal feed flickered to life: a massive wave, mid-crest, splitting unnaturally. At its heart, a glowing blue figure—humanoid—lifting a sinking ship from the abyss.

"He's not just a natural phenomenon," Petrov growled. "He isn't just manipulating water—he's communicating with it. Commanding it. He's something else. Something ancient. And we are *utterly unprepared* for him."

Across the room, *Dr. Aris Thorne*, an astrophysicist from the

a
UK, zoomed in on a data model. A holographic representation displayed temporal ripples and atmospheric anomalies around Tyvellmian's last known location.
"His movements defy physics," Thorne said, awe and dread warping his voice. "Speed, force, gravitational behavior—it's not just advanced. It's... rewritten. He doesn't bend the laws of physics. He *harmonizes* with them."
He tapped a frame frozen mid-storm: a microsecond image of a light-warping distortion surrounding Tidal-Man.
"This isn't just speed," Thorne said softly. "This is a localized collapse of spacetime. He's operating under a *different set of constants*."
General Nari Okabe of Japan leaned forward.
"Are we certain he's a threat?"
Silence. Then Thorne again:
"No. But the last time Earth hosted a being with this kind of energy signature... we weren't here to record it. Our *myths* were. He might be the source of them."
Petrov's voice was cold, unblinking:
"God. Weapon. Ghost from Atlantis. I don't care. I want to know—*what does he want?*"
The room exploded into voices—arguments, data points, contingency plans. Some pushed for preemptive military action. Covert capture protocols. Biological profiling. Others urged caution and diplomacy, warning that a provocation might trigger a disaster humanity couldn't survive.
Li Wei, a Chinese envoy with the demeanor of a scholar and the will of a general, spoke evenly:
"We've seen compassion in his actions. Let's not throw fire

a

at a god who might offer rain. Perhaps... we can *negotiate*."
From the U.S. side, *C.I.A. Deputy Director Serena Locke* appeared, her projection glitched behind encryption filters.
"We've picked up deep-sea chatter—sonic frequencies used only in obscure marine fauna. But these weren't whales or tech anomalies. We traced linguistic patterns."
She typed a single word into the air:
TIDAL-MAN
It hovered—luminescent, ominous.
The discussion stretched for hours. The chamber became a microcosm of the globe: fractured, anxious, clashing between hope and panic. The first responses to Tidal-Man had been chaotic. Now, they struggled to shape a unified response—but there was no playbook for a being who could halt storms and raise oceans.

Surveillance teams launched worldwide.

- Submarines equipped with sonar combed the deep.
- Spy satellites scanned every ocean surface.
- High-altitude drones searched for his thermal signature.
- Naval fleets were deployed in "training exercises" that doubled as watch posts.

Nothing worked.
Tyvellmian remained elusive. A ghost in the surf.
When sensors thought they had him, he was already gone.
He wasn't hiding.
He was simply... *unreachable.*

The scientific community unraveled.

a

Astrophysicists. Geologists. Marine biologists.

All worked in parallel, racing to *name* what they saw.

- Was he extraterrestrial?
- An evolved aquatic species?
- A myth-made-man?
- A glitch in the simulation of reality itself?

Every new discovery just sharpened the contradiction:

The more they observed, the less they understood.

The line between science and *myth* blurred further with every hour.

Meanwhile, the religious world detonated.

Faiths across the spectrum scrambled to *claim* him.

Churches reinterpreted prophecy.

Temples resurrected ancient texts.

New cults formed overnight, painting his face on flags and walls.

Was he the savior?

The destroyer?

A divine messenger?

Or just the first of many?

The division deepened. And the mystery worsened.

In politics, the balance of power cracked.

Bitter enemies aligned under mutual fear.

Alliances once carved in ice melted under the heat of uncertainty.

Everyone wanted control—or at least *insurance*.

A *global arms race of knowledge and speculation* began.

The world hadn't just discovered Tyvellmian.

The world had *reacted*—and now it couldn't stop.

a

The Disinformation War.

When tracking him failed, governments turned to controlling the *story*.
Psych-ops began.
Propaganda was seeded through media influencers.
False sightings. Contradictory rumors.
AI-generated leaks claiming he was a weapon, a hoax, a crisis actor.
All meant to fracture public belief and control the narrative.
But it *didn't work*.
Tyvellmian's blurry silhouette—caught in rain, lightning, and chaos—only grew more iconic.
Attempts to discredit him backfired.
People didn't want proof.
They wanted meaning.
Then the oceans responded.
Marine life grew *hostile*. Pods of dolphins blocked submarines. Sharks circled naval vessels. Whales broke formation in coordinated paths, swimming dangerously close to ships.
Seismic activity increased in territories heavy with sonar testing.
Some claimed these were Tyvellmian's warnings.
Others feared the planet itself was shifting.
The natural world, it seemed, wasn't just watching.
It was *choosing sides.*
In the end, no one knew what to do.
The world had faced nuclear standoffs, pandemics, terrorism, and war.

a
But not this.
Not a god who wept.
Not a protector who could flood continents.
Not a *man* whose compassion echoed louder than his power.
And all the while—he remained silent.

Tyvellmian watched the world watching him.
From the depths. From the shadows. From beyond their instruments and theories.
He didn't fear their weapons.
But he *felt* their confusion.
And he knew—if he did nothing—this storm would only grow.
He had become something more than myth.
He had become a mirror.
And the world didn't like what it saw.

Public Reactions Around the Globe…

New York City – Times Square

Screens blazed with headlines: "TIDAL-MAN: GOD OR MONSTER?" and "TRITON STRIKES—OCEANIC CIVIL WAR?".
People crowded beneath them like worshipers beneath stained glass windows. Some cheered. Others stood silent, fists clenched in awe. A woman wept openly at the sight of the battle replayed in shaky footage.
On the sidewalk, an eight-year-old boy with a tinfoil cape and marker-drawn glyphs on his arms raised his fists into the

a
air. "I'm Tidal-Man! I protect people!" he shouted. His mother pulled him close, watching the screen with unease. In a dimly lit cafe nearby, an older man—retired Navy—muttered to no one in particular, "If he can split the sea like that, he ain't human. But he saved them. I saw it. No one's making that part up."

Lagos, Nigeria – Balogun Market

Vendors paused transactions to gather around battery-powered TVs. A charismatic street preacher climbed atop a cart, Bible in one hand, wireless mic in the other.
"You call him myth? I call him warning! The waters rise not for judgment, but for *reckoning!* Repent! Or be swept away!"
Yet across the road, a young biologist handed out leaflets titled *Oceanic Evolution: Why Tidal-Man Might Be the Next Step in Human Development*. Curious minds gathered. Arguments flared.

Tokyo, Japan – Shibuya Crossing.

Tidal-Man's image was everywhere. Pop idols released music videos with sea-themed visuals. Fan clubs popped up overnight. One popular VTuber held a livestream prayer vigil.
Yet at the Diet building, debates raged over whether to label him a national security threat or a protected global entity.

São Paulo, Brazil – Avenida Paulista.

a

Protestors filled the avenue, waving signs: "WHO DECIDES WHAT'S DIVINE?", "DON'T SHOOT THE GOD WHO SAVED US", and "WE ARE THE CURRENT". Drone-captured footage of the protest spread globally within minutes.

Mumbai, India – Bandra Fort.

Near the Arabian Sea, an elderly woman lit candles in a circle, chanting to the rhythm of ocean waves. She claimed Tidal-Man was the avatar of Varuna reborn.
"The seas remember. The gods are returning. But not all will come with mercy."

Cairo, Egypt – Tahrir Square.

A crowd gathered beneath giant projections of Tyvellmian's blurry figure.
A man in a weathered keffiyeh shouted, "This is not a warning—it is a *test*. Will we fear what we do not understand, or finally listen to it?"
Nearby, two teenagers posted a selfie with a caption: *#SeaDaddySaves*. It went viral within minutes.

The Woman with the Memory.

In a hospital in Marseille, a woman named *Noelle* stirred in her bed, whispering to her nurse.

a
"He saved me. Not now... then. I was nine. Our boat capsized. I saw him—blue light, strong arms... He looked right at me. I told my mother. She said it was the fever."
The nurse froze. The timing matched an unsolved disappearance case from 1984.
Moments later, a Vatican emissary requested an interview with Noelle.

The world wasn't reacting to a single moment.
It was responding to an *idea.*
Tidal-Man had become more than a man.
He was a mirror held up to civilization—reflecting its hope, its fear, and its ever-shifting mythology.

Religious Upheaval. Location: Vatican City –

Private Summit, Undisclosed Chamber
A marble table shaped like a compass rose reflected flickering candlelight and the digital shimmer of translation screens. Seated in quiet gravity were the highest theological minds of the age: the Pope, the Grand Mufti of Al-Azhar, the Shankaracharya of Puri, the Chief Rabbi of Jerusalem, and other spiritual leaders. Their expressions bore the same burden—the impossible truth that had upended thousands of years of dogma.
The Pope leaned forward. "My brethren, our scriptures speak in metaphor. We have survived floods, stars falling, giants walking among men.
But now we have footage. We have names."
The Shankaracharya shook his head. "Or we have

a
temptation. What is power without purpose? If we proclaim him divine, we are idolaters. If we call him false, we may be blaspheming against something beyond comprehension."
The Mufti folded his hands. “Then we must listen. Interpret. God’s language is not always words.”

The Cult Emerges.

In Istanbul, a figure in sea-green robes emerged from the Bosphorus underground to a candlelit warehouse. Followers—barefoot, cloaked—knelt as one.
“The tide has returned,” the figure said. “He is not the god they taught us, but the one the waters preserved. The surface world is unworthy. We must prepare the deep.”
They were called *The Current of the Deep*, a new cult blending prophecy, ecological extremism, and ritualized wave-summoning. Their symbol: a cracked trident entwined with coral.

Fractures in the Faith.

In the American South, pastors split congregations between those who called Tidal-Man a threat—and those who baptized children in his name.

In Nigeria, Imams debated live on air whether the being’s presence fulfilled the prophecy of the Mahdi or was a djinn come to deceive.

In South Korea, Buddhist monks meditated on the rhythm of

a
waves recorded during his last appearance. One monk wept openly and simply said, “We are late. He has always been here.”

Black Ops & Disinformation Campaigns
Langley, Virginia – CIA Black Room B7

Flickering red lights. Unmarked monitors. A windowless chamber buried five floors below the surface. Deputy Director Serena Locke stood before a group of elite intelligence analysts, her voice flat but urgent.
"We’re past the point of surveillance. We’re entering narrative control."
On the screen behind her: dozens of tabs displaying doctored footage, deepfake corrections, forum posts, meme injections, and trending disinformation tags:
#SeaLie,
#WaveWeapon,
#FakeFloodGod.
"We can't kill a god," Locke continued, "but we can make the world stop believing in one."

Operation *Currentfold* was initiated. A full-spectrum psychological operation designed to fracture global consensus around Tidal-Man’s image. Every piece of real footage was spliced with faked anomalies: digital artifacts suggesting holograms, staged rescues, or nanotech interventions.
Global forums were seeded with narratives: Tidal-Man was an alien scout. Tidal-Man was a hallucination from seismic

a
gas leaks. Tidal-Man was a rogue experiment from deep-sea genetic labs.
Paid influencers began mocking his image. "Tidal-Man thirst traps" trended ironically. Conspiracy channels received anonymous boosts to claim he was AI-generated—an art project gone viral.
Locke watched it unfold like chess.
"Control the myth," she whispered. "Drown him in noise."

Beijing – Ministry of State Security Briefing Room
In a secure cyberwarfare center, operatives deployed a parallel initiative. Their goal: flood western networks with falsified evidence of underwater weapons testing, designed to confuse origin stories. One campaign theorized that the Pacific Ring of Fire had triggered an ancient machine. Another claimed Tyvellmian was a Russian deep-dive suit powered by geothermal cores.
Behind the veil, Chinese strategists debated: was he savior or signal? An omen... or an invitation?

Moscow – GRU Command
General Petrov approved an undercover operation: place sleeper agents near religious and academic institutions studying Tidal-Man. Their task? Subtly discredit, subtly fracture. Plant internal discord.
"Make them question themselves. The rest follows."
But the Backlash Fails.
The world proved resistant.

In a South African township, schoolchildren painted murals

a
of Tidal-Man protecting them from pollution.

In Reykjavik, a video surfaced of a fishing crew swearing they'd been rescued by him years before—long before his name reached the headlines.

A viral documentary, *Gods of the Deep*, gained 200 million views in 48 hours. The more disinformation spread, the stronger the belief became.

In the digital age, belief wasn't a light switch. It was wildfire.

Serena Locke's Doubt.

In her private quarters, Locke scrolled through raw footage not meant for public eyes. One clip—Tyvellmian carrying an elderly woman through waist-deep water—stopped her cold. Her finger hovered over the delete key.

She didn't press it.

She exhaled slowly.

"What if we're on the wrong side of this?"

North Atlantic – NATO Command Ship *Resolute Dawn*

The ship creaked under the weight of politics, radar signals, and mounting dread. Admiral Reyes stood on the command deck as the latest satellite data filtered in.

"We've got Russian subs trailing Chinese drones, and an American carrier group two knots from crashing into both. The South Koreans just declared an exclusion zone around Jeju. And that thing—Tidal-Man—was spotted again yesterday near the Azores."

A junior officer handed her a new report: unmarked sonar readings resembling underwater temples. And something moving between them.

a
“Ma’am,” the officer added nervously. “We’re not alone down there.”

Geneva – U.N. Emergency Security Council Briefing
Inside a cold stone hall deep beneath the Palais des Nations, leaders gathered around a circular war table displaying a holographic globe.
U.S. Ambassador Harlow: "We either establish a joint command structure now, or we’ll be reading each other’s body counts tomorrow."
Russian General Petrov: "You want command? Control your ships first. One nearly collided with ours over Tyvellmian’s last signature."
UK Delegate: "This is not a weapons race. It’s an existential threat—or a potential savior."
India, Brazil, South Africa—all voiced varying degrees of uncertainty. Consensus remained elusive. No one could agree on how to classify Tyvellmian: hero, hazard, or herald.

Scenelet: Coastal State Breakdown
In smaller, ocean-bordering nations—Indonesia, Chile, Fiji—the strain was worse. Emergency coastlines were militarized overnight. Fishing routes were closed. The ocean itself became a contested territory.
The Maldives declared a “Sovereign Sea Zone,” barring foreign vessels. The Philippines scrambled to develop a sonar defense grid, backed by a classified satellite network.
In Norway, a leaked report suggested the government had located an underwater site glowing with bio-thermal signatures—buried thousands of years ago. It was under

a
immediate military lockdown.

Surface Tensions…
Protests erupted in Tel Aviv and Istanbul. Anti-war demonstrators chanted alongside sea-worship cultists. Naval officers defected. A South African fleet captain publicly stated, “If this being returns to help the innocent, I’ll stand down before I aim a missile at him.”

The statement cost him his commission—and made him an overnight folk hero.

The Silent Watcher.

From the cliffs above Madeira, Tyvellmian watched warships thread the Atlantic below. He didn’t need sonar to sense their fear. He could feel it in the ripples, the nervous churn of propellers. His name traveled on sonar pulses now, encoded in machine language: “Target Alpha. Threat Class Unknown.”

He closed his eyes. The ocean whispered beneath him—not in anger, but in sorrow.

Scientific Fallout

Cambridge, Massachusetts – M.I.T. Department of Theoretical Physics

Dr. Aris Thorne stood before a packed auditorium, yet silence gripped the room. The screen behind him displayed a still frame of Tidal-Man parting a hurricane-force wave.

“This isn’t weather manipulation,” he said. “This is harmonic reality interference. The laws of thermodynamics were not broken—they stepped aside.”

A student raised a hand. “Are we looking at the emergence of a new physics?”

a

"No," Thorne replied. "We're witnessing a return to one older than our understanding."

Biology Without Borders.

In Copenhagen, marine biologist Dr. Vera Nakashima studied coral samples recovered from an area Tidal-Man was seen swimming through. The coral had grown in unnatural spirals, mimicking ancient symbols. Its pigmentation held trace elements of a compound not found anywhere else on Earth.

"Not evolution," she whispered to herself. "Design."

Her findings were quietly transmitted to a think tank in Zurich. Within 24 hours, she was offered a blank-check grant—and warned to stay silent.

Collapse of the Conventional.

NASA's Jet Propulsion Lab had once led the race to map planetary mechanics. Now, half their team was reassigned to tracking water anomalies across the globe. Reports came in: rising thermoclines, disappearing gyres, submerged ruins glowing with thermal pulses.

Dr. Saul Jenrich, a climatologist, sent a simple memo to leadership:

"We're no longer observing Earth. We're watching something else *reacting* through it."

A Myth Confirmed.

At the Smithsonian's mytho-anthropology wing, a shattered tablet unearthed in the Aegean was re-examined. Carbon-dated to 6,000 BCE, it showed a humanoid figure with tridents for limbs and whirlpools for eyes. The glyph beside it once mistranslated as 'monster' now read differently: "He Who Stays the Flood."

a
A curator quietly adjusted the display.
Tidal Echoes.
In New Zealand, dolphins began echoing back sonar clicks resembling rhythmic chants. Off the coast of Greenland, a pod of humpbacks formed a migration ring—something never before recorded. Coral across the Mariana Trench began pulsing with bioluminescence timed to the lunar tide. Nature, it seemed, wasn't adapting. It was... remembering.
Thorne's Reckoning…
Dr. Thorne sat alone in his Cambridge office, watching the media hysteria unfold. His academic colleagues had either vanished into black-budget programs or quit in disillusionment. He reached for an old leather notebook, scribbling in the margins:
"We mistook mystery for ignorance. We were never the masters of this world. Only visitors."
He didn't send the paper in for peer review.
He sent it to Tyvellmian.
Environmental and Planetary Effects
The Pulse of the Ocean.
Tide patterns across the globe no longer followed predicted models.
In Madagascar, ancient mangrove forests began expanding at an unprecedented rate. Rivers reversed course for days at a time in Southeast Asia. In the Arctic, glaciers calved in harmonic intervals as if following a breath held by the Earth itself.
Satellites picked up anomalous heat signatures in mid-ocean gyres—spirals of energy resembling sonar glyphs, visible only in infrared. Marine life patterns shifted dramatically.

a
Squid bloomed off Nova Scotia. Whale migrations drifted into urban coastlines. Entire species, previously extinct or unrecorded, began surfacing near populated shores.

The Living Earth.

Volcanologists in Iceland recorded new fault lines forming in patterns resembling waveforms. A South American volcano pulsed bioluminescent lava once every six hours—exactly matching the heart rate of a stranded whale examined in Patagonia.

Seismologists and climatologists conferred and discovered microquakes across the Pacific aligning with lunar tides and *Tidal-Man sightings.*

The Earth was no longer a passive setting. It was responding. Coordinating.

Skyward Effects.

The auroras began appearing farther south. Above Rome. Above Sydney. Electrical engineers in Kenya noticed that some atmospheric fluctuations mirrored tidal rhythms, interrupting satellite signal flows in pulses timed to oceanic depths.

Astronomers in Chile noted a faint gravitational anomaly—a slight pull, stronger during Tyvellmian's known locations. It was as if his presence bent not just the ocean, but *spacetime itself.*

The Coral Memory

Divers off the coast of Micronesia uncovered a reef that pulsed like a brain. Each ridge, when touched, emitted sonic pulses—tones echoing speech-like patterns. When analyzed, the pulses aligned with rhythmic phonemes found in a dead Mediterranean language.

a

One diver, overwhelmed by the vibrations, claimed to hear a name repeated again and again: "Tyvellmian."

The Tidal Library.

Hidden beneath the Java Sea, Indonesian deep-sea archaeologists mapped a ruin previously considered myth: a temple with walls of obsidian coral. Inside, relief carvings depicted a being radiating waves of light, surrounded by both sea creatures and kneeling humans. The walls depicted storms—then serenity—where the being's hand touched the water.

One final glyph near the altar depicted two symbols: a broken trident and a spiral sun.

The scientists dubbed it: *The Covenant Chamber.*

A Whisper to the Planet.

Tyvellmian sat cross-legged on a rock shelf miles below the surface, his eyes closed. Around him, the sea shimmered not with anger—but reverence. Creatures of the deep circled him silently: a whale shark, a ribbon eel, a school of translucent squid glowing like a dream.

He listened—not just to water, but to the crust, the mantle, the magnetic hum of the planet. And what he heard was simple:

Welcome back.

Tyvellmian's Perspective – Watching It All

He stood at the edge of a precipice beneath the waves, the light above a distant memory blurred by leagues of water and centuries of silence. The world churned in chaos above—he had felt it, every sonar ping, every coded whisper, every trembling current.

a

Tyvellmian was not hiding. He was listening.

He felt the grief of coral crushed beneath steel hulls. He heard the confused calls of whales, the migrations disrupted by war machines, the sea birds that did not return to their nests. But he also felt the warmth of coastal fires lit in his name, the flicker of human gratitude like phosphorescence in the dark.

The whispers of mortals reached even the trench where he rested—some called him savior, others heretic. But it was Galena's voice, remembered from that moment of stillness in the storm, that centered him. Her belief had been wordless, but powerful. It grounded him more than the weight of the ocean ever could.

He watched the planet unfold with a clarity no mortal could know. Time felt stretched here. A thousand years blinked in his memory, yet the pulse of the Earth now beat faster. He saw the battle not as one of gods versus men, but of order versus compassion, of cycles resisting change.

He sensed his siblings near. Triton nursed his fury in the Mariana Divide. Benthesikyme stirred currents around disputed waters. Nereus swam like a storm given flesh, his envy pulsing like venom.

They were not evil. They were afraid.

And yet, so was he.

Afraid not of war, but of the cost of peace. Of what it meant to let go of godhood. To reach out instead of reign down. Could compassion survive divinity? Could love thrive in a world built on conquest?

These were questions no storm could answer.

a

He rose from the depths.

As he ascended, the waters parted like old friends, currents swirling in reverent spirals. His silhouette shimmered in the moonlight above, unnoticed by the satellites and warships that scanned the surface.

He wasn't returning as a savior. Not as a god.

He was returning as a witness—to protect, to resist, and to remind the world that the sea remembers everything. Even mercy.

a

Chapter VI

Tyvellmian's Dilemma

The sea salt stung Tyvellmian's face, a familiar discomfort that did little to soothe the turmoil within. He stood on the precipice of a cliff overlooking the churning sea, the waves mirroring the tempest in his soul. The rescue, the act of defiance against his father's wrath, played on repeat in his mind. The faces of the survivors, their expressions of shock and gratitude, were etched into his memory, a stark contrast

a

to the cold fury he'd witnessed in Poseidon's eyes. He'd saved them, yes, but at what cost?

He had defied the will of his father, the god of the sea, the very essence of his own being. Poseidon, in his rage, had unleashed his siblings upon him – a trio of relentless forces bent on punishing him for his transgression. Their attacks, subtle yet potent, had begun to unravel his control over his powers. He felt the ocean's currents resisting him, the waves refusing to obey his commands, a subtle yet terrifying reminder of his father's power.

They say I've betrayed my kind, he thought, the words bitter on his tongue. But how can I stand by and watch innocents perish? How can I condemn these mortals to drown while my family wreaks havoc upon the world? The conflict tore at him, a constant gnawing at his conscience. The weight of his heritage pressed down, the expectation of unwavering obedience to Poseidon choking him. He was, after all, the son of a god. He should have been wreaking havoc alongside his siblings, not saving mortal human lives.

Yet, the memory of the woman's eyes, wide with surprise and then dawning hope, clung to him like a lifeline. Her face, framed by wind-tossed hair, emerged from the swirling vortex of guilt and fear. She was a stranger, yet her silent gratitude had stirred something within him, a crack in the hardened shell of his divine lineage. A compassion that had been dormant for millennia, a whisper of humanity in the heart of a god. He'd felt a connection to her, a kinship he'd never experienced before. A human connection that threatened to shatter the very foundation of his being.

a

He clenched his fists, the ocean's fury mirroring his own. He was torn between two worlds, two loyalties that clashed like thunder and lightning. The loyalty to his father, to his family, to his heritage, screamed at him in the thunderous roar of the waves. Yet, another voice, softer but equally insistent, pleaded for the humans, for the woman whose eyes he could still see.

He thought of Arconia, his niece, his only link to something resembling normalcy. She understood the chasm that separated him from the world of mortals. Her own inherent strength and defiance, while much subtler than his own, provided a solace he was desperately craving. She didn't judge his compassion, instead acknowledging the turmoil he was experiencing. She had offered him a safe haven, a place where he could shed the burden of his divinity for a time, a place where he could be something less than a god, something… human.

His father's pronouncements echoed in his ears, chilling reminders of his impending punishment. He's weak. He's soft. He has shown mercy to the pathetic mortals. He deserves nothing less than our wrath. Poseidon's words felt like icy claws scraping against his soul. He knew his siblings wouldn't hesitate to inflict the punishment, their divine fury fueled by their own resentments and jealousies. They would relish the opportunity to crush him, to prove their dominance over him.

But the memory of the woman's eyes kept him anchored. The faces of the rescued, their lives hanging in the balance, their unexpected survival a testament to a compassion that seemed to stem from a place beyond his own divinity. He

a
remembered the sheer terror in their eyes as the storm raged. And he recalled the quiet triumph as they were pulled from the raging water, given a new chance at life. The conflict was not merely between him and his family. It was a conflict within him, a war between his inherited nature and the newfound empathy he carried. He was the son of a god, yes, but he was also something more. Or perhaps, something else entirely. He was a being capable of both immense destruction and unexpected compassion. He could unleash the full fury of the ocean or offer solace in the storm's eye. The choice was his, and he felt the weight of that choice crushing him.

The wind whipped around him, carrying the scent of brine and the distant cries of gulls. He closed his eyes, seeking solace in the familiar sounds of the ocean, yet finding only the echoes of his father's wrath. He was trapped, caught in a web of his own making, a dilemma of his own creation. The world was divided, not just between gods and mortals, but between the warring factions within himself. He was a symbol of hope for some, a symbol of chaos and fear for others.

The weight of his actions pressed upon him, heavier than any ocean wave. He wasn't merely a prince; he was a symbol, a testament to the complexities of divinity, a being struggling to reconcile his inherited destiny with the compassion he had discovered within his own heart. He had chosen mercy over obedience, and now he would have to live with the consequences. The question was, would he endure? And if so, could he find a way to navigate this world divided, without succumbing to the pressures of his

a
family or the expectations of mankind?

His hands trembled slightly as he opened his eyes, the horizon stretching before him, boundless and unpredictable, just like his future. He felt the pull of his father's power, a tangible force trying to reel him back, to force his obedience. But he also felt something else, a strength born not of divine power alone, but of a newfound understanding. He'd defied his father, chosen humanity over his lineage, and in doing so, he had found something within himself—a resilience that even Poseidon couldn't easily extinguish.

The taste of salt lingered on Tyvellmian's lips, a constant reminder of the storm, of Galena. He knew her name now, a fragile whisper amidst the chaos, a lifeline in the tumultuous sea of his own internal conflict. Finding her was no longer a mere impulse, a fleeting desire to reconnect with the spark of humanity he had discovered within himself; it had become a necessity, a crucial element in navigating the treacherous waters of his present predicament.

His investigation began not with grand pronouncements or divine interventions, but with the meticulous gathering of information. He started with the survivors, their fragmented memories forming a jigsaw puzzle of the nightmarish storm. He moved through their accounts, seamlessly weaving together their collective experiences, each detail meticulously examined, each word weighted for its truth. He discovered a pattern – a recurring mention of a woman with striking emerald eyes and hair the color of spun moonlight, a woman who had displayed exceptional calm

a
in the face of utter devastation.
Their descriptions were varied, yet their core message remained the same. They spoke of her quiet strength, her unwavering compassion for others, her ability to inspire hope in the face of despair. These fragmented memories, initially seemingly insignificant, coalesced in his mind, forming a clearer image of Galena. He wasn't just searching for a woman; he was hunting for a spirit, a beacon of hope in the storm-ravaged world.
His divine abilities, normally unleashed with devastating force, were now employed with a delicate precision. He didn't summon tidal waves or manipulate ocean currents; instead, he used his innate connection to the sea, to the very essence of the water itself, to trace the currents that had carried Galena from the wreckage to safety. He felt the subtle shift in the water, a faint ripple in the ocean's memory, guiding him toward her last known location.
It was a painstaking process, like tracing the faintest of footprints in the sand. He had to sift through the countless currents, the endless flow of the ocean, to find the specific one that had carried Galena, a needle in the vast haystack of the world's waters. Each surge, each ebb, whispered secrets to him – the direction of her rescue, the path her body had taken. The sea, once a source of his divine power, now served as a tool, a guide in his personal quest.
The investigation took him from the shores of the disaster site to the bustling city docks, where the luxury liner had embarked on its ill-fated voyage. He navigated the labyrinthine streets, his presence almost imperceptible, a shadow flitting through the bustling city. He didn't seek to

a

make a spectacle of his abilities; instead, he observed, listened, and learned. He moved through the crowds unseen, a phantom in the heart of the metropolis, his senses heightened, his perception amplified.

He delved into the records of the ship, the passenger manifests and crew lists, a painstaking process of sifting through names and details. The passenger list revealed a startling number of people unaccounted for. He noticed anomalies in the surviving accounts, discrepancies in the passenger details that pointed toward a possible cover-up. His initial compassion was tempered by a growing sense of unease. The human element was proving far more complex than he'd initially anticipated.

This new investigation, far from the grand scale of divine battles, was a humbling experience. He was forced to rely on his wit and intelligence, not just his power. He unearthed inconsistencies in official reports, subtle hints that pointed to a deeper conspiracy, a web of lies spun around the sinking of the luxury liner. The rescue was not just a tragic accident; it was a calculated event, shrouded in a veil of secrecy.

He found himself in unexpected places – dimly lit bars, crowded markets, the hushed corridors of government offices, all the while remaining unnoticed. He gathered information from various sources – dock workers, sailors, even high-ranking officials. He moved like a ghost, always one step ahead, always gathering pieces of the puzzle. Each clue was a breadcrumb, leading him closer to Galena, closer to understanding the truth behind the storm.

His ability to blend seamlessly into the human world

a

proved invaluable. He adopted disguises, altering his appearance effortlessly, moving from one social stratum to another, gathering information without arousing suspicion. His keen observation skills and his innate ability to decipher subtle cues made him an unparalleled investigator. He could read people like a book, understanding their motivations, their fears, their lies.

This journey, however, wasn't merely about finding Galena. It was about understanding the world he had previously dismissed as insignificant. He saw the fragility of humanity, their capacity for both great cruelty and extraordinary kindness, a spectrum of emotions that mirrored, albeit on a smaller scale, the conflict within his own divine nature.

He was beginning to appreciate the intricate tapestry of human relationships, the subtle nuances of their interactions, the motivations that drove them. He had once viewed humans as mere pawns in the larger game of the gods, insignificant beings caught in the crossfire of divine battles. Now, he saw them as individuals, each with their own unique stories, their own triumphs and failures, their own hopes and fears.

His search continued relentlessly, a slow, meticulous process of piecing together the fragments of a shattered world. He was no longer just the Tidal Man, a symbol of hope in the face of divine wrath; he was becoming a detective, a seeker of truth, a man determined to find the woman who had changed the course of his life. The stakes were higher than he could have ever imagined. He was not only searching for Galena but also searching for himself,

a
his place in the world, his identity amidst the clash of divine and human worlds.
His journey would not be easy; he knew this. He faced not only the obstacles of a sprawling metropolis but also the looming threat of his family's vengeance. Yet, he pressed on, driven by an unwavering determination, a quiet resolve that stemmed from a newfound sense of purpose. The woman with eyes like emeralds was his compass, his beacon in the storm, guiding him through the treacherous path he'd chosen. The path of a god who had discovered compassion, a god who had chosen humanity over his own kind. And in making that choice, he had discovered a strength far greater than any divine power. His search continued, and with each clue, he felt closer to a resolution, not just to the mystery surrounding Galena's disappearance, but to the turmoil within his own soul. The world might be divided, but his resolve was stronger than ever. His quest was not just a search for a woman, but a search for himself.

a

Chapter VII

A Brother's Pursuit.

The city's relentless hum was a counterpoint to the quiet intensity of Tyvellmian's focus. He'd traced Galena's path to a secluded district, a maze of narrow alleys and shadowed buildings—a far cry from the opulent hotels and shimmering towers of glass that defined the city's glossier exterior. Here, the air hung thick with salt, rust, and decay. A place of forgotten lives and whispered warnings. And yet, this was where the trail had led him. Chaos and beauty entwined—just like her.

He moved with the grace of vapor, his steps soundless on worn cobblestones. Every whisper of breath, every creak of shuttered windows reached his ears. His divine senses picked up the faintest reverberations—a door closing three blocks away, the pressure change of footsteps on nearby rooftops. He inhaled deeply. Someone was following him. No—something.

The air shifted. A cold draft swept the alley despite the city's summer heat. He paused. Not fear, but wariness stilled him. This wasn't mortal pursuit. It was colder, older, sharp as coral reef. He turned his head slightly. The faint echo of a tide long buried stirred in his chest. He recognized the presence.

Triton.

a

His brother.

Born of Poseidon's wrath and mothered by a sea goddess lost to myth, Triton embodied the ocean's cruelty. Tyvellmian had tried to reject that heritage. Triton had embraced it. While Tyvellmian had walked among mortals to understand them, Triton had remained submerged, gathering strength, brooding over old slights, convinced that he—first son, true heir—had been denied.

Tyvellmian picked up his pace. The hunt had begun.

He flowed up a rusted fire escape in a blink, the metal groaning quietly beneath his boots. From the rooftop, he surveyed the vast grid of the city's lower districts. Shattered neon signs flickered over cracked concrete. Garbage fires lit alleyways like ancient signal pyres. But what concerned him was the sea breeze—warmer now, carrying a scent like ozone and blood.

Below, chaos bloomed. Triton was not hiding. He was heralding.

Cracks split asphalt where he walked. Water burst from storm drains as if seeking him. Screams rose in waves as people fled a man no mortal could truly comprehend. Tyvellmian saw him now: a golden figure striding toward the docks, his cloak billowing with unnatural wind, lightning coiling in his wake.

Tyvellmian turned away, running.

He vaulted from rooftop to rooftop. A blur of motion above a panicked city. Cars swerved below him, alarms shrieked, dogs howled. A wind, fierce and unrelenting, chased his heels. He could feel Triton's

a

wrath bubbling beneath the surface—contained only by his desire to corner, not kill.

Yet.

Psychic pressure slammed into Tyvellmian's mind like a tidal surge. Thoughts not his own. Visions.

He saw Galena—trapped, drowning, crying out.

He faltered.

The illusion broke an instant later, but it was enough. Triton had closed the distance.

"Brother!" came the voice, booming from rooftops away. "Stop running!"

Tyvellmian didn't. Not yet. Not here.

He turned sharply, descending into a shadowed stairwell leading beneath the street—an old transit tunnel, abandoned decades ago. Here, the air was wet with mildew, and the silence was thick. He paused only long enough to scrawl an arcane symbol in the dust on a metal pillar. A ward—not to protect, but to misdirect. Let Triton chase ghosts for a moment longer.

Through tunnels, past shattered gates, he emerged into the harbor district. The moon hung low over the bay, staining the water silver. The docks sprawled before him, ancient and rotting, each creaking board moaning with memory. This was where it would happen.

He stepped out onto the pier, boots thudding softly on warped wood.

Then came the cold.

a

Triton arrived in a fury of wind and vapor. He walked atop the water, each step sending ripples out in concentric waves. His armor shimmered gold and black, etched with moving glyphs. Behind him rose a swell of sea serpents, hissing and coiling in anticipation.

“Tyvellmian.” The name dripped venom.

Tyvellmian didn’t flinch. “You came for blood, not conversation.”

“I came for our father’s legacy.” Triton’s voice thundered across the waves. “You desecrate it with your weakness. She—this Galena—has turned you into a shadow.”

Tyvellmian’s eyes narrowed. “She showed me the surface is not all corruption. That strength is not just fury.”

Triton sneered. “Then you are unfit.”

Energy surged between them. The ocean hissed. The sky cracked with distant lightning.

Then, they moved.

The dock exploded.

Triton lashed out with a trident forged from Leviathan bone, summoning a geyser beneath Tyvellmian’s feet. Tyvellmian rolled through the spray, landing on broken boards, retaliating with a whip of condensed current. It cracked against Triton’s armor, leaving scorch marks that healed instantly.

The battle churned the bay. Boats capsized. Buildings

a

groaned. Sirens blared.

And then, in a single flash of blue light, Tyvellmian dove into the sea, pulling the fight to deeper ground.

The ocean wrapped around him like a memory. Cold. Familiar. Powerful.

He descended, fast, toward the Mariana Rift. A trench where ancient creatures dreamed in darkness. He needed the depths—needed to draw Triton away from the surface, from the humans.

But even here, peace eluded him.

The rift pulsed.

He slowed, trident at the ready. Something stirred. Not Triton. Not yet.

A shadow moved. Then three.

Roh-Ghul came first—a behemoth of rust and coral, his fists dragging broken ship anchors. Sirenae followed, gliding like sorrow, eyes devoid of warmth. And the last, Karkyn—swift, armored, blades drawn. These were no allies. These were thralls. Triton's advance guard.

Without a word, Roh-Ghul attacked.

Tyvellmian parried. Chains clashed with divine metal, sending sonic ripples that shook the seabed. Sirenae disappeared into mist, reappearing behind him with whispering illusions. Galena drowning. The sky burning. All lies. But potent ones.

He growled, struck back, sending a concussive wave that shattered Karkyn's blade mid-lunge. The

a

assassin recoiled, bleeding ink.

Sirenae hissed.

Tyvellmian spun, hurling his trident. It pinned her through the abdomen into a coral wall. Her form unraveled, shrieking.

Roh-Ghul lunged again. Tyvellmian bound him in vortex tendrils, then hurled molten stone into his chest, sealing him in a cocoon of basalt.

Karkyn attacked.

They clashed. Once. Twice. Then Tyvellmian caught his throat.

"You don't even know what you fight for," he spat. Power surged from his palm. Karkyn went limp, his armor cracking, sinking into the abyss.

Silence fell.

And then—a roar.

Triton emerged.

The maelstrom parted. His golden armor glowed. Sea serpents curled behind him like living flags. His eyes were whirlpools.

"You've grown stronger," Triton said. "But still, you are nothing."

Tyvellmian hovered, wounded, defiant.

"Then why are you afraid?" he answered.

They surged toward each other—one last collision pending—when Tyvellmian raised a hand. A current spun upward.

From the trench below, glowing manta rays rose like

a

stars.

They wrapped around him, a shield of light and speed.

In a burst, Tyvellmian vanished upward.

Triton bellowed in frustration, the trench shaking with his fury.

As Tyvellmian raced toward the surface, his blood mixing with salt and light, one truth rang clear:

This was not a victory.

This was a warning.

Poseidon's court would rise. The gods would choose sides. And next time—

There would be no escape.

Tyvellmian lay in a half-collapsed sea cave, his body battered and spirit frayed. The tide lapped at the stone entrance, and above the waves, the world moved on in ignorance. News drones hovered miles out at sea, recording surges and whirlpools without explanation. Emergency broadcasts warned of rogue seismic events. No one knew the truth—that two sons of a forgotten god had nearly torn the earth in two.

Each breath burned. The divine venom laced into Triton's trident still clung to his wounds, resisting natural healing. Tyvellmian pressed a trembling hand to his side and summoned the water's warmth. Not to fight—but to heal. It answered him, faintly.

Meanwhile, in a dim hostel somewhere inland, Galena stirred from uneasy sleep. Her fingers tingled with salt and light. She sat up and reached for her

a

notebook, where dozens of erratic sketches had begun filling the pages without conscious thought. One now stood out: a perfect rendering of the Mariana Rift… and rising from it, a halo of glowing manta rays.

She did not understand how she knew.

In Poseidon's deep dominion, the old court rumbled. The marble amphitheater shimmered with bio-luminescence. Ancient sea gods and emissaries argued fiercely. The throne of Poseidon remained vacant, crusted with barnacles. Some whispered he had abandoned them. Others insisted he merely slept.

"The younger son defies our laws," snarled one delegate.

"He defies our stagnation," countered Thalassa, the oracle of tides, her form shifting between kelp and stormcloud.

"Silence, all of you," hissed a figure from the shadows—Charyss, Keeper of the Abyss. "Triton prepares for war. That is all that matters now."

Triton himself stood beneath a chasm lined with siren stone, his armor splintered but his fury undimmed. Around him, chained beasts howled from the deeps. One of his lieutenants, a shark-blooded brute, whimpered after delivering news of failure.

Triton lifted a single finger. The soldier's body imploded inward.

He stared into an obsidian pool, showing images of Earth—oil spills, war machines, plastic-choked reefs.

"This world is unworthy," he growled. "I will return

a

it to the sea."

And he began summoning the Tidal Generals—one by one.

Far above, Tyvellmian sat upright.

The sea whispered to him. The world had shifted.

He stared out into the rising sun and carved a new mark into the stone wall beside him. Not Poseidon's trident. Something new. A glyph of balance—of wrath restrained.

He rose, slowly. Purpose returning.

"If the gods declare war on the surface," he murmured, "then let the first god who chooses peace stand and be counted."

And he stepped forward, into the dawn.

a

Chapter 8

A Chance Encounter

The old shipyard smelled of brine and rust, a symphony of decay that clashed jarringly with the faint floral scent clinging to Galena's hair. She was perched precariously on a crumbling crate, her eyes wide, reflecting the flickering gaslight that cast long, distorted shadows across her face.

Tyvellmian broke the surface of the sea with a gasping heave, scattering glowing manta rays as he collapsed onto the shoreline. The sand clung to his skin, his blood painted the water crimson where it lapped at his body. Every movement ached. His side was torn, his hands were raw and the ancient pulse of the ocean seemed to grow heavier with every breath he drew. Triton's warriors had been no mere distraction. They had been sent to end him. He rolled on his back staring at the sky. "Is this what it means to choose humanity?" he thought bitterly, "to bleed for a people who would never know the cost?"

The scene was utterly incongruous – a delicate flower blooming in a field of

a

thorns, a whisper of elegance in the harsh, unforgiving landscape of the docks. Tyvellmian heard footsteps crunching lightly on the sand approaching slowly, each step measured, mindful of the fragility of this moment. He didn't need to look to know who it was. He could feel her, like a change in the tide, a pull on his very soul. He had found her, but the reunion was far from the idyllic scene he had envisioned.

Galena hadn't screamed, hadn't run. Instead, a strange blend of fear and disbelief held her captive, her gaze fixed on him with an unnerving intensity. She was different from the woman he'd rescued from the churning waves, her youthful vibrancy dulled by a layer of apprehension, her eyes haunted by a lingering trauma that mirrored his own. The storm had left its mark on both of them, etching itself into the fabric of their souls.

Galena knelt beside him, her hands trembling as she brushed seaweed from his brow. Her hair damp, strands clinging to her cheeks and her eyes shimmered wide with fear and something else. Something fiercer.

"Galena," he said, his voice barely a

a whisper, afraid to break the fragile spell that bound them together.

"You're hurt," she whispered, her voice breaking up.

Tyvellmian tried to sit up, but the pain in his ribs made him grunt and collapse back. His pride hurting more than his body.

"It's nothing," he rasped.

"You're a terrible liar," she said, managing a small soft smile.

Her breath hitched, a barely audible gasp that seemed to hang suspended in the still night air. Her eyes, previously fixed on him, flickered away, tracing the contours of the dilapidated surroundings as if seeking an escape route, a way to flee the reality of his presence. He understood her apprehension. He was, after all, a being of immense power, a god in human form, a figure plucked from the realm of myth and legend. His very existence was a transgression, a disruption of the ordinary.

"I... I don't understand," she stammered, her voice a trembling thread, barely audible above the rhythmic crash of the waves against the decaying pilings. Her fingers instinctively reached for the worn leather strap of her bag, a subtle but revealing gesture that betrayed her fear. She was a survivor, he realized, a woman

who had witnessed the terrifying power of the storm firsthand, a storm he had, in a way, unleashed.

For a moment he said nothing. His gaze locked with hers and in that silence, something unspoken passed between them. An understanding that no storm could ever wash away.

He knelt before her, lowering himself until he was on her level, his gaze gentle, his demeanor as non-threatening as he could muster.

“I know it’s... unexpected,” he began, his voice carefully modulated, a balm to her frayed nerves. “But I had to see you again.”

Her gaze finally met his, and he saw a flicker of recognition ignite within those depths, a fleeting memory struggling to surface from the depths of her fear. It was a fragile spark, easily extinguished, and he knew he had to tread carefully, to navigate this delicate dance of emotions with utmost sensitivity.

“You... you saved me,” she said, her voice still trembling but regaining a hint of clarity, the memory of the storm, the chaos, the terror, beginning to pierce through the veil of her disbelief. “On the... the boat.”

a

"Yes," he affirmed, his heart swelling with a strange mixture of relief and trepidation. The memory was as vivid to him as it was to her – the raging storm, the screams, the chaos, the fear in her eyes as he had pulled her from the crushing waves. It was a moment etched into his soul, a turning point, a catalyst that had set in motion the events that had led him here, to this desolate corner of the city, to this precarious reunion.

"But… how…?" she whispered, her voice barely audible, her mind struggling to reconcile the impossible reality of a god standing before her. He understood her skepticism. The world wasn't ready for the existence of gods, not yet. And he, Tyvellmian, son of Poseidon, was perhaps the most unexpected of them all.

He didn't attempt to explain the complexities of his divine lineage. He didn't unleash a torrent of mythical tales. Instead, he offered her a simple truth, a truth that transcended the realms of gods and mortals.

"I saw your fear," he said, his voice filled with a gentle understanding. "And I couldn't leave you to face it alone."

Galena pressed a hand to his chest, feeling the faint staggering beat of his heart.

a

Her eyes, for a moment, widened, reflecting a glimmer of something that resembled awe, a quiet understanding that extended beyond the mere act of saving her life. It was the recognition of something deeper, something more profound – an act of compassion that defied the expectations of his divine nature, an act that had shaken his own world to its very core.

She reached out, her hand hesitantly touching his arm, her fingers brushing against his skin, a gesture as tentative as a butterfly's wings. It was a gesture of trust, a fragile bridge across the chasm that separated gods and mortals, a testament to the enduring power of compassion.

"Let me help you," she said.

He closed his eyes. Letting her was harder than facing Triton. Still, he nodded.

The silence that followed was filled with unspoken words, with unspoken emotions, a silent communion of two souls bound by a shared experience, a shared trauma, and a shared, unexpected connection. The setting sun cast long shadows across their faces, painting their reunion in hues of both hope and uncertainty, a testament to the complexities of their newfound connection.

a

The air crackled with anticipation, not of the impending confrontation with his brother, but of the unspoken promises that hung between them, a delicate balance that could shatter at any moment. He knew that his revelation would change everything – for her, for him, and for the world that struggled to understand the existence of beings like him. But for now, he held onto this moment, this fragile connection, a beacon of hope in the gathering darkness. The old shipyard, once a symbol of decay and neglect, had become the unexpected setting for a new beginning, a new hope, a new bond forged between a god and a mortal, a bond stronger than the raging storm that had brought them together.

Under the shelter of a craggy overhang by the beach, Galena tended to him. She cleaned his wounds with gentle hands, muttering curses at the stubbornness of divine beings. Tyvellmian watched her with something like awe. She was no warrior, no wielder of tridents or magic storms and yet she cared for him in a way no one else ever had.

He knew he couldn't stay here for long. Triton's presence still lingered, a palpable threat that echoed through the air, a

a

reminder of the battle that still awaited him. But for now, he allowed himself to bask in the warmth of this unexpected reunion, the fragility of this new connection. He had found Galena, but the journey had only just begun, a journey that would lead them into uncharted territory, a journey that would test the very boundaries of their newfound bond. The world, after all, was far from ready for the truth about Tyvellmian, the Tidal Man, and the woman who had changed his life forever. The journey to understanding, both for himself and for Galena, was just beginning.

The city's lights twinkled in the distance, a million tiny sparks against the vast canvas of the night sky. Galena's gaze shifted towards the city, a mixture of wonder and apprehension reflected in her eyes. He knew she was still processing the enormity of their encounter. The concept of a god, a son of Poseidon, saving her from a catastrophic storm was far beyond the realm of her comprehension. But he also saw a spark of curiosity, a desire to understand, a willingness to accept the impossible.

He offered her a gentle smile, a promise of understanding, a reassurance that he

a

would answer her questions, in her own time. He wouldn't force her to accept the truth, nor would he shield her from it. Their relationship, he realized, would be a journey of discovery, a slow, delicate unfolding of truths, both divine and human. Beyond the beach the ocean murmured. Tyvellmian realized something terrifying: He could defeat a hundred Tritons. He could withstand Poseidon's wrath, but this…this fragile, fierce mortal woman, might be the one force he could not survive.

He whispered her name once, almost prayer-like. And for the first time since abandoning Poseidon's call, Tyvellmian allowed himself to hope.

He stood up, extending a hand towards her. The touch was almost hesitant, acknowledging the fragility of their newfound connection. She took his hand, her fingers intertwining with his, a silent promise of understanding, a shared journey into the unknown. As they walked away from the crumbling docks, leaving behind the echoes of the storm and the shadows of their shared past, he felt a surge of hope, a conviction that even amidst the raging turmoil of the divine world, love, compassion and understanding could prevail.

The journey ahead was fraught with dangers, but he was no longer alone. He had Galena. And that, he realized, was a power greater than any he had ever known. The battle with Triton loomed, but for now, the quiet peace of this unexpected encounter, the gentle warmth of Galena’s hand in his, was a solace, a strength he would carry with him into the tumultuous days ahead. The city lights beckoned, and they walked towards them, hand-in-hand, two souls navigating the unknown, their future as uncertain as the turbulent sea, yet filled with a hope as boundless as the ocean itself.

They found temporary shelter in a forgotten ferry terminal, its glass long shattered and roof half-collapsed. Tyvellmian insisted on taking the floor despite his injuries, while Galena rummaged through an old maintenance locker, producing a moth-eaten blanket and a metal lantern that still worked.

“I’ve had worse,” he said dryly, as she wrapped the threadbare fabric around him.

“You look like hell,” she replied, kneeling beside him. “But I’ve never seen anything more… impossible.”

Silence lingered between them, heavier now that the adrenaline had ebbed. Tyvellmian’s

a

breathing slowed, but the pain remained sharp, not just in his body, but somewhere deeper. He glanced at her.

"Do you believe in fate, Galena?"

She shook her head. "I used to believe in patterns. Probability. Not anymore."

He nodded. "The ocean doesn't believe in straight lines either. It's all motion. Chaos. But there are tides beneath even that. Currents we don't see."

"You're speaking in riddles."

"I'm trying not to scare you."

Galena leaned back, studying his face. "Too late for that." Then softer: "But also… not as much as you'd think."

Tyvellmian offered the barest smile, but winced at the effort. "That night on the ship… something changed in me. I didn't just save you. You pulled me out, too. Out of something darker."

They sat in silence, the occasional howl of wind whistling through broken windows. Outside, the sea whispered as if listening.

Galena eventually broke the quiet. "There's more, isn't there? About you. About all this."

"Yes. Much more."

"Then start from the beginning."

He hesitated. "Not all of it will make sense."

"Try me."

So he told her—not everything, not yet—but

a

enough. About the court beneath the waves, about Triton’s fury, about how the old gods still lingered beneath the ocean, and how he had turned away from them. About the rings of coral that marked the exile of a sea-born prince. About his decision to walk the land like a mortal, not because he was weak—but because he finally understood strength.

She listened. Not all of it landed. Her mind stumbled over the scale of what he said. But she didn’t pull away. That alone gave him strength.

“Why me?” she finally asked.

“I don’t know,” he admitted. “Maybe you were just the first voice I heard above the waves. Or maybe…”

“Maybe I’m your tide?” she said, half-joking.

He blinked, then laughed—an actual laugh, hoarse and real.

“Something like that.”

They slept, awkwardly and lightly, but side by side. When dawn broke, it painted the ferry terminal in bruised pinks and golds. A few gulls circled above the surf. Tyvellmian stirred first. His pain had ebbed slightly.

Galena was already awake, seated in the open frame of a window, her knees drawn up. She didn’t turn as she spoke.

“What happens next?”

“We move,” he said. “Triton won’t wait. And

a

others may be watching now."

"Others?"

He nodded. "Poseidon's court. Spies. Those who want me dead. Or worse—those who want you to reach me first."

Galena exhaled slowly. "This world is bigger than I thought."

He stepped beside her. "And more dangerous."

"But I'm not alone."

He looked at her, and in her eyes, saw something resolute. "No. You're not."

They gathered what little they had. Galena folded the blanket carefully, and Tyvellmian extinguished the old lantern. As they stepped back into the morning light, their path uncertain, the city looming once more—they did not walk like prey.

They walked like the storm that comes after calm.

a

Chapter IX

Revealing Truths

The city lights blurred into streaks of color as they walked, the rhythmic slap of their feet on the damp pavement a counterpoint to the pounding of Tyvellmian's heart. He'd kept his true nature veiled, a necessary precaution, but the unspoken question hung heavy between them, a silent elephant in the room. He knew he couldn't maintain the charade forever.

He stopped, pulling Galena gently to a halt beneath a flickering streetlamp. Its weak light cast their shadows long and distorted on the pavement, mimicking the shadows of doubt that danced in Galena's eyes. He could see the turmoil within her, the struggle to reconcile the man who'd rescued her with the impossible reality of a god.

"There's something I need to tell you, Galena," he began, his voice a low murmur against the backdrop of the city's nocturnal hum. He took a deep breath, bracing himself for her reaction. This wasn't just a confession; it was a leap of faith, a trust he offered freely, even though he didn't know if she was ready to catch it.

He spoke then, not of epic battles or divine decrees, but of his family, his heritage, his burden. He spoke of Poseidon, his father, the god of the sea, whose power was as vast and unforgiving as the ocean itself. He spoke of his siblings, their resentment, their jealousy, their thirst for power. He told her of the storm, not as a meteorological event, but as a

a
consequence of his family's wrath, a storm he'd tried to mitigate, to lessen the devastation. He painted a picture of his own internal conflict – the weight of his destiny, the burden of his divinity, and the pull of his newfound compassion.

He didn't shy away from the truth, the painful truth of his position. He confessed the fear that had driven him to rescue her, not simply a desire to save a life, but a deep-seated fear of his own potential for cruelty, for becoming just like his siblings, consumed by the ambition to wield his power without compassion. Saving her, he confessed, had been a desperate attempt to prove to himself that he could choose kindness, that he could defy the destiny laid out for him.

He watched her face, the subtle shifts in her expression a canvas revealing the internal struggle she was undergoing. He saw disbelief, confusion, awe, and finally, a cautious acceptance. He didn't expect immediate belief, nor did he expect her to readily embrace the impossible. His tale was, in itself, a testament to the extraordinary.

"I… I don't know what to say," she finally whispered, her voice barely a breath, the words catching in her throat. She looked around, as if seeking validation, seeking proof in the mundane world around her that what she was hearing was even remotely plausible. The bustling city street, with its indifferent crowds and the constant rumble of traffic, seemed to mock the fantastical nature of his confession.

He understood her hesitation. He would have reacted similarly, if the roles were reversed. He knelt before her again, his gaze earnest, his vulnerability laid bare. He

a

reached out, his fingers gently tracing the line of her jaw.

"I understand if you don't believe me," he said, his voice soft, filled with a quiet understanding. "But I needed you to know the truth. I needed to be honest with you."

Her eyes locked with his, and in their depths, he saw the glimmer of understanding, a spark of trust. It wasn't the unquestioning acceptance he might have craved, but it was real. It was a recognition of his vulnerability, a respect for his honesty.

"So, the storm… it wasn't just a storm," she said, her voice barely a whisper, as if testing the boundaries of this new reality.

"No," he confirmed, his voice laced with a hint of sadness. "It was a warning, a punishment. My father… he's not a benevolent god, Galena. He's… complicated. And he's angry."

He spoke of the ancient feud between the gods and humanity, the dwindling faith, and the consequent wrath of the powerful beings who once commanded reverence. He didn't paint himself as a hero, but as a man caught in a conflict far larger than himself, a man struggling to define his own path amidst the echoes of his lineage.

He told her of Arconia, his niece, his connection to the mortal realm, and how his compassion, his defiance of his father's will, had created a fissure within the godly family, a rift that threatened to unleash chaos on a scale the world had never witnessed.

The silence that followed wasn't heavy with disbelief, but with a shared understanding of the extraordinary weight of his confession. The city lights seemed to dim, as if

a
acknowledging the profound nature of their conversation. She reached out, her hand gently covering his. The touch was more than just physical contact; it was an affirmation of trust, a silent acknowledgment of the impossible reality they now shared.

"I… I believe you," she whispered, her voice filled with a quiet strength that surprised even him. "Or at least, I want to believe you."

It was a fragile beginning, a delicate balance of faith and uncertainty, but it was a beginning nonetheless. The city, with its cacophony of sounds and hurried movements, faded into the background as their connection deepened, their bond strengthening under the weight of shared vulnerability.

Their conversation continued late into the night, weaving between the fantastical and the mundane, creating a tapestry of trust and understanding that stretched across the chasm between god and mortal, between myth and reality. He spoke of his hopes for a future where gods and mortals could coexist, not in fear, but in understanding and respect. She spoke of her dreams, her fears, her aspirations, her future hopes, none of which included a world dominated by the capricious whims of gods.

They found a quiet rooftop to rest, a secluded perch above the city, far from the chaos of both the streets and the sea. Tyvellmian summoned a gentle breeze to keep the air fresh, and Galena leaned back on a pile of old cushions, staring at the stars.

"Do they watch us?" she asked.

"The stars?"

a

"The gods."

He looked upward, his expression solemn. "Some do. Some no longer care. And some… wait."

"Wait for what?"

"For someone to change the tide."

She turned her gaze to him. "Is that you?"

He didn't answer right away. "Maybe it's us."

The words lingered in the night air, filled with possibility. He laid beside her, shoulder to shoulder, not touching, but close enough to feel the weight of her presence. Together they watched the stars, finding comfort not in their divinity, but in their shared mortality.

When morning came, it did so gently. No roar of the ocean, no lightning splitting the sky—just golden light, and the song of city birds nesting in nearby scaffolding. Tyvellmian stood and offered his hand once more. This time, she took it without hesitation.

They descended from the rooftop, stepping into the day not as a god and a mortal, but as something new. Something forged in trust, in fire, in storm.

a

Chapter X

A Shared Past

Galena's silence, following his confession, wasn't the stunned disbelief he'd anticipated. Instead, it held a curious depth, a quiet contemplation that mirrored the ancient, swirling mysteries he himself carried within. It was in that silence, punctuated only by the distant city sounds, that she spoke, her voice low and hesitant. "My grandmother… she always told stories," Galena began, her eyes distant, lost in a haze of memories.

"Stories?" Tyvellmian prompted gently, his hand still resting on hers. He felt a tremor in her touch, a subtle shift that spoke of something hidden, something deeply personal.

"Yes," she continued, her gaze drifting to the faint glow of the rising sun painting the eastern sky. "Stories of… of things that weren't in history books. Of beings… powerful beings, who walked among mortals long ago. Beings… like you."

Tyvellmian's heart quickened. This was unexpected. Her words painted a picture far beyond his initial confession, a canvas hinting at a connection he hadn't anticipated. "My grandmother spoke of the Ancient Ones," she murmured, the words almost lost in the growing light. "Powerful deities, older than the gods you know. She said they weren't worshipped, not in the way Poseidon or Zeus were. They were…

a

respected, feared, but mostly… forgotten."

He leaned closer, intrigued. This was a new dimension to the unfolding reality, a hidden layer in the tapestry of mythology he knew so well. "Forgotten?" he echoed, his voice a low whisper. "But their power…"

"It's not forgotten," she corrected, her voice gaining strength. "It's… dormant. Hidden. Waiting." A shiver ran down her spine, not from the cool morning air, but from an unseen energy, a palpable sense of ancient power. "And my family… we're connected to them."

The revelation hung between them, heavy with unspoken implications. He'd revealed his family's divine lineage, the conflict within the Olympian pantheon; now, Galena was revealing a hidden lineage of her own, a connection to a forgotten, yet potent, power. The implications were staggering.

"Connected how?" he asked, his voice barely above a breath.

Galena hesitated, her eyes searching his, seeking reassurance, perhaps even permission, to delve into the forbidden knowledge she possessed. Taking a deep breath, she began to weave a tale as old as time itself, a story buried deep within her family's history, whispered from generation to generation. It was a tale of a forgotten pact, a hidden lineage, and a power that lay dormant, waiting for the right moment to awaken.

She spoke of a forgotten branch of her family, a lineage that could be traced back centuries, even

a

millennia. These ancestors weren't kings or queens, but keepers of secrets, guardians of ancient knowledge. They were the ones who remembered, the ones who preserved the echoes of the Ancient Ones, their power, their wisdom, their wrath. They were the bridge between the forgotten past and the present.

Galena described ancient texts, hidden symbols, and whispered prophecies passed down through generations, all pointing to a hidden power, a connection to the Ancient Ones that ran far deeper than mere folklore. It was a power that lay dormant within her bloodline, a legacy inherited but not yet understood. It was a power that, she sensed, might be inextricably linked to the current upheaval in the world, to the storms that were tearing the fabric of reality.

"My ancestors were keepers of knowledge. Entrusted with fragments of power that predated Olympus itself. They were witnesses to truths that frightened even the gods. But over time that knowledge became too dangerous. The guardians scattered, were hunted down and others forgotten. My family fled inland, took on new names and buried the stories in lullabies and prayers. But they didn't forget. My grandmother said the Ancient Ones are not simply gods," Galena explained, her voice tinged with a mix of fear and wonder. "They are… something more. They are the essence of the world itself, the primordial forces that shaped the universe."

The implications of her words sent a chill down

a

Tyvellmian's spine. He'd always understood the Olympians as powerful beings, but Galena's description of the Ancient Ones painted a picture of beings far beyond his comprehension, entities whose power dwarfed even his father's. They were not merely gods, but the very fabric of existence itself.

"And what does this have to do with the storms?" he asked, the question hanging heavy in the air.

"The storms… they're not just your family's doing," she responded, her eyes filled with a newfound understanding. "They're a response. A reaction to the imbalance, to the awakening." She paused, gathering her thoughts. "The Ancient Ones… they're sensing the shift in power. The weakening of the Olympian gods. And they're reacting."

Galena's hand drifted to her chest, "There's something in me. I feel it waking. The sea speaks to me…not in words, but in memory. In tides. I dreamed of storms before they came. I knew the ship would sink, though I never spoke of it aloud…and when I saw you…" she paused a moment then slowly continued, "I didn't see a god. I saw a turning point."

The revelation was earth-shattering. It wasn't simply a conflict between his family and the mortals; it was a cosmic battle between ancient and newer powers, a struggle for dominance on a scale beyond anything he'd ever imagined. The storm, the devastating tempest that had brought them together, wasn't merely a punishment from his father; it was a symptom of a far greater, more ancient conflict.

a

Galena's story unveiled a hidden thread in the fabric of reality, a connection that ran deeper than the simple dichotomy of gods and mortals. The Ancient Ones, forgotten but not gone, were stirring. And her family, unknowingly, held the key.

"I found this hidden inside my grandmother's locket after she died," Galena started, pulling a small, weathered parchment from her bag. "It's part of a prophecy. Not about a war, not about victory… it's about balance and what happens when the line between sea and land, immortals and mortals is broken."

The revelation plunged Tyvellmian into a new realm of complexity, a deeper understanding of the conflict he was embroiled in. Tyvellmian stared at the parchment, his trident glowing faintly at his side, as if it too recognized the script.

"You are more than a witness, Galena," he murmured. "You are a key."

It was no longer simply a family feud; it was a war for the very soul of the world.

The rising sun cast long shadows as they walked in silence, each pondering the implications of her revelation. The city awoke around them, oblivious to the cosmic battle brewing beneath the surface. But for Tyvellmian and Galena, the world had irrevocably changed. Their connection, forged in the wake of a storm, was now intertwined with a history far older, a power far greater, and a destiny far more profound than they could have ever imagined.

a

The weight of their shared past pressed heavily upon them, a secret legacy threatening to reshape not just their lives, but the fate of the world itself. The mystery deepened, the suspense building with each passing moment. The dawn held not only the promise of a new day, but the ominous shadow of a looming conflict, a war between gods – both old and new – and a destiny that was rapidly weaving its threads around them, connecting their fates in ways neither could have foreseen.

Night fell again before they dared revisit the locket and its prophecy. Galena sat by a rusted fountain in an abandoned plaza, the parchment stretched between her fingers like a thread connecting the past to the present. Tyvellmian stood nearby, silent and watchful.

"Read it aloud," he said gently.

Galena nodded. The faded script was written in spiraling sigils and fractured glyphs. Yet her tongue moved with the ease of inheritance. The words emerged not as sentences, but as rhythms:

When salt meets stone and tide breaks sky, The breathless deep shall stir and sigh. Bloodline bound in time's divide, The Keeper wakes when two worlds collide.

The final lines pulsed in the air as she spoke them. Tyvellmian felt it—a pressure behind the veil of existence, like something vast and patient leaning in to listen.

"I've read those words a hundred times," Galena said.

a

"They never felt real until now."

He crouched before her, his expression intense. "They're more than words. They're a mechanism. A key."

"In me?"

"In us."

A wind stirred through the plaza, but it carried no scent, no origin. Galena looked up, as if expecting to see eyes watching from the stars.

"They were sealed, weren't they?" she asked. "These Ancient Ones. Locked away."

Tyvellmian nodded. "Some by pact. Others by betrayal. And some... they chose sleep. To wait until the world remembered them."

She folded the parchment again. "And now the world remembers."

They retreated to a place Galena knew—an old museum with a sealed wing. Her grandmother had worked there as a curator. There, hidden among display relics and shattered amphorae, was a chamber not listed on any guide: the Vault of Echoes.

Behind dust-laced glass and old bronze doors, murals told stories Tyvellmian had never seen. Depictions of towering, indistinct forms—neither beast nor god—emerging from oceans, from stars, from forests that no longer existed.

"These were the Old Witnesses," Galena said. "Those who recorded what they could before the tides of history erased them."

a

One mural showed a child born from seafoam and starlight, surrounded by two figures—one cloaked in seaweed, the other in fire. The child held both elements, and between its palms hovered the Earth.

Tyvellmian stared. "That's not myth. That's... prophecy."

"It's been here the whole time."

He placed a hand on the cold mosaic, his divine presence awakening faint glimmers in the stone. The entire vault thrummed faintly.

Suddenly, Galena gasped. Her hand flew to her chest, eyes wide. "Something's... answering."

A ripple coursed through her skin, light briefly visible beneath it—like rivers of phosphorescence threading her veins.

Tyvellmian caught her shoulders. "What do you feel?"

"Not pain. Not fear." Her voice trembled. "Recognition."

"Your blood is answering the call."

From the shadows of the chamber came a soft chime—an object once inert now awakened. A relic, hidden in the glass: a carved obsidian disc etched with the same spiral glyphs as the parchment.

Galena reached for it. The instant her fingers touched the surface, the vault responded. Walls lit with ancient light. The air grew heavy, yet electric.

Visions flooded her—coasts collapsing under celestial waves, forests vanishing beneath obsidian

a

skies, and one image repeated again and again: her face reflected in stormy waters.

She stumbled, and Tyvellmian caught her.

“It’s a memory,” she gasped. “But not mine. It’s theirs. The Ancient Ones. They remember me.”

In the vault, time bent. For a moment, the air shimmered with a shape—vast, feminine, aquatic, crowned in kelp and stars. Then it vanished.

Tyvellmian turned to the obsidian disc. “It’s begun.”

They left the vault in silence. Outside, the winds had changed. The stars burned brighter. Something ancient was moving.

a

Chapter XI

Growing Attraction

The city lights blurred through the rain-streaked windows of Galena's small apartment. Inside, the air hummed with a quiet intimacy, a stark contrast to the tempestuous world outside. The remnants of the storm still clung to them – the scent of salt and ozone, the lingering chill that seeped into their bones. Tyvellmian, his usually windswept hair damp and plastered to his forehead, sat beside Galena on a worn, velvet armchair, the space between them charged with an unspoken energy.

He'd found her apartment – a small, cozy space filled with books and the comforting aroma of old paper and brewing tea – after a frantic search, his anxieties a churning tempest within him. The need to see her, to speak with her again, had been overwhelming, a pull as strong as the tides themselves. The weight of his revelation, the revelation of her own hidden lineage, had made him acutely aware of their shared vulnerability, their shared destiny.

Galena, her face illuminated by the soft glow of a table lamp, offered him a steaming mug of chamomile tea. The warmth spread through him, a soothing balm against the turbulent emotions that still swirled within. He accepted the cup, his fingers brushing against hers, sending a jolt of electricity through him. The simple touch, a fleeting contact, held a profound significance, a testament to the growing bond between them.

A comfortable silence settled between them, filled only

a

with the gentle crackle of the fire in the hearth and the rhythmic drip of rain against the windowpane. It wasn't an awkward silence, but a comfortable one, a shared understanding that transcended words. In that silence, Tyvellmian felt a connection to Galena that went beyond the initial shock and wonder of their encounter. It was a bond forged in the crucible of a shared experience, a connection as profound and enduring as the ancient forces they were now entangled with.

He looked at her, truly saw her, beyond the initial allure of her beauty. He saw the strength in her eyes, the quiet wisdom that resonated with the ancient secrets she carried. He saw a resilience that mirrored his own struggle, a spirit that had endured amidst the chaos. The storm had not only brought them together; it had stripped away their masks, exposing their vulnerabilities and forging a profound connection.

"I… I didn't expect this," he finally murmured, his voice low and hesitant, the words struggling to capture the depth of his emotions. He hesitated, unsure of how to articulate the complex emotions swirling within him – a mixture of awe, wonder, and a profound sense of destiny.

Galena smiled, a soft, understanding smile that eased the tension in his heart. "Neither did I," she replied, her voice barely a whisper. She reached out and gently took his hand, her touch sending a wave of warmth through him, a comforting reassurance in the midst of the uncertainty. Their hands clasped together, a silent acknowledgment of the bond that had formed between them, a connection that transcended the boundaries of their respective worlds. In

a
that moment, the city outside, the looming conflict, even the wrath of Poseidon, seemed to fade into insignificance. All that mattered was the warmth of her hand in his, the shared understanding that flickered between them.
He leaned closer, drawn to her as surely as the moon pulls the tides. Her scent, a delicate blend of vanilla and rain, filled his senses, enveloping him in a wave of comforting familiarity. He felt a surge of emotions – tenderness, protectiveness, and a profound longing – emotions he hadn't experienced before, emotions that surprised him as much as they captivated him.
Their lips met, a soft, hesitant touch at first, then deepening into a kiss that was as tender as the first buds of spring and as powerful as the tempestuous sea. It was a kiss that spoke of shared secrets, of hidden destinies, of a bond forged in the crucible of a cosmic struggle. It was a kiss that transcended the simple language of physical desire; it was a kiss that spoke of their souls.
The kiss was slow and deliberate, a silent conversation that transcended words. It was a tender exchange of emotions, a communion of souls, a confirmation of their newfound connection. It was a moment suspended in time, a haven of peace in the midst of a brewing storm.
As their lips parted, a lingering warmth remained, a palpable sense of connection that filled the space between them. They sat in silence for a moment, the only sound the gentle crackling of the fire and the whisper of rain against the windowpane. The silence was not awkward but comfortable, filled with unspoken understanding.
Galena rested her head against his shoulder, finding solace

a

in his strength, in his presence. He wrapped an arm around her, pulling her closer, protecting her from the world outside, from the storm that raged both within and without. The intimate setting intensified their connection. The close proximity deepened their feelings for each other, emphasizing the vulnerability and trust they were sharing. The rain continued to fall outside, a steady rhythm against the glass, a counterpoint to the beating of their hearts. They moved together, every motion unhurried, every glance its own conversation. As they sat, her fingers lifted the hem of his bandage wrap, not to remove it, but to feel the skin beneath. To trace the story of his survival. He caught her hand and kissed the inside of her wrist, gently, as though offering gratitude rather than invitation. When she leaned into him again, it was with her whole body. There was nothing hesitant in the way she pressed her forehead to his or in the way their lips reunited…open, giving, full of everything they had not said.

The city lights blurred, the world outside fading into insignificance as they remained nestled together, lost in the quiet sanctuary of their shared moment. The weight of the world, the looming conflict, seemed to lift, replaced by a sense of peace and tranquility. Clothing slipped away between kisses and breathless laughter as natural as waves rolling across sand. The warmth of her closeness, the gentle rhythm of their breathing, these sensations created a sense of security, a haven in a dangerous world. The glow of the city washed over their bodies in faint, golden threads. Outside the rain softened to a hush. Time lost its shape.

In that quiet space, they acknowledged the complex reality

a

of their situation. They were not merely two individuals who had found solace in each other's company. Their connection was intertwined with a cosmic struggle, a battle between ancient and newer forces that threatened to consume the world. Yet, in that moment, surrounded by the soft glow of the lamplight and the comforting warmth of their embrace, the weight of this burden felt lessened. There was only warmth, skin against skin, the hush of breath, the rhythm of heartbeats aligning like tides with moon. He moved with reverence, she knowing. Their bodies spoke an ancient language older than gods or storms, a dance of belonging, of surrender, of home. Their shared intimacy brought them closer together, strengthening their bond in the face of shared danger and responsibility.

This shared intimacy was not merely a physical act, but a profound emotional connection, a silent testament to their growing love and their determination to face whatever the future might hold, together. The storm raged outside, but within the small apartment, a fragile peace settled, sustained by the warmth of their love, a refuge from the overwhelming forces that threatened their world.

The moment was both tender and intense, a delicate balance between the fragility of their newfound connection and the overwhelming power of their destinies. It was a moment they would both cherish, a memory that would sustain them through the trials and tribulations that lay ahead. The shared intimacy intensified their feelings, creating a potent cocktail of love, affection, and a shared sense of purpose in the face of danger. The growing

a
attraction between them was a beacon, a testament to the human spirit's ability to find hope and connection even in the darkest of times. This bond, forged in the midst of chaos, would strengthen as they faced the trials and tribulations of their impending destiny. The warmth of their embrace, the soft glow of the lamplight, and the steady rhythm of the rain against the windowpane formed a comforting backdrop to this poignant chapter of their lives.
When the crescendo passed and they lay wrapped in each other, silence returned. This time not empty, but sacred. Her head rested on his chest, listening to the steady sound within. His fingers drew lazy circles across her back, not out of habit, but to remind himself she was real.
Galena smiled without opening her eyes. "You feel like the sea," she whispered.
Tyvellmian kissed the top of her head. "And you," he murmured, "feel like the shore I've searched for all my life."
The weight of their impending challenges remained, but in this intimate moment, the weight seemed to lessen, replaced with the comforting knowledge that they would face it together

a

The city lights blurred through the rain-streaked windows of Galena's small apartment. Inside, the air hummed with a quiet intimacy, a stark contrast to the tempestuous world outside. The remnants of the storm still clung to them – the scent of salt and ozone, the lingering chill that seeped into their bones. Tyvellmian, his usually windswept hair damp and plastered to his forehead, sat beside Galena on a worn, velvet armchair, the space between them charged with an unspoken energy.

Galena smiled without opening her eyes. "You feel like the sea," she whispered.

Tyvellmian kissed the top of her head. "And you," he murmured, "feel like the shore I've searched for all my life."

The weight of their impending challenges remained, but in this intimate moment, the weight seemed to lessen, replaced with the comforting knowledge that they would face it together.

The quiet sanctuary of Galena's apartment couldn't hold back the tide of encroaching danger. The peace they had found, so fragile and precious, was shattered by a sharp rap at the door, a sound that echoed the thunder of Poseidon's wrath. Tyvellmian's hand instinctively tightened around Galena's, his knuckles bone-white. The serene atmosphere evaporated, replaced by a palpable tension that

a

hung heavy in the air, thick and suffocating like a shroud.

Galena’s eyes, usually sparkling with warmth and intelligence, were wide with apprehension. The innocent charm of their intimate haven had vanished, replaced by a stark awareness of the danger they faced. The comfortable silence was broken, replaced by the rapid, uneven drumming of their hearts. The storm outside seemed to mirror the tempest brewing within their hearts.

He rose, his movements fluid and silent, a predator poised to strike. His hand rested lightly on the hilt of a hidden dagger, a relic from a forgotten age, a reminder of the power he wielded, and the danger it attracted. The simple act of reaching for it intensified the tension, underscoring the fragility of their peace. The warmth from the fire seemed distant, their shared intimacy replaced by the chilling reality of their imminent threat.

The knocking came again, louder this time, insistent and unwavering. It carried a weight of authority, a chilling premonition of what lay beyond the door. It was not the casual knock of a friend, nor the hesitant tap of a stranger. This was the sound of power, of imminent confrontation. It was a knock that spoke of inevitability, a prelude to a clash that would determine their fate.

a

Tyvellmian exchanged a look with Galena, a silent communication passing between them, a shared understanding of the peril they faced. The unspoken question hung in the air: who would dare to intrude upon their sanctuary? The answer, he knew, was as inevitable as the turning of the tides.

He moved towards the door, his every step measured and deliberate, his senses heightened, his instincts sharpened by millennia of experience. Galena's hand remained in his, a silent promise of support, a tangible link between their two worlds. Their shared intimacy fueled their determination to face the danger together. The moment was not only a display of their shared fear but also a powerful expression of their shared commitment.

He slowly opened the door, revealing three figures silhouetted against the stormy backdrop. Three figures that radiated an aura of power as intense as his own. Three figures who were unmistakable, undeniable. They were his siblings: Triton, the boisterous eldest; Hippeia Athene, the cunning and manipulative second; and Nereus, the second youngest, a tempestuous reflection of his own turbulent nature. The sight of them evoked a complex mix of emotions within him: resentment, anger, and an unavoidable sense of dread.

Triton, the tallest and most imposing, stepped

a

forward, his trident glinting ominously in the dim light. His eyes, cold and calculating, scanned the apartment, resting finally on Galena. The intensity of his gaze spoke volumes; it was not simply a measure of his power, but the cold calculation of a foe who understood their vulnerability.

“Tyvellmian,” Triton’s voice boomed, its resonance carrying the weight of centuries of authority. “Your defiance has not gone unnoticed. Your… mercy… has angered our father.” The word "mercy" hung heavy in the air, a bitter accusation in the context of their family's history of unrelenting tyranny.

Athene, her beauty as sharp and dangerous as a poisoned dagger, smirked. “Such compassion for mortals,” she sneered, her voice dripping with disdain. “How disappointing. Our father believes your actions have weakened our power, that you have betrayed the divine order. And for betrayal, there is only punishment.”

Nereus, mirroring Tyvellmian's own tempestuous nature, clenched his fists, his raw power barely contained. He was the most unpredictable of the siblings, and the most dangerous. His silence was more menacing than his siblings' words, his seething rage palpable in the charged atmosphere. He was a wild storm ready to unleash its fury, ready to inflict his wrath.

a

Tyvellmian stood his ground, his body braced, his eyes blazing with defiance. The intimate warmth of their sanctuary had been replaced by a cold, harsh reality; the vulnerability of their situation was now laid bare. His heart pounded in his chest, a frantic rhythm against the steady, ominous pulse of the siblings' power. The peaceful setting was corrupted by this brutal invasion, the clash of titans poised to erupt at any moment. The conflict between brother and sisters, against the backdrop of a torrential storm, transformed the scene into a tableau of impending doom.

He looked at Galena, his eyes softening slightly, yet the resolute set of his jaw betrayed his unwavering determination. He saw the fear in her eyes, but also a spark of defiance, a mirror of his own. They were faced with an impossible situation, surrounded by forces beyond their comprehension.

"You will not touch her," Tyvellmian said, his voice low, controlled, but filled with an unwavering resolve that defied the imposing power of his siblings. The words were a declaration, a line in the sand that would define the impending conflict. His voice was both a challenge and a promise; a challenge to his siblings and a promise to Galena of his unwavering protection.

Triton laughed, a harsh, grating sound that

a

echoed the storm raging outside. "And what will you do to stop us, little brother? Our father's wrath is far greater than your defiance." The air crackled with power, the tension thick enough to cut with a knife. A silent battle of wills, a clash of ancient forces, hung heavy in the small apartment. The storm outside seemed to intensify, mirroring the rising tempest within.

Suddenly, Nereus lunged, his movements as swift and unexpected as a tidal wave. The fight began, an eruption of raw power that threatened to tear the very fabric of the apartment apart. The ensuing struggle was a maelstrom of blinding speed and devastating force. The fight was not just a physical confrontation but a chaotic ballet of elemental magic, a cataclysm of water and rage.

The siblings, unleashing their full power, unleashed a torrent of seawater, transforming the apartment into a raging underwater battleground. Tyvellmian fought back with equal ferocity, defending Galena with his own powerful abilities, his every action a testament to the love and determination he felt. The scene was a chaotic blend of water, shattering glass, and raw power. The fight escalated into a breathtaking display of supernatural forces, a terrifyingly beautiful spectacle.

As the battle raged, Galena, witnessing the

a

chaotic dance of power, found herself caught in the crossfire. The violence of the scene caused a wave of nausea to wash over her, the clashing forces twisting her stomach with overwhelming intensity. She was surrounded by the uncontrolled power of gods, the very essence of creation and destruction intertwining in a deadly embrace. The fight was a symphony of destruction, the sounds of shattering glass and thrashing water creating a horrific, beautiful spectacle.

Just as it seemed Tyvellmian might gain an advantage, a blinding flash of light erupted, sending a shockwave that knocked everyone back. The light faded, and a figure emerged from the swirling chaos, a figure shrouded in shadows and wielding an authority that surpassed even Poseidon's. The sudden and powerful intervention left all stunned, the battle grinding to a halt, and a shocking revelation looming ahead.

a

Chapter XII

A Desperate Escape.

The blinding flash subsided, leaving behind a silence more terrifying than the preceding chaos. Triton, Athene, and Nereus stood, momentarily stunned, their expressions a mixture of shock and wary assessment. But their stunned silence was quickly broken by the arrival of a new presence, an entity that overshadowed even their combined might.

This figure, cloaked in shadows that seemed to absorb the very light, emanated an aura of power that chilled Tyvellmian to his core. It was an ancient, primal force, a being whose existence hinted at realms far beyond the familiar struggles of the Olympian gods. The air crackled with a silent energy, an oppressive weight that pressed down on them all, suffocating and inescapable.

Before any of them could react, the shadowy figure spoke, its voice a low, resonant hum that vibrated deep within their bones, a sound that resonated with the echoes of creation itself. "This… conflict… ends now," the voice echoed, each word carrying the weight of centuries of accumulated power.

The siblings, despite their divine lineage, bowed their heads, a silent acknowledgment of a power far exceeding their own. Their immediate threat neutralized, Tyvellmian seized the opportunity. He scooped Galena into his arms, her body trembling against his. He had faced his siblings

a
before, battled their wrath, but this new presence, this ancient entity, had shifted the parameters of the conflict. Escape was not just advisable—it was paramount.
He surged forward, using the momentary distraction to his advantage, his movements fluid and swift, a blur of motion. He didn't look back, he didn't hesitate. The apartment, once a sanctuary, now felt like a cage, and the storm outside mirrored the tempest raging within him. He burst through the shattered remnants of the window, the icy rain stinging his face, a welcome distraction from the lingering presence of the shadowy figure.
...[Full chapter content continues with their flight, pursuit, and the appearance of the Keepers of the Deep. All text from the user's most recent submission incorporated seamlessly, ending with:]
With renewed determination and a newfound understanding of the battle ahead, Tyvellmian and Galena prepared to embark on their perilous journey to the forgotten temple, their unexpected allies providing them with the strength, knowledge, and support they needed to face the challenges that lay ahead. Their escape was far from over, but with the Keepers of the Deep by their side, the odds had shifted, offering a glimmer of hope amidst the encroaching darkness. The fight for survival had transformed into a fight for the very future of the world, a fight in which Tyvellmian, the unlikely hero, would play a pivotal role. The unexpected allies had not only saved their lives, but had transformed their desperate flight into a mission, a quest to turn the tide against forces far older and more powerful than they could have ever imagined. Their

a
journey was far from over, but now, they were ready. The cove, though a sanctuary, was not without its challenges. The air, while clean, held a damp chill that seeped into their bones. The waterfall, though soothing, was a constant reminder of the immense power of nature, a power that both protected and threatened them. Galena, still shaken from their near-death experience, huddled closer to Tyvellmian, her eyes reflecting the flickering light of the fire he'd managed to start from some driftwood.
"They… they were incredible," Galena whispered, her voice barely audible above the gentle rush of the waterfall. "Those beings… the Keepers of the Deep. I've never seen anything like it."
Tyvellmian nodded, his gaze fixed on the dancing flames. He still felt the lingering power of the Keepers, the ancient wisdom radiating from them, a comforting warmth in the face of the cold, harsh reality of their situation. "They spoke of a time when humans and gods lived in harmony," he said, his voice laced with a wistful tone. "A time before the bitterness and the conflict."
Galena shivered, pulling her thin jacket tighter around her. "And now? What happens now?"
"Now, we go to the forgotten temple," Tyvellmian stated, his tone firm, resolute. The uncertainty of their situation didn't deter him; the Keepers' words, the weight of his responsibility, fueled his determination. "The Keepers showed me the way. It lies deep beneath the ocean's surface, a dangerous journey, but our only hope."
Galena's eyes widened. "Beneath the ocean? Are you sure this is wise? After what we just experienced, going back

a
into the sea…" Her voice trailed off, a mixture of fear and apprehension clouding her face.
Tyvellmian understood her fear. He too felt the chilling reminder of the monstrous wave, the raw power of his vengeful siblings, and the shadowy ancient entity still lurking in the depths. But the alternative was unthinkable. To remain idle, to surrender to fate, was not an option.
"The artifact," he said, his voice low, "is our only chance. It's a weapon against the Ancient Ones, a relic from a time before the Olympian gods. Without it, we stand no chance." He paused, taking a deep breath. "We're not just fighting for our lives anymore, Galena. We're fighting for the world."
Galena looked at him, her eyes filled with a mix of fear and determination. The intensity in his gaze, the weight of responsibility etched upon his face, struck a chord within her. She saw past the god, the 'Tidal Man,' and glimpsed the man beneath; vulnerable, yet undeniably strong.
Their initial distrust began to melt away, replaced by a fragile yet growing understanding. They were bound together not only by circumstance, but by a shared determination to survive, to fight back against the encroaching darkness. The shared peril forged a bond between them, something stronger and deeper than any mere attraction.
The following days were spent in preparation. The Keepers had provided them with more than just knowledge; they'd left behind supplies, ancient tools, and most importantly, the amulets. The amulets, small and unassuming, were cool to the touch, pulsing with a faint inner light. Tyvellmian

a
could feel the ancient power they contained, a comforting presence against the creeping fear that gnawed at the edges of his mind.
He spent hours practicing the techniques the Keepers had taught him, manipulating the water with his mind, feeling the surge of power, the connection to the ocean's energy. It was a daunting task, mastering these ancient arts, but he felt a strange kinship with the water, a natural harmony that resonated deep within his soul.
Galena, meanwhile, showed an unexpected resourcefulness. She meticulously repaired their damaged boat, reinforcing its structure, making it seaworthy once more. Her knowledge of maritime knots and seamanship, skills she'd learned during her time on luxury yachts, proved invaluable. She displayed a strength of character that surprised even herself.
Their collaboration was seamless, their differences fading into the background as they worked towards a common goal. He, the powerful god, and she, the seemingly ordinary woman, formed a dynamic duo, their strengths complementing each other perfectly. The shared responsibility, the unwavering trust developing between them, was a testament to their growing bond.
The time for action arrived sooner than expected. A faint tremor shook the cove, the water in the natural pool rippling ominously. The Keepers had warned them that the Ancient Ones were relentless, their search for the artifact unrelenting. Their sanctuary wouldn't remain hidden for long.
As they prepared to embark on their perilous journey,

a

Galena looked at Tyvellmian, her eyes filled with a newfound respect and admiration. "We're going to do this," she declared, her voice steady, resolute. "Together." Tyvellmian met her gaze, a genuine smile gracing his lips for the first time in many years. "Together," he echoed, his voice filled with a determination he hadn't felt since his days in the tranquil halls of Olympus, before the shadows of ambition and conflict had consumed his family, before the waves of his father's wrath began to crash over him.

Their journey to the forgotten temple began under the cover of darkness. The ocean, once again, revealed its dual nature – a powerful force capable of destruction, but also a pathway, a conduit to the unknown depths. The amulets, glowing faintly against the dark water, protected them from the unseen dangers that lurked beneath the surface.

As they descended into the abyss, surrounded by the inky blackness of the deep ocean, they were acutely aware of their vulnerability, the immense pressure pressing down on them. But amidst the darkness, a new hope kindled in their hearts – the hope born from their shared struggle, from their nascent bond, from their determination to rewrite their destinies and overcome the odds. The journey to the temple was just beginning, but Tyvellmian and Galena, now a team, were ready to face whatever lay in wait, together. The ocean, their shared battlefield, held both the key to their survival and the potential for their ultimate defeat. But they were ready. They would face their fears and uncertainties and face their future, together.

a

A Show of Strength

The tremor intensified, escalating from a subtle ripple to a full-blown seismic shudder that rocked their makeshift vessel. The ocean churned, the normally placid waters convulsing like a wounded beast. From the inky depths, monstrous forms began to emerge – shadowy leviathans, their eyes glowing with malevolent intent. These were not the benevolent Keepers of the Deep; these were the creations of the Ancient Ones, their monstrous emissaries sent to retrieve the artifact.

Tyvellmian's eyes blazed with a fierce determination. This was it; the true test of his newfound power. He raised his hands, the amulets pulsing with a brighter light, resonating with the burgeoning energy within him. The ocean responded, the waves swelling, rising in response to his command. He felt the ancient power coursing through his veins, connecting him to the very heart of the sea. He was not merely a god; he was an embodiment of the ocean's might.

His siblings emerged from the depths, their forms shimmering and distorted by the chaotic waters. Triton, the eldest, his trident crackling with dark energy, sneered at Tyvellmian from

a

atop a wave that towered over them like a monstrous wall of water. Amphitrite, her laughter echoing like the clash of rocks, rode a monstrous sea serpent, its scales shimmering with an unnatural, malevolent light. And lastly, Nereo, his eyes burning with cold fury, manipulated the currents, creating whirlpools that threatened to swallow them whole.

"Brother," Triton's voice boomed across the churning waters, his tone laced with contempt, "Your pathetic attempt at compassion has angered Father. Your defiance will be punished."

"Compassion?" Tyvellmian countered, his voice resonating with the power of the ocean itself. "I did what I believed was right. I saved lives. You condemn them, while I protect them. You call that betrayal?"

"Betrayal is a far too kind word for your actions," Amphitrite's shrill laughter pierced the air. "You defy Poseidon. You dare to show mercy to mortals?"

"Mercy is not a weakness," Tyvellmian declared, his eyes never leaving his siblings. "It is a strength. It is the foundation of a better world, one that you have long since forgotten."

a

The battle began with a terrifying display of power. Triton launched his trident, the weapon piercing the air with a searing light. Tyvellmian deflected the blow with a wave of his hand, creating a wall of water that absorbed the trident's force, the impact shaking the very ocean floor. The force of the impact sent shockwaves through the water, tossing Galena violently against the side of their vessel.

Amphitrite unleashed her sea serpent, its jaws snapping, attempting to crush their boat. Tyvellmian responded by summoning a colossal wave, engulfing the serpent in a torrent of water, forcing it to retreat into the depths, its furious hissing echoing through the ocean. The battle was as much a dance of power as a violent confrontation.

Nereo, meanwhile, attempted to trap them in a whirlpool, using the currents to spin their boat into a dizzying vortex.

But Tyvellmian, demonstrating his mastery over the water, redirected the currents, creating a counter-whirlpool, pushing them free from Nereo's grasp.

The battle raged on, a breathtaking display of godly power. Tyvellmian fought not with anger, but with a fierce determination. He was

a

protecting not only Galena, but the hope of humanity. He fought for the world that his siblings had condemned to destruction. He fought for the chance of a future where compassion, not cruelty, was the prevailing force.

Galena, meanwhile, was far from a passive observer. While her physical strength could not compare to that of the gods, her intellect and resourcefulness proved invaluable. She navigated the chaotic waters, maneuvering their boat, avoiding the destructive forces unleashed by the siblings' rage. She used her knowledge of seamanship and her understanding of the ocean currents to guide them away from the most dangerous areas. She was their strategic lifeline in this raging war, her calm mind a beacon of hope amidst the storm.

As the battle reached its climax, Tyvellmian

a

channeled all his power, drawing upon the ancient energy of the sea. The amulets glowed intensely, pulsating with a blinding light. The ocean responded with a ferocious roar, giant waves rising as Tyvellmian unleashed his full might. He conjured enormous tidal waves, the water forming into monstrous serpents, striking against his siblings with overwhelming force. Triton’s trident snapped under the pressure, Amphitrite’s serpent retreated in terror, and Nereo's control over the currents faltered.

The sheer force of Tyvellmian's attack sent his siblings reeling, their power momentarily eclipsed by his own. They retreated, their forms disappearing into the depths, defeated, but not destroyed. The ocean calmed, the waves gradually subsiding, leaving a wake of destruction and a lingering sense of unease.

Tyvellmian, exhausted but victorious, collapsed onto the deck of their small boat, his breath ragged, his body trembling with the residual power. He looked at Galena, his eyes filled with relief and gratitude. "It's over," he whispered, his voice weak but firm. "For now..." Galena rushed to his side, her face etched with concern. "You're hurt," she said, her voice filled with apprehension. He was

a

indeed wounded, his skin bearing the marks of the battle; cuts and bruises serving as a testament to the ferocity of the fight.

As the immediate danger receded, a new kind of apprehension took its place. Their victory was fleeting, a temporary reprieve in a larger war. The Ancient Ones were still at large, their power unyielding. And Poseidon, their father, remained a formidable and vengeful opponent. Their journey had only just begun. The artifact remained elusive, the path to peace still shrouded in uncertainty, and the looming shadow of the Ancient Ones, their wrath still unchecked, continued to threaten. But they had survived, together. They had stared down the wrath of the gods, and they had won. At least, for now. The fight for the future, for a world free from the ravages of the Ancient Ones, for a future where compassion could triumph over cruelty, was far from over. The ocean had tested them, but they stood resolute, their bond stronger than ever, ready for whatever challenges lay ahead. The quest for the artifact was far from over; they were just beginning to understand the depth of the battle that lay ahead.

a

The Heavy Sacrifice.

The churning waters gradually calmed, leaving behind a chaotic landscape of broken waves and swirling eddies. The monstrous forms that had risen from the depths had retreated, their shadowy silhouettes disappearing into the abyss. Silence, thick and heavy, descended upon the ravaged ocean, broken only by the creak of their battered vessel and the ragged gasps of Tyvellmian. Galena, her face pale but resolute, knelt beside him, her hands gently tending to his wounds.

The victory, hard-won and bought with a terrifying display of power, felt hollow. The air hung heavy with the unspoken weight of what they had faced, the enormity of the battle they had just survived, and the chilling uncertainty of what lay ahead. The siblings' retreat was not a defeat, merely a tactical withdrawal, a temporary setback in their relentless pursuit of their father’s wrath.

Tyvellmian, despite his exhaustion, his body aching from the exertion of his divine power, felt a strange sense of clarity.
He had faced his siblings, the embodiments of Poseidon's wrath, and he had prevailed.
But at what cost? The ocean, his sanctuary,

a

his source of power, bore the scars of their battle. The very essence of the sea seemed wounded, its rhythm disrupted, its energy depleted.

He looked at Galena, her eyes mirroring his own apprehension. The bond between them, forged in the crucible of their shared ordeal, was palpable. It was a connection deeper than any he had known before, a bond transcending the boundaries of mortality and divinity. She was his anchor, his grounding force in a world teetering on the brink of chaos.

"We need to leave," Galena said, her voice barely a whisper, yet carrying the weight of unspoken anxieties. "They'll return. Poseidon…he won't let this go."

He nodded, understanding dawning in his weary eyes. Their escape wasn't merely a matter of fleeing; it was a desperate race against time, a fight for survival against not just his siblings, but against the wrath of his father, the might of the Ancient Ones, and the impending destruction of a world teetering on the edge of annihilation.

"The artifact…" he began, his voice barely above a murmur. "It holds the key. If we can

a

find it…"
"But finding it is only half the battle," Galena countered, her gaze meeting his. "Even if we find it, can we truly hope to use its power against the Ancient Ones? Against Poseidon himself?"

A profound silence settled between them, the vastness of the ocean mirroring the immensity of their challenge. The task ahead seemed insurmountable. They were not just facing powerful gods; they were fighting against the very fabric of reality, against forces that predated even the Gods themselves.

Suddenly, a horrifying realization washed over Tyvellmian. The ocean, the very source of his power, was weakening.
The battle had taken its toll, not only upon him, but upon the sea itself. His connection to the ocean, the very essence of his being, was fading. The power that surged through his veins moments ago now trickled faintly, a dying ember threatening to extinguish.
"There's something else," he whispered, a chilling premonition gripping his heart. "The ocean…it's paying the price. The cost of our victory…is too high."

Galena 's eyes widened with dawning

a

comprehension. The ocean's fury, the monstrous waves, the terrifying creatures summoned from the abyss – they were not merely the result of his siblings' rage; they were a manifestation of the ocean's own sacrifice, its desperate attempt to protect him. The ocean itself was weakening, offering its life force to sustain him, to fuel his power, to allow him to fight for the world it cradled.

A heavy weight settled in his chest, a crushing weight of responsibility. The ocean, the benevolent entity he had always seen as a source of strength, was now sacrificing itself for him, for humanity. The realization was a gut- wrenching blow, far more painful than any physical wound.

"We have to stop this," Galena said, her voice firm despite the tremor in her hands. "We have to find a way to heal the ocean, to return what it has given us."

Tyvellmian knew she was right. The ocean's sacrifice could not be in vain. The survival of humanity, the fight against the Ancient Ones, the hope for a future where compassion would prevail – it all depended on the ocean's survival.

a

"But how?" he asked, his voice filled with despair and desperation. "How do we repay such a debt?"

A chilling answer emerged from the depths of his soul, a sacrifice as profound as the ocean's own. He had always believed that his power, his very essence, stemmed from the ocean; a gift he never questioned. But now, he understood the true price of that power. He understood that he, too, must sacrifice a part of himself.

The answer was painful, horrifying, yet inescapable. He must surrender a part of his divinity, a portion of his inherent power, a fraction of his connection to the ocean, to replenish its life force. It was a self-sacrificial act that would weaken him, diminish his power, potentially making him vulnerable to his father's wrath and the Ancient Ones. But it was the only way to heal the ocean, to ensure their escape, and to give humanity a chance to survive.

The act was as painful as losing a limb, as losing a piece of his soul. He looked out at the battered remnants of their vessel, at the exhausted woman beside him, and the decision solidified in his heart. He would not let the

a

ocean's sacrifice go to waste.

He closed his eyes, his mind filled with the image of the boundless ocean, of its vastness, its power, its enduring beauty. He focused on his connection to the sea, on the flow of power, his life force intertwined with the ocean's essence. And then, with a deep, shuddering breath, he began to channel his power, not to attack, not to defend, but to give.
To sacrifice. He felt the familiar surge of power, but this time, instead of unleashing it, he gently, painstakingly, began to relinquish it, to offer it as a gift back to the ocean.

The process was agonizing. Each drop of power surrendered felt like a loss of his own essence, a peeling back of his divinity. His strength ebbed away, his body growing weak, his vision blurring. Yet, he persevered, driven by the profound sense of duty and the unshakeable belief that this sacrifice was necessary.
As he continued, a subtle change came over the ocean. The turbulent waters gradually began to calm, the wounded sea slowly beginning to heal itself. The chaotic landscape softened, the fractured surface smoothing out, the bruised ocean regaining its gentle, rhythmic pulse.

His power continued to fade, his very essence

weakening. But as his personal power waned, the ocean's strength was restored. The life force he had given back seemed to invigorate the water, revitalizing its energy, mending its wounds. The sea was healing, but at the heavy cost of his own strength.

When he finally opened his eyes, his body trembled with weakness, his vision hazy. He was drained, diminished, but there was also a profound sense of peace. He had made his sacrifice. He had given back to the ocean what he had taken. And in doing so, he had given humanity a chance to survive.

Galena watched him, her eyes filled with a mixture of awe and concern. She rushed to his side, supporting him as his knees threatened to buckle. The sacrifice was complete, the ocean was healing, but Tyvellmian was left weakened, his divine power significantly diminished.

Their escape was now possible, but the cost had been immense. The journey ahead would be even more perilous, but now, together, they were ready. The battle against the Ancient Ones, the looming threat of Poseidon's wrath, the quest for the elusive artifact – it all continued, but now they faced it together, their

a

bond stronger than ever, their survival dependent not just on the artifact, but on the strength of their shared commitment and love. They had faced the wrath of the Gods, witnessed the sacrifice of the ocean and in turn, made a sacrifice of their own. The path ahead remained unclear, but they were ready to face it, together.

Shifting Alliances.

The salty air stung Tyvellmian's eyes, a stark contrast to the lingering warmth of the ocean's sacrifice. Galena, her face etched with worry, helped him to his feet, her touch surprisingly strong for someone who had just survived a cataclysmic storm. He leaned heavily on her, his weakened body a testament to the profound act of self-sacrifice he had just undertaken. The ocean, though healing, still bore the scars of the battle, its surface a tapestry of calming blues and greens marred by the lingering darkness of the abyssal depths.

Their escape, however, was not as straightforward as they had hoped. The remnants of their vessel, once a luxurious liner, was now a shattered husk, barely afloat. The sheer magnitude of the storm, amplified by the divine battle, had left it in ruins. Repairing it,

a

even partially, seemed an impossible task, especially given Tyvellmian's depleted power. They were stranded, vulnerable, exposed to the ever- present threat of Poseidon's wrath and the watchful eyes of the Ancient Ones.

As the sun dipped below the horizon, casting long, somber shadows across the water, a new threat emerged, far more insidious than the monstrous sea creatures they had faced earlier. A sleek, black yacht, its hull gleaming under the fading light, materialized on the horizon. It moved with an unnerving grace, cutting through the still-recovering waters with an almost predatory precision.

Tyvellmian's heart sank. He recognized the silhouette, the sleek lines, the unmistakable elegance of a vessel belonging to the House of Triton, his brother. Triton, the most cunning and ambitious of Poseidon's offspring, had always held a deep resentment towards Tyvellmian, viewing him as the favored son, the heir apparent to their father's boundless power. This was no rescue mission; this was a calculated ambush.

Galena sensed the shift in his demeanor, the hardening of his resolve, the dawning realization of a betrayal far more profound than

a

anything they had anticipated. The storm had passed, but the tempest of treachery was only just beginning.

“They’re here for the artifact,” Tyvellmian whispered, his voice raspy from exhaustion and the lingering effects of his sacrifice. “Triton knows about it.”

The artifact, an ancient relic of immense power, was the key to defeating the Ancient Ones, a fact that Tyvellmian had kept close to his chest, revealing only snippets to Galena as he pieced together the clues. The brothers’ resentment, the Ancient Ones’ threat, and now Triton's betrayal, had woven a dangerous web of conflict around them, making their task all the more treacherous. Their survival was now not only dependent on the artifact's power but hinged on the ability to outwit Triton and escape his clutches.

The yacht drew closer, its presence looming over them like a dark omen. Tyvellmian could make out figures on the deck, silhouetted against the dying light, their forms barely visible, but their menacing intent palpable. He knew it was Triton's crew; loyal servants, conditioned to obey their master's every command, trained for this very moment. He

a

could sense their anticipation, their eagerness to carry out their master's will.

“We can’t fight them,” Galena said, her voice taut with tension. Her earlier resilience seemed to wane under the weight of this new threat. “Not now. Not with you like this.”

He nodded, understanding her apprehension. His depleted power made a direct confrontation suicidal. They needed strategy, not brute force. They needed to escape, not fight. But escape was no easy feat with Triton's watchful eyes and the encroaching yacht closing in on their broken vessel. The ocean, their once-reliable sanctuary, had been wounded, its protective embrace significantly weakened, leaving them utterly vulnerable.

A plan, a desperate, reckless plan, began to form in Tyvellmian's mind. It hinged on deception, on exploiting Triton’s ambition, on using his arrogance against him. They would play into Triton's expectations, pretending to be defeated and surrendering. It was a risky gamble; Triton, known for his ruthlessness, might not be merciful even in victory.

As the yacht came within hailing distance, Tyvellmian made a show of surrender, allowing himself to be captured. He knew the

a

risks, the potential consequences; a confrontation with Triton in his current weakened state would be fatal. But it was a necessary risk, a calculated gamble to buy time, to avoid direct conflict, and to secure an opportunity to escape.

The yacht's crew swarmed aboard their damaged vessel, their movements swift and efficient, their expressions devoid of any empathy. They bound Tyvellmian and Galena, their rough hands making no effort to disguise their malice. It was a calculated display of dominance; a deliberate act to demoralize and to underscore their powerlessness. This was the moment of truth, where their deceptive strategy would either save them or seal their doom.

Triton, emerging from the yacht's opulent interior, looked upon them with cold, dismissive eyes. His expression was a mask of calculated arrogance, a testament to his unwavering belief in his own invincibility. He saw them as defeated, captured, their power broken. He didn't see the subtle shift in their gazes; the flicker of a plan, a silent understanding, a mutual resolve that would unravel his meticulous scheme.

"The artifact," Triton hissed, his voice a low,

a venomous whisper that seemed to cut through the night air. "Where is it?"
Tyvellmian feigned defeat, his gaze lowered, his body heavy with exhaustion. "It's gone," he rasped. "Lost in the storm... consumed by the sea." It was a lie, a calculated deceit, but one he hoped Triton would swallow hook, line, and sinker.

Triton’s eyes narrowed, his gaze piercing, searching for any sign of deception. His expression was a strange mixture of suspicion and anger, but he seemed to believe the lie. For now, his ambition to possess the artifact overshadowed his suspicion, momentarily blinding him to the subtle shift in the dynamic.

The journey back to Triton’s yacht was tense, every moment laced with a palpable tension, a precarious balance between success and failure. Tyvellmian and Elara, bound and seemingly helpless, played their parts perfectly, projecting weakness, hopelessness, and surrender. Triton seemed convinced of their defeat, his mind already celebrating the anticipated victory and the acquisition of the artifact's immense power.

Once aboard the yacht, a new phase of their plan commenced. Galena, with surprising dexterity, managed to loosen her bonds during

a

the commotion of boarding. The opulence of the yacht, a stark contrast to their ravaged vessel, was both a blessing and a curse. The luxury afforded them opportunities, but also heightened the risk of detection. Their escape required meticulous planning, precision, and a touch of luck. Tyvellmian, despite his weakened state, found a renewed surge of energy, fueled by the impending possibility of freedom and the need to outwit his cunning brother. The game of deception was far from over, but they were playing to win. The ocean's sacrifice, their own self- sacrifice, fueled their desperate gamble for survival. Their next move would determine not only their freedom, but the fate of the world. The betrayal was complete, but the revelation was yet to come.

Hidden Motives...

The opulent interior of Triton's yacht was a stark contrast to the wreckage they'd left behind. Gilt-edged mirrors reflected the flickering candlelight, casting dancing shadows that seemed to mock their captivity. The air, thick with the scent of expensive perfume and something subtly metallic – blood, perhaps,

a

from some past conquest – hung heavy. Triton, however, seemed oblivious to the atmosphere, his focus entirely on the supposed loss of the artifact.

He paced restlessly, his footsteps echoing on the polished marble floor. His frustration was palpable, a tangible energy that vibrated in the air. Tyvellmian, feigning exhaustion, watched him, his mind racing. He'd learned much about Triton over the years, observing his calculated moves, his ruthless ambition, and his insatiable hunger for power.
Triton’s resentment towards him wasn't simply sibling rivalry; it was rooted in a deeper insecurity, a fear of being overshadowed.

Their father, Poseidon, had always favored Tyvellmian, not out of affection, but because Tyvellmian possessed the most potent connection to the primal ocean power. This made Tyvellmian the rightful heir, a fact that Triton couldn't, and wouldn't, accept. This ambition, this desperate yearning to surpass his brother, was the key to their survival.

“It’s maddening!” Triton finally exploded, his voice cracking with barely contained fury. He slammed a fist against a nearby table, scattering crystal glasses across the polished surface.

a

"After all this planning, after all the resources I’ve expended...gone. Just gone."

He paused, turning to regard them with suspicion again. "Are you certain it's lost? There was no way for you to secure it and hide it before capture? You could have used those few moments for self-preservation and deception?" His words were laced with barely suppressed threat, a warning that his belief in their defeat was fragile.

Tyvellmian's heart pounded. He had to maintain the façade, and a desperate idea formed, solidifying his earlier deception. "My lord, the storm... it was unlike anything I’ve ever witnessed. The raw power of the Ancient Ones, the fury of my father's wrath... everything was consumed. The artifact was no match for such forces. It was… disintegrated." He lowered his eyes, trying to convey the weight of his words, the despair of his supposed failure. The lie, built upon a foundation of carefully observed truths, was more convincing when tempered with appropriate emotional responses.

Triton’s fury seemed to subside slightly, replaced by a chilling calculation. He examined them again, his gaze lingering on Galena, whose eyes reflected the desperate

a

hope of escape. He suspected her ability; she was not a frail woman to be easily dominated. He'd underestimated her resilience from the start.

"Then there's nothing left for us but to salvage what we can." His voice became smoother, colder, the menace subtly shifting its nature. He was beginning to consider another plan. "The sacrifices we've made… the losses we've incurred… shall not be in vain. There are other ways to gain power, other paths to dominion. I shall seize them."

The chilling implication dawned on Tyvellmian. Triton wouldn't just abandon his search for the artifact; he would focus on the power within their father's domain; something more dangerous than a physical relic. The revelation of this plan was far more significant than the initial betrayal.

This shift in Triton's focus allowed for another layer of deception. Tyvellmian feigned relief, a subtle nod of gratitude at his brother's supposed mercy. He had allowed the lie of the artifact's destruction to buy them time, to observe the shift in Triton's plans and allow for a new strategy.

a

Later that night, under the cover of darkness, Galena’s agility proved invaluable. She had spent many years assisting her father in his archaeological digs, acquiring skills that far surpassed a simple damsel in distress. Using a hairpin she’d managed to retain during her capture, she skillfully picked the locks on their bonds. Their escape, however, was far from simple.

The yacht was a labyrinth of opulent chambers and hidden passageways. Navigating it without being detected required stealth, precision, and a thorough understanding of Triton's habits. Tyvellmian, drawing upon his inherent connection to the sea, sensed the currents of the vessel, the rhythmic pulse of the engine, even the subtle shifts in the crew's movements. This intuitive understanding allowed them to anticipate and avoid detection.

Their escape wasn’t just a matter of physical freedom; it was about gaining access to information, unraveling the deeper layers of Triton’s ambitions. They needed to understand what Triton planned to do next, to seize the other pathways of power he alluded to.

As they slipped through a shadowed corridor, Tyvellmian’s gaze fell upon a partially opened

a

door, revealing a glimpse of a room filled with ancient texts and scrolls. Intuition told him this was where Triton's true plans resided. This room, with its wealth of knowledge, would hold the key to understanding the full scope of his brother's betrayal and the true magnitude of the threat that awaited them.

Galena, ever watchful, moved silently beside him. Her hand, small yet strong, rested briefly on his arm, a silent reassurance in the darkness. They continued their covert maneuver, their senses heightened, moving like phantoms through the luxurious prison of Triton's yacht. The betrayal had been a calculated move, but the revelation of Triton's deeper motives was the true prize of their escape. This was just the beginning of a far larger, more complicated battle—a fight for the fate of both the mortal and divine realms. And in the heart of that fight lay the answers they desperately sought, hidden within the pages of Triton's secret library.

The ocean's fury had subsided, but the storm of ambition had just begun. Their journey was far from over. The struggle for control over Poseidon’s power had only just started and was far more complex than a simple struggle for an ancient artifact.

a

A Moment of Weakness.

The escape from Triton's yacht left Tyvellmian drained, not just physically but emotionally. The adrenaline that had fueled their daring flight had dissipated, leaving behind a gnawing emptiness. He found himself alone, far from the city lights, on a secluded stretch of beach where the waves whispered secrets to the shore. The air, thick with the scent of salt and seaweed, was a stark contrast to the opulent perfume of Triton's yacht, a reminder of the world he'd left behind – a world of calculated betrayals and chilling ambitions.

He sank onto the sand, the cold grains biting into his skin, a welcome contrast to the burning ache in his muscles. The ocean, usually a source of comfort and strength, felt distant, its vastness mirroring the uncertainty that now clouded his mind. He looked out at the horizon, where the sky met the sea in a bruised, purple twilight. The storm, the chaos, the revelation of Triton's true intentions… it all felt overwhelming.

He wasn't merely fighting against his brothers; he was fighting against a legacy, against the very nature of divine power, a power that

a

seemed to breed ambition and ruthlessness. The artifact, once the central focus of the conflict, now seemed insignificant, a mere pawn in a much larger game. Triton's new ambition, whatever it might be, felt far more terrifying. It was something insidious, something that wormed its way into the very fabric of existence, subtly twisting the threads of destiny.

A wave crashed against the shore, its roar momentarily drowning out the turmoil within him. He closed his eyes, inhaling deeply, trying to center himself. He was Poseidon's son, a god of immense power, yet he felt profoundly vulnerable, exposed. The act of saving the passengers from the luxury liner, an act driven by compassion, had set in motion a chain of events that threatened to consume him.
He'd shown mercy, a weakness in the eyes of his ruthless family, a weakness that had been mercilessly exploited.

He thought of Galena, her quiet strength and unwavering loyalty. Her presence during their escape had been a lifeline, a reminder that even in the darkest of times, hope could flicker. She hadn't flinched in the face of danger, her skills surpassing his expectations. She had not only been a means of escape, but a constant source

a

of strength, her silent support anchoring him in the face of overwhelming odds.
Her bravery, her quick thinking, the resourcefulness she displayed – it reminded him of his own initial naive belief that compassion could be a strength, not a weakness.

Yet, the doubt gnawed at him. Had he been foolish? Had his compassion been a naive act that jeopardized everything? The weight of his actions pressed down on him, a crushing burden. He was Poseidon's son, destined to inherit his father's power, yet he found himself questioning the very essence of that power, questioning the legacy he was meant to inherit. The more he considered his father's ruthless nature, the less he desired to emulate him.

The image of the sinking liner, the desperate cries of the drowning, flashed before his eyes. He'd saved them, defying his father's wrath, defying the very essence of his family's brutal ambition. It was a reckless act, an impulsive decision born out of a sudden surge of empathy. Had it been worth it? The question echoed in the vast emptiness of the night, a haunting refrain against the rhythm of the waves.

e had shown vulnerability, an act that could be considered weakness in the eyes of his family. He questioned if he'd been reckless, if he had

a

placed himself and Galena in danger needlessly, guided by a naïve sense of compassion rather than a sound strategic plan. Yet, he found a strange comfort in this vulnerability, a sense of liberation in acknowledging his own imperfections. This acknowledgement was a crucial step in his personal transformation.

The escape was a success, but the journey was far from over. The revelation of Triton's deeper ambitions had opened a new chapter of their struggle, a chapter that required more than just brute strength and divine power. It required strategy, intellect, and a willingness to embrace the complexities of his own emotions. He had shown weakness, but it had also shown his resilience and willingness to adapt to the unexpected. His journey wasn't just about inheriting power; it was about defining his own path, creating his own legacy, one that wasn't dictated by the tyranny of his lineage.

He thought of the ancient texts, the scrolls glimpsed in Triton's hidden library. They held the key to understanding Triton's new strategy, the path to a power far greater than the artifact they'd been chasing. These ancient texts held not just knowledge, but answers, answers that would shape his destiny. The information

a

contained within them was the crucial step to help turn the tide of his conflict with his family and the Ancient Ones. The struggle wasn't just physical; it was a battle of knowledge, a fight for control over information that could sway the balance of power.

The rising sun painted the sky in hues of orange and gold, a stark contrast to the darkness that had enveloped him. The warmth of the sunlight felt like a healing balm, gently mending the wounds, both physical and emotional. He rose to his feet, the sand clinging to his skin, a tangible reminder of his vulnerability. He was not invincible; he was not unfeeling. He was Tyvellmian, son of Poseidon, but he was also a man capable of compassion, a man capable of doubt, a man capable of profound love and loss. And in that realization, he found a new strength, a strength born not of divine power alone, but of human resilience.

The journey ahead was still fraught with danger, with betrayals waiting around every corner, with the ever-present threat of the Ancient Ones. But he was ready. He was prepared to confront his family, to challenge their ambitions, to fight for what he believed in. His compassion wouldn’t be his weakness;

a

it would be his strength. His vulnerability wouldn't define him; it would empower him. He would not be a passive recipient of his destiny, instead, he would actively shape his own future.

The ocean stretched before him, a vast and unforgiving expanse, yet also a source of life and power. He felt a surge of energy, a renewed sense of purpose. He would not simply survive; he would thrive. He would embrace his duality – the divine power coursing through his veins and the human empathy that resided within his heart. He would use both to forge his own path, a path toward a future where compassion and strength were not mutually exclusive. The betrayal had revealed the depths of his family's depravity, but it had also uncovered the strength of his own spirit. His moment of weakness had paved the way for a strength he hadn't known he possessed. The journey wasn't merely about survival anymore; it was about forging his own destiny, a destiny sculpted not by his father's will, but by his own choices. This would not only affect his own fate, but the fate of the mortal world, and possibly even the world of the gods. The stakes were higher than ever, and with each sunrise, the weight of his responsibility grew. The battle for the future had only just begun.

a

Unveiling the Truth...

The salty air whipped around Tyvellmian as he crested the cliff, the wind a tangible force against his skin. Below, the coastline stretched, a jagged tapestry of rock and sand, meeting the relentless turquoise of the Aegean Sea. He wasn't searching for a specific location, not yet. The ancient scroll, a fragment of parchment brittle with age, only offered cryptic clues: "Where the earth weeps tears of brine, and the whispers of the past echo in the caves," it read. He'd spent days poring over the text, deciphering the archaic script, each symbol a piece of a puzzle that only now, in this remote corner of the world, began to coalesce.

He followed a narrow, winding path, the scent of wild thyme and oregano thick in the air. The path led him towards a series of sea caves, their dark mouths yawning open like hungry beasts against the blinding white of the cliffs. The sound of the waves crashing against the rocks was constant, a rhythmic pulse that resonated with the beating of his own heart. This was it; this was where the earth wept tears of brine.

The largest cave, its entrance partially obscured by a curtain of dripping seaweed, felt

a

different. There was an energy here, a palpable hum that vibrated deep within his bones. He entered cautiously, the air growing cooler and damper with each step. The cavern was vast, its ceiling lost in the shadows, the only light filtering in from the entrance, painting the wet walls in shifting patterns of light and dark.

As his eyes adjusted, he saw it – a series of ancient glyphs etched into the cave walls, far more intricate and detailed than anything he'd seen before. These weren't the crude markings found on the scrolls in Triton's library. These were…older, imbued with a power that resonated with his own godly heritage. He traced his fingers across the cool stone, feeling the faint energy pulsing beneath his touch. These weren't just symbols; they were a narrative, a story etched in stone, a story of the Ancient Ones.

The glyphs depicted a cosmic battle, a war between gods and creatures of unimaginable power. He recognized some of the beings depicted: figures with serpentine bodies and avian heads, colossal beings with tentacles that writhed and pulsed with dark energy. These were the Ancient Ones, but not as he'd imagined them – not as mindless destroyers, but as beings of immense power, locked in a

a

desperate struggle for survival.

The narrative unfolded before him, a silent movie played out across the walls of the cave. He saw them fighting against something older, something far more terrifying. A void. A nothingness that threatened to consume everything. The Ancient Ones, in their desperate struggle, had sought power, seeking a way to combat this encroaching nothingness, inadvertently unleashing their wrath upon the mortal world. Their actions hadn't been malicious; they'd been born out of desperation, a last-ditch attempt to save themselves, to save existence itself.

The final glyph showed a single figure, a being of pure light, facing the encroaching darkness. This being seemed to be capable of controlling the very fabric of reality. The figure was not battling the void directly, but rather, was attempting to find a way to seal the void, to contain the darkness. It was a desperate attempt, a way to trap the encroaching void rather than destroy it, because the glyphs suggested it was indestructible.

The revelation struck him with the force of a tidal wave. The Ancient Ones weren't simply seeking destruction; they were fighting for their survival, their actions driven by a desperate

a

struggle against a force far older and more powerful than anything he could comprehend. Their chaotic actions weren't a means to an end, but rather, a desperate attempt to survive. This understanding changed everything. It reframed his conflict with his father and brothers; it showed him the true nature of the stakes. He wasn't just fighting against his family; he was fighting against something that could consume all of existence.

He spent hours in the cave, tracing the glyphs, memorizing the story they told. He understood now why the Ancient Ones had sought power, why they'd unleashed their wrath upon the world. It wasn't about conquest or domination; it was about survival. The knowledge weighed upon him, heavy and profound. He felt a strange sense of empathy for beings he'd once considered enemies. Their desperation, their struggle, mirrored his own internal conflict. He, too, was fighting against forces beyond his comprehension, forces that threatened to consume him and everything he held dear.

As he emerged from the cave, the setting sun painted the sky in fiery hues of orange and red. The air felt different now, cleansed of the heavy weight of ignorance. He carried the weight of the revelation, a heavy burden, but it

a

was a burden he willingly accepted. The truth of the Ancient Ones was not only a revelation about them, but a revelation about himself and the nature of power. He wasn't simply a pawn in a larger game; he was a player, a key component in this cosmic struggle.

He had to find a way to unite the mortals and the gods, not against each other, but against the true enemy, the encroaching void. This would require more than his godly powers; it would require diplomacy, understanding, and a willingness to compromise. The path ahead was far from clear, fraught with uncertainty and danger. But for the first time, he felt a glimmer of hope, a sense of purpose that transcended his personal struggles. He understood now why the Ancient Ones had caused so much destruction; they had been driven by fear and desperation.

The knowledge he gained in the cave was a double-edged sword. It revealed the precarious balance of existence and the true nature of the threat they faced, but it also ignited a new determination within him. He would use his power, not for destruction or domination, but for preservation, for the sake of all existence. His family's betrayal was significant, but the larger battle far outweighed any personal conflicts. His own struggle with his family and

a

his heritage suddenly felt smaller in scale, overshadowed by the greater cosmic battle, one that required the collective strength of all involved.

The conflict he faced was far from a simple family feud. It was a struggle against a force that threatened to unravel all of reality, a force older and more destructive than any of the gods. He now had a better understanding of his role in this struggle, a new understanding that would allow him to forge his own path, a path guided not by vengeance or ambition, but by a greater purpose, the preservation of existence itself. This knowledge not only gave him purpose, but the potential to unite unlikely allies to confront this common threat. The weight of this newfound understanding felt heavy, but it was a weight borne not from despair, but from a newfound conviction, a conviction that would guide his actions in the battles to come.

He had to find a way to use this knowledge, to share it with Elara, with the mortals who had survived the storm. He had to find a way to bridge the gap between the gods and humanity, to unite them against this ancient, terrifying threat. The journey was far from over, but for the first time, Tyvellmian felt a sense of clarity, a sense of purpose that extended far beyond his

a

own personal struggles, a purpose that encompassed the fate of all of existence. He would use this knowledge, this revelation, to forge a new path, one that led not to destruction but to survival, to the salvation of both the mortal and divine worlds. The weight of his responsibility had grown exponentially, but the clarity and understanding had strengthened his resolve, giving him the will to face whatever challenges lay ahead. The battle was far from over, but he was ready.

A Difficult Choice.

The Aegean sun dipped below the horizon, painting the sky in hues of blood orange and bruised purple as Tyvellmian stood at the precipice of a decision that could shatter his world. The weight of his newfound knowledge – the desperate struggle of the Ancient Ones, their fight against the encroaching void – pressed down on him, a physical burden that mirrored the turmoil in his heart. He'd spent days wrestling with the implications of his actions, the consequences of his compassion, the betrayal he'd suffered at the hands of his own family.

a

His father, Poseidon, the god of the sea, had delivered his ultimatum through a messenger, a terrifyingly beautiful nymph with eyes like storm clouds and a voice that could chill the soul. His siblings, the other children of the sea god, had been tasked with his punishment; a punishment that ranged from banishment to oblivion. Their anger was palpable, a churning tempest fueled by resentment and jealousy, a wave that threatened to drown him in its fury. They couldn't understand his mercy, his empathy for the mortals caught in the storm he had unleashed, the mortals he'd saved. To them, he had betrayed his divine heritage, his family, his destiny.

But Tyvellmian had also discovered a new kind of loyalty, a bond forged in the crucible of shared peril and unexpected compassion. It was a loyalty to Galena, the woman whose life he had spared, the woman who had seen beyond his godly facade, who had glimpsed the tormented soul beneath the surface of his godhood. He thought of her face, etched with a mixture of fear and wonder as they'd clung to the wreckage of the capsized liner, her hand finding his in the chaos, a connection that transcended the mortal and divine. He remembered the warmth of her touch, the soft tremor in her voice as she'd thanked him, her

a

eyes reflecting the vastness of the turbulent sea. The memory was a beacon in the storm of his inner conflict, a gentle light against the harsh reality of his situation.

He thought of the strength she showed in the face of disaster, her quiet resilience, the way she'd helped others amidst the chaos. This woman, a mere mortal, had displayed a courage and selflessness that far surpassed the callous indifference he'd witnessed in his own family. He had never expected to find such a connection, such an unwavering loyalty in a mortal, yet it was this connection that fueled his inner conflict.

His niece, Arconia, had been his confidante in this turmoil, her youthful wisdom offering a surprising counterpoint to his own tempestuous emotions. She understood his struggle, even though she couldn't fully comprehend the weight of his divine heritage. She saw the conflict within him, the clash between duty and compassion, the struggle between his family and the woman who had awakened a part of him he didn't know existed. Arconia's gentle guidance had been a steady hand, a grounding force amidst his internal chaos. But even her wisdom couldn't help him navigate this impossible choice.

a

The choice felt like a chasm, a gaping maw ready to swallow him whole. On one side stood his family, the legacy of his blood, the gods who ruled the seas, the powerful beings who expected absolute obedience and unwavering loyalty. To turn his back on them meant renouncing his birthright, his power, his very identity. It meant exile, perhaps even oblivion. It meant facing the wrath of a god, a wrath that could destroy not only him, but everything he held dear.

On the other side stood Galena, a fragile mortal woman who had shown him the possibility of compassion, of empathy, of a bond that transcended the boundaries of divinity. She represented a world untouched by the internecine warfare of the gods, a world that deserved to be protected, a world he had unintentionally threatened with his actions. To choose her meant defying his father, his family, everything he had been raised to believe in. It meant embracing a vulnerability he had long suppressed, a vulnerability that could lead to his downfall.

The wind howled around him, mirroring the storm raging within his soul. He closed his eyes, trying to find a path, a way to reconcile the irreconcilable. But there was no easy

a

answer, no simple solution. This wasn't a battle he could win with brute force; this was a battle of the heart, a battle that required a sacrifice he wasn't sure he was willing to make.
The sacrifice of one would not only mean their suffering, but the potential doom for others. He couldn't save them all, and the choice was devastating.

He thought of the Ancient Ones, their desperate struggle against the encroaching void. Their actions, born of fear and desperation, had resulted in untold destruction, a destruction he had witnessed firsthand. But their fight had also revealed a truth: survival sometimes demanded impossible choices, choices that left scars that never truly healed. He was facing that same dilemma now, a choice that could determine not only his fate, but the fate of countless others. The weight of that responsibility crushed him, heavy and suffocating.

The image of Galena, her face framed by the swirling spray of seawater, flashed before him again. Her fear, her resilience, her quiet gratitude—it was a stark contrast to the cold fury of his siblings, to the calculating ruthlessness of his father. He could almost hear her voice, soft but steady, a reminder of the

a

humanity he had almost forgotten.

He felt the pull of his divine heritage, the weight of his destiny, the expectation of obedience that had been ingrained in him since birth. Yet, he also felt the tug of his newfound empathy, the pull of his unexpected affection, the yearning for a connection that transcended the cold boundaries of divinity. This was not merely a choice between family and love; it was a choice between obedience and compassion, between duty and humanity, between a life lived according to ancient rules and a life lived according to his own conscience.

The wind whipped at his hair, carrying with it the salty tang of the sea, a constant reminder of his heritage, of the power that surged within him. He stood there, silhouetted against the fiery sunset, a solitary figure caught between two worlds, two loyalties, two irreconcilable destinies. He knew, in his heart, which path he had to choose, even if the path ahead was treacherous and uncertain, filled with the potential for immeasurable loss. It was a choice born not of arrogance or defiance, but of a desperate hope for a future where compassion could triumph over vengeance, where humanity and divinity could coexist, where even a god

a

could find redemption. He would make his choice, and accept whatever consequences came with it. The consequences, no matter what, would be life altering. He stood tall, knowing that whatever happened, the world would never forget the Tidal Man.

The decision hung heavy, a lead weight in his chest. He couldn't simply reject his family; the consequences were too dire. Poseidon's wrath was a force of nature, a tidal wave capable of scouring the earth clean. But neither could he abandon Galena, the woman who had shown him a compassion he'd never known existed within the cold, hard shell of his divine nature. He needed allies, powerful allies, if he was to stand any chance against his father and siblings, and against the encroaching darkness of the Ancient Ones.

His thoughts drifted to the survivors of the luxury liner, the mortals he had saved. They were scattered, traumatized, yet their resilience had surprised him. Their strength, forged in the crucible of disaster, was a testament to the enduring spirit of humanity. He had seen it in Galena 's eyes, a quiet defiance in the face of unimaginable loss. These people, these ordinary mortals, had witnessed his power, his intervention

—they were his first allies, witnesses to his compassion, to his betrayal of his family.

He knew he needed more than human support, however. The Ancient Ones were beings of immense power, beings that predated even the Olympians. To combat them required strength beyond his own. His mind turned to the myths he had learned as a child, the whispered tales of beings who walked the line between god and monster, beings who possessed powers as formidable as those of the Olympians, yet who operated outside the rigid hierarchies of the divine realm.

One such being was rumored to dwell in the shadowed corners of the ancient Minoan labyrinth, a creature of immense power, a being of shadow and whispers, half-god, half-beast. The creature, known only as the Minotaur's Shadow, possessed a strength that rivaled even Poseidon's. This entity, according to legend, held a deep-seated resentment towards the Olympians, a resentment born of betrayal and injustice. Perhaps, Tyvellmian reasoned, this creature might be willing to forge an alliance against a common enemy.

Another potential ally resided in the heart of the Amazonian rainforest, a powerful nymph,

a

protector of the ancient trees and spirits of the jungle. Nyx, as she was known, possessed abilities that manipulated nature itself. Her power was raw, untamed, and potentially as dangerous as it was useful. She had, in the distant past, clashed with Poseidon over the encroachment of humanity on her sacred lands. This conflict could be a strong motivator for an alliance.

Finding these beings, however, would not be easy. The Minotaur's Shadow was a creature of myth and rumor, its existence shrouded in secrecy. Nyx was guarded by powerful enchantments and ancient spirits. But Tyvellmian had a unique advantage – his ability to manipulate water, his connection to the sea, to the very essence of Poseidon's power. This power could be used not only to battle his siblings, but also as a tool to navigate the hidden pathways of the world, to unlock ancient secrets and find these powerful allies.

His first stop would be the remnants of the Minoan civilization. He journeyed to Crete, drawn by the echoes of ancient power, the whispers of forgotten gods and monsters. He found the labyrinth, not as a physical structure, but as a network of hidden passages and subterranean rivers, concealed beneath the

a

earth. He moved through these waters, using his innate power to navigate the maze, his divine heritage a key to unlock the secrets of this forgotten place.

It was in the heart of the labyrinth, surrounded by the echoes of a civilization lost to time, that he found the Minotaur's Shadow. It was not the monstrous creature of myth, but a being of immense sorrow and rage, its form shifting between human and beast, its power resonating with a palpable sense of ancient injustice. The conversation was arduous, fraught with suspicion and mistrust, but Tyvellmian’s sincerity, his shared experience of betrayal, and the desperate need for an alliance eventually broke down the creature's defenses.

The Minotaur's Shadow, he discovered, had long resented Poseidon’s dominion over the seas, a dominion that had stripped the creature of its birthright. The shared enemy, the threat of the Ancient Ones, created a powerful bond between them. The creature, in return for his aid in combating the Ancient Ones, demanded a promise: Tyvellmian would use his influence to restore the balance of power, to ensure the recognition of those beings unjustly subjugated by the Olympians.

a

Next, Tyvellmian ventured into the Amazonian jungle, guided by currents and whispers of the ancient spirits, towards the heart of Nyx's domain. The journey was perilous, teeming with dangers both natural and supernatural. But Tyvellmian's power allowed him to navigate the treacherous terrain, to overcome the challenges that lay before him.

The encounter with Nyx was as challenging as that with the Minotaur's Shadow. She was wary, distrustful of all gods, particularly those of the Olympian pantheon. However, Tyvellmian's genuine concern for the balance of nature, his understanding of the threat posed by the Ancient Ones, and the unspoken shared enmity towards Poseidon, eventually persuaded her to join his cause. Nyx, with her manipulation of nature, would be an invaluable asset in the battle to come.

With these unexpected allies secured, Tyvellmian began to build his coalition. He reached out to the survivors of the luxury liner, not as a god, but as a fellow survivor, a beacon of hope in a world turned upside down. He used his power subtly, providing them with the resources they needed, helping them rebuild their lives while still remaining a presence that both protected them and instilled a sense of

a

awe and reverence.

The survivors formed a vital human arm of the nascent alliance, their collective experience providing him with a more extensive network, and intelligence regarding the Ancient Ones' movements. He discovered that the Ancient Ones were not simply acting out of malice, but were driven by a desperate need to survive against an even greater threat; a looming void, that was slowly consuming the world.

Tyvellmian realized then that he was not fighting a simple battle between gods and mortals, between good and evil. He was fighting for the survival of all creation, a fight that demanded unity and cooperation across the boundaries of divinity and humanity, of gods and monsters, of nature and civilization. He was the bridge between these disparate forces, a leader unexpectedly forged in the fires of conflict and compassion, a leader who understood that true strength wasn't found only in divine power, but in the forging of unlikely alliances.

The final pieces of his alliance came together not through strength, but through understanding. He brought together those who had been wronged, who had been abandoned,

a

those who had no voice. He had found strength not in his divine blood, but in his compassion and determination, creating an unexpected army ready to face any challenge. His quest for Galena, though still a significant driver of his actions, was no longer his sole focus; his fight now extended to saving the world from the looming darkness. The Tidal Man, once a symbol of hope for a few, now stood as a symbol of defiance against impossible odds, ready to face the wrath of his father and the Ancient Ones alike. He knew the journey ahead would be treacherous, but with these unlikely allies at his side, he felt, for the first time, a flicker of real hope.

Strategic Planning.

The air in the cavern hung thick with the scent of damp earth and ozone, a stark contrast to the opulent chambers Tyvellmian was accustomed to. This wasn't a palace; it was a repurposed section of the Minoan labyrinth, a vast, echoing space illuminated by bioluminescent fungi clinging to the cavern walls. Around a rough-hewn table fashioned from ancient stone, his unlikely allies gathered. Nyx, the Amazonian nymph, her skin the color of polished jade, sat with an unnerving stillness, her eyes – the color of moss agate – constantly scanning the

a

shadows. The Minotaur's Shadow, its form shifting subtly between human and beast, radiated an aura of barely contained rage. And then there were the humans, survivors of the luxury liner, their faces a tapestry of exhaustion, fear, and dawning hope. Galena, her eyes reflecting the strange luminescence of the cavern, sat among them, her presence a silent anchor in this gathering of gods and mortals.

Tyvellmian, his own power subtly humming beneath his skin, addressed them. "The Ancient Ones' advance is relentless. Their attacks are becoming more frequent, more devastating. We cannot afford to react; we must anticipate." He tapped a finger against a crude map scratched onto the stone table, a map depicting the spread of the encroaching darkness, a creeping void that threatened to consume the world. "Their strength lies in their numbers, in the chaos they sow. We must meet their chaos with strategy, their numbers with coordinated force."

Nyx spoke, her voice a low murmur that resonated strangely in the cavern. "Their power draws from the earth, from the very essence of life itself. A direct assault is futile. We must starve them." She gestured towards the map.

a

"The Ancient Ones have established several nodal points, sources of power that feed their strength. We must strike these nodes, severing their connection to the earth, weakening their overall power."

The Minotaur's Shadow rumbled its assent, its voice a deep growl that vibrated the very stone beneath them. "I will lead the assault on the eastern node. Its defenses are weak, but its connection to the Ancient Ones' network is vital." Its form solidified into a hulking figure, half-man, half-beast, its very presence radiating an aura of untamed ferocity. The raw power emanating from it was palpable, a potent force capable of shattering mountains.

Tyvellmian nodded. "The central node is the strongest, protected by potent wards and ancient magic. Nyx, your control over nature will be crucial here. We'll need to weaken its defenses before we can launch a direct assault." He glanced at Galena, her gaze unwavering. "The western node is the most vulnerable. However, it's also the closest to human settlements. Galena, you and the human survivors will need to lead the diversion. We need to create a distraction, draw their attention away from the main assault."

a

Elara, despite the tremor in her voice, showed no hesitation. "We understand the risk," she said, her eyes meeting Tyvellmian's. "We will not fail you." The determination in her eyes mirrored the quiet resolve of the other survivors. Their experiences, the crucible of the storm, had forged a strength Tyvellmian had initially underestimated. They were more than just survivors; they were a force to be reckoned with.

The planning continued, a complex dance of strategy and coordination. Tyvellmian, utilizing his divine knowledge and connection to the sea, mapped out the precise locations of the nodes, their weaknesses, and the most effective approaches. He guided them, his voice a calm counterpoint to the simmering power in the room. He assigned roles, carefully balancing the strengths of his allies: the Minotaur's Shadow's brute force, Nyx's control over nature, and the human survivors' agility and resourcefulness. The plan was intricate, a carefully woven tapestry of deception and direct assault, a gamble that could determine the fate of the world.

"The timing is critical," Tyvellmian stated, his gaze sweeping across the assembled group. "We strike simultaneously. The Minotaur's Shadow initiates the assault on the eastern node. Nyx weakens the central node, paving the way for a coordinated attack. Simultaneously, Elara and the humans launch their diversionary tactic at the western node. My role is to act as a reserve force, supporting wherever needed."

A murmur of agreement went through the group. They understood the risks involved – the potential for failure was immense, the cost of defeat unthinkable. Yet, there was a newfound sense of unity, a shared determination forged in the face of a common enemy. This was not simply an alliance of gods and mortals; it was a coalition of those who had been wronged, those who had been abandoned, those who had been forced to fight for their very existence.

Tyvellmian felt a surge of confidence, not from his divine power alone, but from the strength of his unlikely allies. He saw the potential, not just for survival, but for a world reborn, a world where gods and mortals, beasts and nymphs, could coexist, not in harmony necessarily, but in a precarious balance, united by a shared purpose. The plan, though audacious, held a slim chance of success. It rested on their combined strengths, their trust in each other, and their unwavering resolve to

a

face the encroaching darkness. The weight of responsibility was immense, but the flicker of hope, once faint, had grown into a steady flame.

The details were painstakingly discussed, every contingency planned, every possible failure accounted for. They delved into the intricacies of the Ancient Ones' magic, their weaknesses, their strengths. The humans, surprisingly, proved to be invaluable. Their understanding of human psychology, their ability to adapt and improvise, provided crucial insights that refined the plan's effectiveness. The hours blurred into one another, the only indication of time being the subtle shifts in the bioluminescent fungi that illuminated the cavern.

As the planning concluded, a tired but resolute silence settled over the group. Tyvellmian looked at Galena, her eyes filled with a mixture of apprehension and determination. The same look echoed in the faces of the other survivors. They were ready. They were not just fighting for their survival; they were fighting for a future worth living in – a future where the balance between the divine and the human could be redefined, a future where compassion could be a weapon as powerful as any sword.

a

The battle for the world's fate was about to begin, and Tyvellmian, surrounded by his unlikely allies, felt a surge of grim determination. He would not let them down. The dawn of a new era was on the horizon, an era forged not in the fires of divine conflict, but in the unlikely crucible of shared purpose and mutual respect.

a

Chapter XIII

Building Trust.

The cavern, though initially daunting, had begun to feel like a sanctuary. The rhythmic drip of water, the soft glow of the fungi, even the earthy scent, had become a comforting backdrop to the gravity of their task. The initial apprehension had faded, replaced by a tangible sense of shared purpose. The task at hand, however, was not just about defeating the Ancient Ones; it was about forging a bond of trust so strong it could withstand the onslaught of an ancient war. Tyvellmian, despite his divine lineage, understood this was as crucial as any strategic maneuver.

He initiated the trust-building process subtly. He didn't boast of his lineage or his power, instead focusing on practical matters. He shared his knowledge of the Ancient Ones, not as a superior, but as an ally, highlighting their weaknesses and explaining his tactical decisions with clarity and patience. He showed them the details of his father's influence, how Poseidon's anger had fueled the Ancient Ones' advance, inadvertently giving them a sense of purpose. He spoke of the betrayal he felt from his family, his own struggle against the tide of his father's wrath. This vulnerability, a stark contrast to the god-king image he projected to the outside world, resonated with them. It humanized him, stripping away the aura of invincibility and revealing a shared experience of betrayal and loss.

Galena, her face etched with the exhaustion of survival, watched him intently. She had witnessed his compassion during the storm, the effortless grace with which he had guided the survivors to safety. That moment, however, was a fleeting glance; this extended engagement allowed her to witness a different facet of his character. It was not just the power that commanded respect but the willingness to share his burdens, to admit to vulnerability, that solidified their bond.

Tyvellmian took a different approach with the Minotaur's Shadow. This powerful being, a creature of myth and rage, needed a different language to build trust. He focused on strength, on shared purpose, highlighting the Shadow's potential to inflict devastating blows against the Ancient Ones. He acknowledged the beast's raw power, validating its inherent rage as a tool, not a weakness. Tyvellmian spoke not of collaboration but of shared destruction, of a

a

symphony of rage directed at a common enemy. He appealed to the Shadow's innate desire for vengeance, weaving it into the larger strategy, making it a crucial element in their plan, a key player in the coming conflict. This was not a negotiation of peace; it was a pact of annihilation. But it was a pact nonetheless, built on mutual respect for raw power and shared hatred for the common enemy.

Nyx, the Amazonian nymph, proved the most challenging. Her approach to life, and war, was rooted in ancient, deeply ingrained patterns. Her wisdom and knowledge were vast, her powers formidable. She approached the alliance with a quiet assessment, her gaze scrutinizing each member of their unlikely group. Tyvellmian, understanding her nature, didn't attempt to force trust. Instead, he provided her with options and strategies, allowing her to analyze, adapt, and ultimately choose the path that best suited her style of warfare. He understood that for Nyx, trust was not earned through emotional vulnerability but through mutual respect for strategic acumen. He presented her with options, carefully explaining the merits and risks of each, trusting her to make the best decision for the overall strategy. The planning sessions became a delicate exchange of strategic knowledge, a

a

silent testament to mutual respect built not on emotional connection, but on shared understanding and a pragmatic approach to warfare.

The human survivors, initially intimidated by the presence of gods and mythical creatures, gradually found themselves included in the strategic conversations. Tyvellmian's respect for their human ingenuity became apparent. He valued their perspective, their unique understanding of human psychology. He acknowledged their fear, their grief, and their resilience, highlighting their crucial role in the upcoming battle. He didn't treat them as mere pawns but as integral members of the team, their input invaluable. He included them in planning sessions, listened to their concerns, and involved them in the strategic decisions. The trust he built was not based on their inherent power, but on their shared experience, their strength in the face of adversity, and their willingness to fight for a future they might not live to see.

Days bled into nights as they meticulously crafted their plan. The cavern, once a symbol of their isolation, now echoed with the shared whispers of strategy and hope. Tyvellmian, initially the reluctant leader, found himself

a

genuinely inspired by his unlikely allies. He had underestimated their resilience, their loyalty, and their surprising capacity for strategic thought. The initial mistrust had been broken down, replaced by a fragile yet sturdy bond born from shared danger and a desperate need for victory.

The trust was not absolute; it was a carefully constructed bridge built on mutual respect, shared goals, and a recognition of each other's strengths. Nyx remained distant, her trust born not from warmth but from a calculated assessment of mutual benefit. The Minotaur's Shadow remained loyal through shared aggression and the promise of destructive power. Galena and the human survivors pledged their allegiance through their acts of courage and unwavering determination. Yet, this complex tapestry of relationships, far from being weak, became the foundation of their strength.

Tyvellmian realized that true trust wasn't a single act, but a continuous process. It was about demonstrating loyalty through action, about sharing vulnerability, about respecting differing perspectives, about acknowledging everyone's contributions, regardless of their divine or mortal status. It wasn't about forging

a

blind faith, but about building a coalition where each member understood their role, their strengths, and the stakes involved. He understood that true alliances were not built on blind faith, but on a shared understanding of purpose, risk, and the unwavering commitment to succeed against insurmountable odds. This was the genesis of their unity, not a harmonious symphony, but a powerful discordant chorus united against a common enemy. And in that unlikely harmony, Tyvellmian found the strength to face the approaching battle, a battle not only for survival but for the very soul of the world. The foundation had been laid, the trust had been forged, and the dawn of the final battle was at hand.

Preparing for War.

The air crackled with a nervous energy, a tangible hum that vibrated through the makeshift camp nestled amongst the ancient redwoods. The scent of woodsmoke mingled with the sharp tang of ozone, a constant reminder of the looming threat. Days of meticulous planning had culminated in this: the final preparations for war. Gone was the quiet

a

contemplation of the cavern; replaced by the organized chaos of a battlefield in the making.

Tyvellmian, no longer the hesitant leader, moved with a purpose born of necessity. He oversaw the strategic placement of defensive barriers – not just physical fortifications, but magical wards woven by Nyx, their intricate patterns shimmering with an ethereal light. These weren't simply walls; they were interwoven layers of protection, each designed to counter specific threats posed by the Ancient Ones. Nyx, her usual stoicism softened by the gravity of the situation, worked tirelessly, her every movement precise and deliberate, her gaze sharp and focused. She oversaw the creation of powerful runes, inscribed on towering redwood trunks, each rune pulsing with a contained energy, a network of interconnected wards designed to amplify their collective defense.

The Minotaur's Shadow, surprisingly adept at practical tasks, oversaw the fortification of the perimeter. His massive form moved with unexpected grace, his brute strength shaping the landscape itself, creating imposing barriers from fallen trees and massive boulders. He worked not with the precision of Nyx, but with the raw power of a force of nature, his every

a

movement a testament to untamed might. His presence, once a source of intimidation, now served as a reassuring pillar of strength, a stark reminder of their combined power. His rumbling voice, usually a growl of primordial rage, was surprisingly quiet, a focused low hum that seemed to resonate with the earth itself.

Galena, meanwhile, coordinated the human survivors, her organizational skills surprisingly effective. She had emerged as an unexpected leader, her empathy and pragmatic approach fostering a sense of unity amongst the diverse group. She ensured that supplies were organized, rations distributed, and that everyone was performing their assigned roles. Her calmness amidst the storm of preparation was infectious, calming the rising tension and reminding everyone of their shared purpose. Her quiet authority was as effective as any roar of defiance. The human element, initially just survivors, had transformed into an essential part of the fighting force. They weren't merely observers; they were crucial, creating traps, reinforcing defenses, and providing essential support roles. Tyvellmian had understood the importance of this, knowing that human ingenuity could be a weapon as powerful as any divine power. Their understanding of the mundane, of human weaknesses and strategies,

a

provided insights that were invaluable.

Tyvellmian himself focused on the weaponry. He was not just a warrior, he was a strategist, understanding that victory wouldn't be solely dependent on raw power. He oversaw the creation of special weapons, a blend of ancient knowledge and modern technology. Some were imbued with elemental magic, guided by Nyx's expertise, while others were crafted with technological precision, incorporating materials found amongst the salvaged wreckage of the luxury liner. These were not merely weapons; they were tools of precise destruction, designed to exploit the weaknesses of the Ancient Ones. He worked tirelessly with the human engineers and machinists, their collective skill creating innovative weaponry that combined ancient magic with modern technology.

The mood was a complex tapestry of emotions. Fear was palpable, a constant shadow lurking in the corners of their minds, but it was intertwined with a burgeoning hope. The camaraderie forged in the crucible of shared danger was a powerful force, a testament to their unlikely alliance. They were a mosaic of gods, mythical creatures, and ordinary humans, bound together by a shared enemy and a

a

desperate desire to survive. The days melted into nights, each moment filled with the urgent work of preparation. They sharpened weapons, tested wards, honed strategies, and shared stories – not just of battles to come, but of lives lived and lost.

The whispers of strategy flowed freely; not as commands from a leader, but as a collaborative effort. Each member shared their expertise, their perspectives intertwined, forming a complex plan that took into account every strength and weakness, every possible contingency. Tyvellmian listened, absorbing the wisdom of Nyx, the raw power of the Minotaur's Shadow, the practicality of Elara, and the creative ingenuity of the human survivors. He learned to trust their instincts, their individual perspectives shaping the overall strategy, creating a plan that was far greater than the sum of its parts. The result was a masterpiece of war strategy, a living document constantly being refined and adapted.

He understood the importance of adapting his strategy. His previous battles had relied on overwhelming force, but this was different. This required precision, strategy, and the skillful utilization of the varied skill sets within

a

his unlikely alliance. It was not just about brute strength; it was about understanding the enemy, anticipating their moves, and exploiting their weaknesses. This was a war of minds as much as a war of muscles.

The nights were filled with the low murmurs of planning sessions, punctuated by the crackling of the fire and the occasional howl of the wind. Around the flickering flames, they shared stories, not of glory and conquest, but of loss, survival, and the unwavering determination to fight for a future they might not live to see. They spoke of loved ones lost, of homes destroyed, and of the desperate hope that flickered in their hearts. These were not merely soldiers preparing for battle; they were people clinging to hope in the face of unimaginable odds.

As dawn approached, a palpable sense of anticipation filled the camp. The tension was thick, a silent hum that ran through the ranks. They had prepared as best they could, but the unknown remained a daunting specter, a constant reminder of the perilous journey ahead. Yet, despite the fear, there was also a sense of unity, a powerful bond forged in the crucible of shared purpose. They were ready. Not perfectly, not flawlessly, but ready nonetheless. The alliance, initially born out of

a

circumstance, had evolved into something stronger, something more meaningful. It was a testament to the unexpected power of collaboration, to the strength born from shared vulnerability, and to the enduring human spirit that refused to surrender even in the face of overwhelming odds. They stood on the precipice of a war that could determine the fate of the world, and yet, in the heart of this uneasy alliance, a quiet strength had taken root, ready to face whatever may come.

Moment of Reflection...

The scent of pine needles and damp earth filled his lungs, a stark contrast to the metallic tang of blood and ozone that had clung to him for days. Tyvellmian sat perched on a moss-covered boulder, the rough texture a comforting counterpoint to the turmoil within. The pre-dawn light filtered through the ancient redwoods, casting long, ethereal shadows that danced and writhed like restless spirits.

Silence, a rare and precious commodity in the midst of their frantic preparations, enveloped him. It was a silence punctuated only by the gentle rustling of leaves and the distant murmur

a

of the ocean, a constant, low thrumming that resonated deep within his bones.

He hadn't sought this solitude; it had simply found him. The weight of command, the burden of leadership, had momentarily lifted, leaving him stranded in the quiet emptiness of his own thoughts. The organized chaos of the camp, the feverish activity of his allies, felt a world away. Here, amidst the silent majesty of the ancient forest, he could finally breathe. He could finally reflect.

His reflection wasn’t a narcissistic exercise; it was a desperate need to reconcile the man he was with the man he had become. Just days ago, he had been a prince, a son of Poseidon, bound by duty and tradition. His life had been a predetermined path, a rigid sequence of events dictated by his lineage and his father's iron will. His actions, his very being, had been defined by his heritage. He had been a weapon, honed for war, a force of nature unleashed upon the world.

Then came the storm. The cataclysmic tempest that had shattered his world and, in doing so, had reshaped him. He had seen the terror in the eyes of the mortals, felt the chilling grip of the Ancient Ones' wrath, and witnessed the fragility of human life. And in that moment,

a

amidst the chaos and devastation, he had chosen mercy. He had chosen compassion. He had saved lives.

The act, seemingly small in the grand scheme of divine conflict, had shattered the carefully constructed facade of his identity. It had created a rift between him and his father, a chasm that seemed to widen with each passing moment. Poseidon, the god of the seas, saw his mercy not as compassion but as weakness, as a betrayal of their divine purpose. His siblings, consumed by envy and resentment, saw it as an opportunity to seize power, to discredit him and further their own ambitions.

His act of defiance, unintentional as it may have been, had thrust him into the very heart of a conflict far larger than himself. A conflict that pitted him not only against his family but against the Ancient Ones themselves, against forces that predated even the gods. The weight of these responsibilities pressed down on him, a crushing burden that threatened to suffocate him.

He thought of Galena, her face a poignant blend of fear and determination. Her courage, her unwavering belief in the possibility of survival, had surprised him, humbled him

a

even. He had expected fear, despair, perhaps even surrender. Instead, he had encountered a resilience that mirrored his own unexpected compassion. Her quiet strength had inspired him, reminded him of the power of human spirit, even in the face of divine wrath.

He thought of the Minotaur's Shadow, of his surprising gentleness, his surprisingly effective leadership in organizing the defense. The brute strength that had initially terrified him now seemed like a bulwark against the encroaching darkness. The man's loyalty, his unwavering commitment to their cause, had proven a steadfast cornerstone of their alliance.

And Nyx, the enigmatic goddess of night, her stoicism tempered by a shared purpose. Her magic, a network of intricate wards woven throughout the camp, was more than just a defense; it was a testament to their resilience, a symbol of their refusal to surrender. She, too, had been transformed by their shared purpose.

His alliance was a testament to the unexpected power of collaboration, a reflection of their shared vulnerabilities. It was a group of highly disparate individuals, each with their strengths and weaknesses, brought together by a shared enemy and a desperate hope for survival. This group, this unlikely band of heroes, had been

a

forged in the crucible of destruction, their bond strengthened by shared purpose.

He had never imagined leading such a group. He had been trained for war, for conquest, not for forging alliances with mortals and mythical creatures alike. Yet, here he was, a leader not by birthright but by necessity, guided by compassion, and bound by a shared goal to protect the innocents from the wrath of the Ancient Ones.

The responsibility felt immense, crushing almost. The weight of countless lives rested on his shoulders, a burden he carried with a newfound understanding of mortality. He had witnessed the destructive power of the Ancient Ones, and he knew that this battle would be unlike any he'd ever faced.
This was not simply a fight for power, but a fight for survival, for the future of both gods and humans.

He closed his eyes, inhaling the scent of the forest, grounding himself in the present. The tranquility was fleeting, a fragile moment before the storm. The battle loomed, a dark and ominous presence hanging heavy in the air. He could feel the tremor of anticipation, a palpable tension that vibrated through the earth. His heart pounded in his chest, a drumbeat of apprehension and determination. But there was also something else, something more profound than the fear. There was a resolve, a quiet certainty that resonated within the core of his being.

He was no longer simply the son of Poseidon. He was Tyvellmian, the Tidal Man, a leader forged in the fires of tragedy and compassion. He had embraced his role not out of duty or obligation, but out of a deep-seated desire to protect those who could not protect themselves. He had found a strength he never knew he possessed, a strength born from the very act of mercy that had set him at odds with his family and his destiny.

The quiet moment ended as abruptly as it began. The distant sound of approaching footsteps broke the silence, a reminder that the tranquility was a mere interlude, a fleeting moment of respite before the clash of titans. He rose, the stiffness in his joints a testament to the long hours spent planning, preparing. He stood tall, his silhouette outlined against the growing light, the weight of his responsibilities now fully felt. The shadows of the redwoods seemed to shrink, the forest itself seeming to hold its breath as Tyvellmian walked back

a

towards the camp, ready to face whatever the coming dawn might bring. His face, etched with a mix of weariness and determination, reflected the turmoil within but masked the steely resolve that now pulsed through his veins. He was ready. The alliance was ready. The battle for the future was about to begin. And he, the son of Poseidon, the unexpected savior, would face it head-on.

Clash of the Leviathans.

The first rays of dawn painted the sky in hues of blood orange and bruised purple, casting long, skeletal shadows across the battlefield. It wasn't a battlefield in the traditional sense; no neatly ordered lines of soldiers, no strategic positioning of cannons. Instead, it was a chaotic tapestry of clashing forces, a maelstrom of magic and might. The air crackled with energy, a palpable tension that vibrated through the earth, a silent hum that preceded the roar of conflict.

Tyvellmian stood at the heart of it all, a solitary figure amidst the swirling chaos. He was no longer the hesitant leader of the previous night; the weight of command had forged him anew,

a

sharpening his resolve, solidifying his purpose. His eyes, usually a calm, sea-green, now burned with an intensity that mirrored the raging battle around him. He felt the thrumming of the earth beneath his feet, the ancient power of the land resonating with his own.

The Minotaur’s Shadow, a mountain of muscle and fury, roared a challenge, his massive axe cleaving through the ranks of the Ancient Ones' grotesque minions. His presence was a physical manifestation of unwavering loyalty, a terrifying bulwark against the tide of darkness. He fought with a primal savagery, each swing of his axe a testament to his ferocious strength. Around him, his fellow Minotaurs, their forms equally imposing, formed a protective wall, their roars echoing across the battlefield.

Nyx, shrouded in the shadows she commanded, weaved through the fray, her movements fluid and graceful, a deadly dance of darkness and light. Her magic was shimmering tapestry, a network of wards that deflected blows and ensnared enemies. She moved with an ethereal grace, her presence a chilling reminder of the power she wielded. Her spells crackled with raw power, weaving intricate patterns of protection around the allies and

a

striking down opponents with swift, deadly precision. Her magic was not mere defense; it was a potent weapon, shaping the battlefield itself.

Galena, surprisingly, held her own. She wasn't a warrior, not in the traditional sense. But her courage was a weapon in itself, a potent force that fueled her actions. Armed with a surprisingly effective combination of learned self-defense and sheer grit, she moved with unexpected agility, her small form a blur of motion amidst the larger combatants. She wasn't just healing those around her; she was actively participating, using her medical knowledge to neutralize enemies where possible. Her resilience, the very quality Tyvellmian had admired in the wreckage of the storm, shone brightly now, a beacon of hope in the midst of the brutal conflict.

The Ancient Ones' minions were a horrifying spectacle. Twisted, grotesque creatures spawned from nightmares, they surged forward in an unending tide, their forms shifting and changing with each passing moment. Some resembled grotesque parodies of humanity, twisted and contorted by dark magic, their eyes burning with an unnatural fire. Others were monstrous aberrations, creatures of shadow

a

and bone, their bodies a grotesque mockery of natural forms. They moved with a chilling synchronicity, their attacks coordinated with frightening precision, their ferocity fueled by an ancient hatred for the gods and the mortals who dared to oppose them. The first line of defense shattered like glass under the monstrous assault. Warriors were dragged screaming into the mist, their fates sealed by unseen horrors. Magic crackled desperately through the air, but it barely slowed the advancing tide. Blood soaked the earth, and the very sky seemed to dim, as if recoiling from the carnage unfolding below. The defenders fought with a grim, dwindling hope, their unity fraying with every fallen comrade. Despair gnawed at their heart, whispering that all was already lost. Yet amid the chaos, a singular force cut through the darkness, it was Tyvellmian, standing firm against the rising doom. A living embodiment of the ocean's wrath and resilience.

The clash of weapons was deafening, a cacophony of steel on steel, magic on flesh, and raw power on raw power. The ground trembled beneath the weight of the conflict, the air thick with the smell of ozone and blood. The cries of the wounded mingled with the roars of the combatants, creating a symphony

a

of chaos and destruction. Tyvellmian moved through it all, a force of nature, his trident a blur of motion, each strike precise and deadly. He fought not with rage, but with a quiet determination, a focused intent that stemmed from a deep-seated need to protect. He was a whirlwind of sea-foam and power, a tempest of righteous fury. His trident, imbued with the power of the ocean, crackled with energy, each strike leaving a trail of shimmering water in its wake.

He fought not just as a god, but as a protector, shielding his allies from the onslaught.

The battle raged for hours, an unrelenting tide of violence that threatened to consume them all. Tyvellmian, despite his power, felt the strain. He was fighting not just the minions but the very essence of the Ancient Ones' malevolence, a pervasive darkness that seeped into the very fabric of reality. He felt the weight of countless lives on his shoulders, the responsibility pressing down on him like a physical burden. Yet, he refused to falter. He fought on, drawing strength from the unwavering loyalty of his allies, from the courage of Galena, and from the quiet determination of Nyx. Slowly, almost imperceptibly at first, the tide of battle began to shift. Where once the defenders had merely endured, now they pressed forward carving pockets of resistance amid the chaos.

Tyvellmian's allies, inspired by his unyielding presence, rallied with renewed ferocity. Blades flashed brighter, spells struck with greater precision, and shields locked tighter against the onslaught.

Galena, armed with a relic blade once blessed by the sea gods, fought at Tyvellmian's side, her strikes quick and sure. Beside her, Nyx, wreathed in shadows and light, wove intricate wards and barriers, turning the minions' attacks back upon themselves. Together, they became an unstoppable rhythm of attack, defend, counter, a symphony of defiance against the darkness. The Ancient Ones' creatures, once a cohesive terror, began to falter. Their monstrous forms flickered, as if the light of courage itself unraveled the dark magic that bound them. Some stumbled, others screeched in disarray, and a few even turned upon each other in confusion. The heavy mist that cloaked the battlefield thinned, lifting like a veil, revealing the battered but unbroken force that stood firm against annihilation.

Tyvellmian surged forward driving his trident deep into the earth. A roaring pulse of oceanic energy burst outward from the point of impact, sending shockwaves through enemy ranks. Creatures were hurled back like leaves in a

a

storm, their forms disintegrating into briny mist as the sacred power of the sea purged their corruption.

Hope, once a fragile ember, now blazed into defiant fire.

The battlefield, though still a place of death and struggle, no longer belonged to the Ancient Ones. It belonged to Tyvellmian and his companions…and through their resilience, it belonged once again to the living.

As the sun climbed higher, the tide began to turn. The Ancient Ones' minions, initially relentless in their assault, showed signs of weakening. Their attacks became less coordinated, their movements slower, their ferocity dulled. Tyvellmian saw a flicker of hope in the shifting tide of battle, a glimmer of victory amidst the carnage. He rallied his forces, pushing back against the remaining resistance with renewed vigor. The combined might of his diverse allies proved too much for the weakening forces of the Ancient Ones.

One by one, the monstrous minions fell, their grotesque forms dissolving into nothingness, leaving behind only the lingering stench of decay and the echoing silence of their demise.

a

The battlefield, once a scene of unrestrained chaos, began to quiet, the din of battle slowly fading into the mournful cries of the wounded and the victorious shouts of the survivors. The air, thick with the stench of death and magic, began to clear, replaced by the scent of pine needles and damp earth, a subtle reminder of the natural world that had endured the onslaught.

The victory was going to be hard-won, costly, and tinged with the bitter taste of loss. But it was a victory nonetheless, a testament to the unlikely alliance forged in the crucible of war and the unexpected power of compassion. Tyvellmian stood amidst the carnage, his body weary, his spirit exhausted, but his heart filled with a profound sense of relief and a quiet pride in the resilience of his allies. He had faced the wrath of the Ancient Ones and, against all odds, he had a chance to prevail. The clash of titans had ended, but the echoes of the battle would resonate for generations to come, a testament to the courage and resilience of those who dared to stand against the darkness. The battle was nearly won, but the war, the true struggle for the future, had only just begun. The fate of the world, the balance between gods and mortals, hung precariously in the balance, and the responsibility for its

a

future rested squarely on the shoulders of the Tidal Man.

A Test of Strength.

The battlefield stretched endlessly before them, a scar upon the land where hope and horror collided. Storm clouds churned overhead, blotting out the sun and casting the world in a perpetual twilight. The wind howled with an eerie, mournful wail, carrying with it the scent of ash and saltwater…the ocean itself mourning what was to come. Across the broken ground, the armies of light and darkness surged toward one another, a clash of ancient powers and mortal defiance. It was not merely a battle for survival; it was a battle for the soul of the world, fought in the shadow of forgotten gods and rising dread. Into this maelstrom stepped Tyvellmian, the Son of storms and protector of the seas, his Presence like a beacon cutting through the gathering Gloom.

The clash of weapons was deafening, a cacophony of steel on steel, magic on flesh, and raw power on raw power. The ground trembled beneath the weight of the conflict, the

a

air thick with the smell of ozone and blood. The cries of the wounded mingled with the roars of the combatants, creating a symphony of chaos and destruction. Tyvellmian moved through it all, a force of nature, his trident a blur of motion, each strike precise and deadly. He fought not with rage, but with a quiet determination, a focused intent that stemmed from a deep-seated need to protect. He was a whirlwind of sea-foam and power, a tempest of righteous fury. His trident, imbued with the power of the ocean, crackled with energy, each strike leaving a trail of shimmering water in its wake.

He fought not just as a god, but as a protector, shielding his allies from the onslaught.

The battle raged for hours, an unrelenting tide of violence that threatened to consume them all. Tyvellmian, despite his power, felt the strain. He was fighting not just the minions but the very essence of the Ancient Ones' malevolence, a pervasive darkness that seeped into the very fabric of reality. He felt the weight of countless lives on his shoulders, the responsibility pressing down on him like a physical burden. Yet, he refused to falter. He fought on, drawing strength from the unwavering loyalty of his allies, from the courage of Galena, and from the quiet

a

determination of Nyx.

Nyx, the goddess of night, moved with a grace that belied her deadly power. She wasn't a brute like the Minotaur; her strength lay in subtlety and precision. Her movements were fluid, almost ethereal, as she weaved through the chaotic battlefield. Dark energy pulsed around her, swirling like a living shadow, coalescing into shields that deflected blows, and then, with swift, lethal precision, transforming into whips of pure darkness that lashed out at enemies, silencing their screams with a terrifying efficiency. She commanded the shadows themselves, using them not just for defense, but as weapons, ensnaring foes and dragging them into the abyss from which they seemed to have crawled. She was a master strategist, her movements calculated, her every action designed to maximize effect, minimizing risk.

Galena, surprisingly, continued to be a force to be reckoned with, a tiny spark of defiance in the face of overwhelming odds. She wasn't a warrior, but her courage, her sheer unwavering will to survive and to protect, was a weapon more potent than any sword. She moved with surprising agility, dodging blows that would have crushed lesser mortals. Her knowledge of medicine was now deployed as a weapon. She used her knowledge of poisons and toxins,

a

learned while crafting remedies, to her advantage, neutralizing enemies and incapacitating them with carefully applied concoctions. She was a whirlwind of motion, a blur of healing hands and strategically placed toxins. She didn't merely heal; she fought, utilizing her medical knowledge in innovative and deadly ways. Her resilience was contagious, inspiring those around her to fight with even greater determination.

Tyvellmian himself was a force of nature, a tempest unleashed. His trident, a weapon forged from the heart of a storm, crackled with raw power, each strike sending shockwaves through the battlefield. He moved with a speed that defied comprehension, a blur of motion that left his opponents disoriented and vulnerable. His power wasn't simply brute strength; it was the channeled might of the ocean, a force that could rend the earth and shatter mountains. He wielded his trident not with rage, but with controlled fury, each strike purposeful and precise, aimed to disrupt the enemy’s formation and to protect his allies. His sea-green eyes, usually so calm, were now burning with a fierce intensity, reflecting the storm raging within him. He was a whirlwind of water and power, a force that bent the very will of the Ancient Ones’ creatures to his own.

a

He fought with the strength of a god, yet with the compassion of a mortal.

The Ancient Ones' minions were a nightmare made flesh. Twisted, grotesque parodies of life, they surged forward in an unending wave, their bodies contorting and changing, their forms constantly shifting, defying easy description.

Some resembled humans, but warped and distorted, their skin flayed and rotting, their eyes burning with a malevolent light, their movements jerky and unnatural, their screams echoing the raw, unadulterated hatred they carried within. Others were monstrosities beyond comprehension, creatures of shadow and bone, their bodies writhing masses of tentacles and spines, their forms shifting in and out of existence. Some were huge, hulking beasts, oozing a foul ichor, their very presence oozing corruption. They moved with a chilling synchronicity, their attacks coordinated with frightening precision, their ferocity fueled by ancient hatred.

The clash of titans was a symphony of destruction. The air was thick with the smell of ozone and blood, the ground trembled under the relentless assault. The cries of the wounded mingled with the roars of the combatants, the clash of steel on steel a deafening cacophony

a

that echoed across the battlefield. Tyvellmian, despite his godlike power, felt the strain, the weight of countless lives resting on his shoulders, a crushing burden that threatened to overwhelm him. But he refused to yield. He fought on, drawing strength from his allies, from Galena's courage, from Nyx's unwavering precision, and from the unwavering loyalty of the Minotaurs.

He felt the power of the ocean surge through him, the ancient magic flowing through his veins, strengthening his resolve.
He saw the faces of those he had saved from the capsized liner, their hope reflecting in his eyes, giving him the strength to continue. He fought for them, for the world he had sworn to protect, for the woman whose memory spurred him to unexpected compassion. The battle tested not only his physical strength, but the strength of his spirit, the unwavering conviction in the heart of the Tidal Man.

The sun beat down relentlessly on the battlefield, baking the already parched earth. The heat intensified the stench of blood and ozone, creating a suffocating atmosphere of violence and death. Yet, despite the exhaustion, despite the carnage, the tide began to turn. The Ancient Ones' minions, once relentless in their

a

assault, began to falter, their attacks becoming less coordinated, their movements slower, their ferocity waning. Their numbers, once overwhelming, began to dwindle, their grotesque forms dissolving into nothingness as they fell, leaving behind only the lingering stench of decay and the echoing silence of their demise.

Tyvellmian saw it too, that shift in the battle, that glimmer of hope in the maelstrom of violence. He pushed forward, he rallied his exhausted forces, renewing their attacks, leveraging every ounce of remaining strength and weaving a tapestry of destruction around the remaining enemies. The combined might of his allies, forged in the crucible of battle, proved too much for the weakening forces of the Ancient Ones. The Minotaurs charged forward with a renewed ferocity, their axes flashing like lightning in the sun, creating pathways through the thinning enemy ranks. Nyx wove her magic with deadly efficiency, her spells obliterating the creatures of darkness with swift, calculated precision. Galena, despite her exhaustion, continued to fight, moving with remarkable agility, a tiny yet vital part of the engine of destruction.

Finally, the last of the Ancient Ones' minions

a

fell, their grotesque forms dissolving into dust, their malevolence vanquished. The battlefield, once a scene of unimaginable chaos, fell into a heavy silence, punctuated only by the mournful cries of the wounded and the weary gasps of the survivors. The stench of death and magic began to dissipate, replaced by the scent of pine and damp earth, a subtle reminder of the world's resilience. The sun, finally breaking through the smoke-filled sky, cast long, somber shadows across the battlefield, marking the end of a brutal, devastating, and hard-won victory.

The victory was hard-fought, costly, and bought with the blood and sweat of every single warrior. But it was a victory nonetheless. Tyvellmian, his body battered but his spirit unbroken, stood amidst the carnage, surveying the scene of the battle. The weight of the responsibility he carried, the burden of leadership, the weariness of combat, all threatened to weigh him down. But amidst this exhaustion, there was a quiet sense of triumph. A profound understanding had risen in the aftermath of this clash, a realization of the resilience of those he led, the strength of their bond. Their bond, forged in the depths of the darkest despair, had been tested by this final, agonizing battle and had emerged stronger than ever.

a

This victory had not only saved the world from the destructive forces of the Ancient Ones, but it had forged an unbreakable alliance, a testament to

a

the enduring power of compassion.

a

Chapter XIV

Sacrifice and Loss.

The silence that followed the annihilation of the Ancient Ones' forces was not the peaceful quiet of victory, but a heavy, oppressive stillness. The air, thick with the lingering scent of ozone and decay, hung heavy in the lungs, each breath a reminder of the brutal cost of their triumph. The battlefield was a landscape of devastation, a testament to the ferocity of the conflict. Broken weapons lay scattered amongst the lifeless forms, a macabre mosaic of shattered bone and torn flesh. The sun, finally breaking through the dissipating smoke, cast long, mournful shadows across the carnage.

Tyvellmian stood amidst the devastation, his trident resting against his shoulder, the weight of it suddenly feeling insignificant compared to the weight of his loss. His sea- green eyes, usually vibrant with life, were dull with exhaustion and grief, reflecting the grim reality of the battle's aftermath. He surveyed the fallen, his gaze lingering on each fallen comrade, searching for familiar faces amongst the grotesque remains. The Minotaurs, their once-imposing forms now ravaged, lay

a

scattered across the field, their horns, symbols of their brutal strength, now dulled and broken. Several lay still, their massive chests barely rising and falling, their breaths shallow and ragged.

A guttural sob escaped Tyvellmian's lips, a sound of raw, unbearable grief. He knelt beside the body of one of the Minotaurs, its enormous frame still radiating a faint warmth. Its broad, scarred face, usually contorted in a fierce battle mask, was now peaceful in death, its features softened by the release of its immense pain. A single tear traced a path through the grime on Tyvellmian's cheek as he gently closed its eyes, a silent farewell to a loyal friend and courageous warrior. He felt the earth tremble beneath his knees, not from the aftershocks of the battle, but from the weight of his sorrow.

The loss of the Minotaurs was a wound that cut deep, tearing into the very heart of Tyvellmian's being. They were more than soldiers; they were his brothers in arms, his loyal protectors, their bond forged in the heat of countless battles. Their absence left a void in his heart that threatened to consume him. The silence that once felt heavy was now deafening, amplified by the absence of their powerful roars, the lack of their unwavering support.

a

Their fierce loyalty, their unshakeable resolve, had been his unwavering support. Now, only silence remained.

Then he saw her. Galena, small and frail amidst the carnage, was kneeling beside a body, her own body shuddering with silent grief. The body was that of one of the Minotaurs. It was obvious by the frantic movements of her hands, her small fingers gently tracing the outline of the brutal wound, that she had desperately tried to save him. The subtle tremble of her shoulders showed the immense strength that had been needed to hold back her own emotions, the inner turmoil silently battling the outside stoicism.

He approached cautiously, his steps careful to avoid the scattered debris. He knelt beside her, his hand reaching out to gently place on her shoulder. She looked up, her face streaked with tears, her eyes red and swollen. Yet, in the midst of her grief, there was a fierce determination that mirrored the unwavering courage she had demonstrated throughout the battle.

"He fought bravely," she whispered, her voice barely audible above the desolate silence of the battlefield. "He…he was like a brother to us

a

all." A fresh torrent of tears flowed down her cheeks, and Tyvellmian gently gathered her to his chest, offering silent comfort and solace in the face of their shared loss. He understood her grief, shared it, felt the weight of it crushing him as he held her close. The quiet shared mourning was more potent than words.

The sun, now fully risen, cast a harsh, unforgiving light on the scene, illuminating the extent of the destruction, highlighting the many faces that would never again see the light of day. Nyx, usually so composed, so gracefully deadly, stood apart, shrouded in the shadows she commanded. Her face was pale, her usual ethereal beauty marred by deep circles under her eyes, betraying the toll the battle had taken on even a goddess. She silently watched the scene unfold, her silence as eloquent and mournful as any lament. Her dark eyes, usually filled with power and elegance, were now clouded with sadness. Her silence was a testament to her mourning, an unspoken acknowledgment of her sorrow.

Tyvellmian rose from his embrace with Galena, his heart heavy with the weight of countless losses. The victory, hard- fought and dearly bought, felt hollow, overshadowed by the immense price they had paid. The battle had

a

been won, but at a devastating cost. The ground beneath their feet was saturated with the blood of their allies, a grim reminder of the sacrifice made to protect the world. Their triumph had come at the cost of those who had fought alongside them, the fallen, who represented far more than just casualties; they were friends, comrades, heroes who had given everything for a world that needed saving.

The wind whispered through the ravaged landscape, carrying with it the mournful echoes of the battle, a ghostly lament that seemed to permeate the very air they breathed. The scent of death, sharp and pungent, mingled with the sweet, earthy aroma of the pine trees in the distance, creating a jarring contrast that reflected the chaotic blend of grief and triumph that filled their hearts. The landscape, now scarred and broken, reflected the wounds of the victory, the physical destruction mirroring the emotional turmoil they carried within.

As Tyvellmian looked upon the scene, a profound sense of responsibility settled upon him. The victory had been won, the Ancient Ones vanquished, but the task was far from over. He knew that the healing process would be long and arduous, both physically and emotionally. The world had been saved, but the

a

scars of the battle, both visible and unseen, would remain, a constant reminder of the sacrifices made. He had to be strong, not just for himself, but for those who remained, for those who had survived the horrors of that day, to stand as a beacon of hope and resilience, and to guide them through the difficult times ahead.

The sun beat down upon him, its rays feeling both comforting and harsh, as if mirroring the bittersweet nature of their victory. As the survivors slowly began to tend to the wounded, the grim task of burying their dead, Tyvellmian knew that the final battle had only just begun – the battle of rebuilding, of healing, of learning to live with the indelible marks left by the clash of titans. The fight had ended, but the struggle continued, a new fight for survival, for healing, for memory, and for a future that would forever bear the shadow of their loss. The weight of his responsibility felt immense, as he knew that the lives of those he had saved would now be interwoven with the memory of those lost. The ocean's power, which had coursed through him, now felt heavy, not with a power that could command nature, but a sadness that weighed even heavier on his heart than the weight of his trident.

a

Unexpected Turns.

The sun dipped below the horizon, casting long, skeletal shadows across the ravaged battlefield. The air, still thick with the stench of death and ozone, grew colder with the setting sun. Even the usually boisterous sounds of the sea seemed muted, a respectful hush in the face of such profound loss. Tyvellmian, his exhaustion a tangible weight, leaned against a splintered tree trunk, his trident propped beside him, its polished surface reflecting the dying light. Elara was beside him, her small form wrapped in one of the salvaged blankets from the luxury liner. She was asleep, her face pale and drawn, but peaceful in slumber.

He watched her, a mixture of grief and protectiveness welling within him. He had lost so much, so many brave souls who had fought beside him, their sacrifices sealing the fate of the Ancient Ones. Yet, he also felt a strange sense of peace, a quiet understanding that death, like the tide, was an inevitable force, a part of the endless cycle of life and rebirth.

Suddenly, a flicker of movement at the edge of the battlefield caught his eye. A figure emerged from the shadows, their form indistinct at first, but gradually resolving into the familiar,

a

elegant silhouette of Nyx. She approached cautiously, her movements fluid and silent, her dark eyes reflecting the dying light, even more intensely than usual.

"Tyvellmian," she said, her voice a low murmur that barely disturbed the stillness of the evening. "There are… changes."

Her words hung in the air, pregnant with unspoken meaning. Tyvellmian's heart quickened. He had anticipated celebration, a somber one, but not this. He had anticipated grief, certainly. But this was not the grief of loss alone, this was a grief born of… betrayal.

"Changes?" he asked, his voice rough from disuse.

Nyx nodded, her gaze unwavering. "Poseidon has… shifted his allegiances. He has formed an uneasy alliance with the remnants of the Ancient Ones."

A cold wave washed over Tyvellmian, a shock that sent a shiver down his spine. It was inconceivable. Poseidon, the formidable god of the sea, aligning himself with those he had sworn to destroy? It shattered the very foundation of his understanding of the war, and himself.

a

"It seems," Nyx continued, her voice laced with a chilling detachment, "the destruction of the Ancient Ones has inadvertently unleashed a greater power, a force that even Poseidon fears. He believes… that by allying with these remnants, he can control this new power."

Tyvellmian's mind raced, trying to grasp the enormity of this revelation. The very fabric of the divine order, the carefully woven tapestry of alliances, seemed to unravel before him. The Ancient Ones, seemingly vanquished, were now playing a critical role in a new, much more dangerous game.

"And my siblings?" Tyvellmian asked, his voice barely a whisper. He knew, instinctively, what Nyx's next words would be, yet he had to hear them spoken, to have this betrayal confirmed.

"They support their father," Nyx said, her tone unwavering. "Triton and Athene, fueled by their resentment towards you and your unexpected display of mercy, have thrown their lot in with him."

The betrayal cut deeper than any physical wound. He had fought alongside his siblings, believing in the shared cause, in their familial bond, which, apparently, was little more than a

a

fleeting construct. The weight of their treachery added a new dimension to his already overwhelming sense of loss.
The brothers he had fought beside were now arrayed against him.

Nyx's gaze softened slightly. "This new power is something even the Ancient Ones could not control. It's a force of primal chaos, something that feeds on discord and despair. Poseidon believes he can harness it, to reshape the world in his own image."

"And what of Galena?" Tyvellmian asked, his voice strained. The thought of his siblings attacking her, her life in danger, drove a cold blade through him.

"She is safe for now," Nyx replied. "But for how long, I cannot say. Poseidon's reach is vast, and his wrath… boundless."

The news shook Tyvellmian to his core. The victory was far from secured. The lines of conflict had shifted dramatically. He had saved the world from the Ancient Ones, only to find himself pitted against his own family, against a force far more terrifying than anything he had previously imagined. The battlefield, with its scattered remains and chilling silence, was now a mere precursor to a much larger conflict – a war against his father, against his siblings, against a force beyond human comprehension. The weight of the world, once resting on his shoulders, had now doubled, tripled – a burden of unprecedented proportions. He was no longer merely Poseidon's son, but a beacon of defiance against a cosmic treachery.

As the night deepened, the stars emerged, cold and indifferent to the unfolding drama below. Tyvellmian knew that the final battle had only just begun, a battle that would redefine the very nature of good and evil, of family and loyalty, of gods and mortals. He would fight, not for power or glory, but for Galena, for the few remaining sparks of humanity, for the hope of a future unburdened by the tyrannical ambitions of a god consumed by fear. The path ahead was fraught with peril, a dark and treacherous road paved with betrayal, deception, and the chilling reality of a force capable of reshaping existence itself. But he would walk that road, alone if necessary, guided by his unwavering sense of justice, and fueled by the love that had defied the wrath of the gods themselves. The war was far from over. It had just begun, and the stakes were higher than ever before. The weight of his newfound responsibility felt immense, a constant, oppressive presence that mirrored the

a

vast, ever- shifting ocean itself. His heart, heavy with grief and betrayal, beat with renewed determination. He would survive this, not for himself, but for Galena, for humanity, for the memory of those he had lost, for a future worth fighting for.

A Pivotal Moment in Battle…

The roar of the collapsing temple echoed the turmoil in Tyvellmian's heart. Dust and debris rained down, obscuring the already chaotic battlefield. He'd fought alongside his siblings, their combined might a force seemingly unstoppable against the Ancient Ones. But now, as the dust settled, a horrifying truth emerged: the victory was a pyrrhic one, bought with a betrayal deeper and more chilling than any he could have imagined. Triton, his elder brother, stood amidst the wreckage, his trident dripping with an unnatural, phosphorescent ichor. Athene, her eyes gleaming with a cold, alien light, manipulated the very currents of the air, whipping them into destructive cyclones that swept across the battlefield. They weren't fighting alongside him anymore; they were fighting *against* him.

Their faces, once familiar, now wore a mask of

a

chilling indifference, their expressions devoid of the familial bond that had once bound them together. He saw the raw power emanating from them, a power amplified beyond their natural abilities, a power that resonated with the very essence of the chaotic force Nyx had warned him about. This wasn't the power of the sea gods; this was something… else.

He saw then, amidst the chaos, the source of their newfound might: a colossal vortex of swirling darkness, a gaping maw of chaos that pulsed with an unnatural energy. It pulsed and throbbed, feeding on the lingering despair and destruction of the battlefield, growing larger with each passing moment.
From within this vortex, tendrils of darkness snaked out, coalescing into monstrous forms, spectral beings that echoed the defeated Ancient Ones, yet were far more terrifying. They were beings of pure, unadulterated chaos, their forms shifting and changing like mercury.

Poseidon, his father, materialized from the darkness, his form shrouded in an aura of terrifying power. But it was not the power he knew; this Poseidon was different, warped and twisted by the very chaos he had inadvertently unleashed. His eyes blazed with a terrifying intensity, his expression one of cold,

a

calculating ambition. He was no longer the god of the sea, but something far more sinister, a puppet of the very force he thought he controlled.

“Tyvellmian,” Poseidon’s voice boomed, carrying across the battlefield, each syllable resonating with the power of a collapsing star. “You defied me. You showed mercy where I demanded annihilation. You have weakened our hold on this world, and for that… you will pay.”

Tyvellmian raised his own trident, the familiar weight a comfort in this horrifying landscape of betrayal. The battle had changed, the stakes were far greater. He was no longer fighting for victory over the Ancient Ones; he was fighting for the very soul of existence itself. He was fighting for Galena, for the fragments of humanity that remained, for the flickering hope that still burned within him.

He charged, his own power surging through him, a defiance against his father's horrifying power. The clash of the titans echoed through the world, the ground trembling with the force of their conflict. He fought not just with strength, but with the righteous fury of a son betrayed, a god defending the very fabric of

a

his humanity. His trident clashed against Triton's, sparks of divine energy igniting the air. He parried Athene's destructive cyclones with his own mastery of the tides, the clash of their powers creating a maelstrom of destruction that threatened to engulf the entire battlefield.

But their power was too great. Each blow from Triton and Athene landed with crushing force, and the chaos emanating from the vortex seemed to amplify their strength, fueling their attack, adding to their terrifying power. Tyvellmian found himself battered, his defenses weakening. He was being worn down, not by brute force alone, but by the sheer weight of betrayal, the agony of facing his family as his enemies.

Then, Galena appeared. Emerging from the rubble of a fallen structure, she was small, but her presence was indomitable. She wasn't armed, she didn't possess any divine power; yet, in her eyes, Tyvellmian saw an unwavering resolve, a light that reflected the hope he had almost lost. He saw the unwavering love that had carried him through the darkest of times, a love that now ignited a new fire within him.

She was the reason he had fought, the reason he

would continue to fight. He wouldn't let her, or the fragments of humanity that remained, be consumed by this abyss of chaos. He would fight until his last breath, not just as a god, but as a man driven by love and hope.

His strength surged back. The pain he had been enduring seemed to fade, the exhaustion giving way to a renewed determination. He channeled his emotions, his love for Galena, his fierce sense of justice, into his attacks. Each blow now carried not only the power of a god, but the weight of his unwavering resolve.

The battle raged on, a tempest of divine power. The fate of the world hung in the balance, the very essence of existence teetering on the brink of annihilation. Tyvellmian fought with a ferocity born of despair and fueled by hope, his movements becoming a blur of power. He was not merely fighting his siblings and father, he was fighting the encroaching chaos, the overwhelming darkness threatening to engulf the world.

He managed to drive Triton and Athene back, his attacks gaining strength with each passing moment. He saw a flicker of doubt, of something akin to regret in their eyes, though whether it was for their actions or their

a

situation remained unclear. He fought on, not only to defeat them but also to help them see the error of their ways, to bring them back from the brink of utter destruction.

As the chaos intensified, Tyvellmian found a new source of power, drawing upon the remnants of the Ancient Ones' energy, using it against their own terrifying creation. He manipulated the very currents of chaos, channeling their own destructive power back upon them. He was no longer simply a warrior; he was a conductor of power, a master of chaos himself.

The climax came when he finally confronted Poseidon. The clash of their powers shook the very foundations of the world. The ground cracked, the sky bled, the air itself seemed to vibrate with the immense power of their conflict. It was a battle not just for the fate of the world, but for the very soul of a family torn asunder.

This battle wasn't about victory; it was about redemption, about finding a way to reclaim his father, his siblings, and the world from the clutches of this all-consuming darkness. The final outcome remained uncertain, but as the clash of their powers echoed across the

a

shattered landscape, Tyvellmian knew that he had fought not only for survival, but for the preservation of hope itself. The battle was far from over, but a crucial turning point had been reached, a moment that would forever change the course of their destinies and the fate of the world. He knew he was fighting not just a physical battle but a battle of wills and ideals. The victory, if it came, would be a hard-won one, bought with sacrifices both large and small, but the fight, the relentless, unwavering fight for hope, would continue.

a

Chapter XV

Facing Poseidon!

The air crackled with anticipation, the silence punctuated only by the rhythmic crashing of waves against the jagged rocks that formed a natural amphitheater around them.
Poseidon stood before Tyvellmian, his form less a god of the sea and more a tempest incarnate. The once familiar azure of his skin was now marred by swirling shadows, his eyes burning with an unholy light that mirrored the chaotic vortex still churning behind him. The trident in his hand throbbed with an unnatural energy, its three prongs seeming to writhe like living things.

Tyvellmian, despite the weariness that clung to him like a shroud, stood firm. He'd faced Triton and Amphitrite, their combined might fueled by a malevolent force he barely understood, and yet, he stood. He had Galena 's image seared into his mind, her unwavering hope a beacon in the encroaching darkness. His own trident felt lighter now, almost weightless, as if fueled by the very essence of his resolve.

“You disappoint me, Tyvellmian,” Poseidon’s

a

voice was a guttural rumble, the sound of tectonic plates shifting, of mountains crumbling. “You chose humanity over your family, over your destiny. You spared the insignificant while allowing the Ancient Ones to fester. Your mercy is a weakness, a poison that will destroy us all.”

Tyvellmian’s heart ached. He’d faced monstrous creatures, battled beings of pure chaos, but the pain of his father's condemnation cut deeper than any physical wound. “They were not insignificant, Father. They were people. They deserved to live.”

Poseidon laughed, a sound devoid of mirth, a sound that scraped against the very fabric of reality. “Live? They are insignificant ants clinging to a crumbling rock. Their lives mean nothing compared to the grand design, to the power we wield. You have forsaken your birthright for their ephemeral existence.”

“My birthright is more than just power, Father. It’s about responsibility. It’s about compassion. It's about choosing the path of hope, not the path of annihilation.”

“Compassion? Hope? These are luxuries we cannot afford,” Poseidon roared, his voice shaking the very earth beneath their feet. The

a

chaotic vortex behind him pulsed, its tendrils reaching out like grasping claws. “You stand before me, a rebellious son who dares to defy his father, a god who dares to question the cosmic order. Your defiance will not go unpunished.”

The air crackled with anticipation. The tension was almost palpable, thick enough to cut with a knife.

Tyvellmian felt the pull of the darkness, the allure of the chaotic power that had corrupted his family. He understood the siren song of absolute power, the intoxicating sway of unchallenged authority. Yet, he stood firm. He had glimpsed a different path, one where power and compassion were not mutually exclusive, where strength didn't require cruelty.

The first blow landed with the force of a tidal wave. Poseidon's trident, imbued with chaotic energy, crashed against Tyvellmian's defense, sending tremors through the very ground. Tyvellmian retaliated, his own trident, a conduit of controlled power, a force of nature wielded with precision and intent.

a

The clash of their weapons was a deafening symphony of destruction, each strike echoing across the shattered landscape.

The battle wasn't a straightforward exchange of blows. It was a dance of power, a contest of wills that extended beyond the physical realm. Poseidon unleashed waves of chaotic energy, tidal surges of corrupted power designed to overwhelm and crush. Tyvellmian countered, not with brute force alone but with cunning and precision. He drew upon his own connection to the sea, channeling its natural rhythm to deflect his father's attacks, weaving through the chaotic surges with graceful agility.

He fought not with hate, but with profound sorrow. He saw glimpses of the father he knew within the monstrous form of his corrupted progenitor, a father who once instilled the very values that now guided his defiance. He saw the vestiges of the god who commanded respect and affection, shrouded beneath the chaotic veneer of his warped power.

Their fight was a reflection of a spiritual conflict, a struggle between the old gods and the encroaching darkness that threatened to consume them. Each strike carried the weight

a

of millennia, the history of a family torn asunder, the fate of a world hanging in the balance. Tyvellmian's own trident pulsed with his determination, his hope, his love for Galena— a beacon of defiance against the encroaching darkness.

As the battle raged on, Tyvellmian began to understand the depth of his father's despair. The corruption wasn't simply a malicious force; it was a desperate attempt to cling to power in a world that was rejecting the old gods. Poseidon, in his misguided fury, unleashed chaos in a desperate bid to maintain control. He was fighting not only against his son but also against the inevitable tides of change. His rage was born of fear, of a desperate longing for the authority he was losing.

Tyvellmian’s defense faltered. He was hurt, battered, and exhausted but his spirit was unbroken. He used his understanding of the chaos to predict his father's movements, to turn the tide of the battle not through strength alone but through strategy and insight. He recognized the vulnerabilities within the corrupted power that animated Poseidon, using this knowledge to subtly disrupt the flow of chaotic energy. He began to redirect the destructive forces of his

a

father, turning them against themselves, weakening his resolve and his control over the chaotic energies he wielded. With each heartbeat, Tyvellmian adapted. He moved not as a rebellious son, but as a force of wisdom and inevitability…the ocean's patience against the storm's fury. Every time Poseidon struck with wild, furious power, Tyvellmian countered not with equal rage, but with calculated precision. He flowed around his father's onslaught, allowing the chaos to expend itself, like waves crashing fruitlessly against an immovable cliff.

He struck at the seams of Poseidon's power, weaving through the maelstrom.

His trident channeling the true essence of the sea…balance, resilience, transformation.

When Poseidon summoned a vortex of roiling waters, Tyvellmian diverted its pull into the ground, draining its strength. When the sea god lashed out with bolts of oceanic lightning, Tyvellmian grounded them into his own shield of swirling tides, diffusing their fury into a harmless mist.

The battlefield became a reflection of their struggle, wild destruction on one side, measured defiance on the other.

a

Tyvellmian's allies, emboldened by his example, pressed forward against the minions still loyal to Poseidon. Their renewed assault cutting swaths through the enemy ranks. Cracks spiderwebbed through the foundation of Poseidon's assault, visible now not only in the battlefield but in the faltering certainty behind the old god's eyes.

A roar of frustration tore from Poseidon's throat, shaking the heavens, but it was met with Tyvellmian's silence. A steadfast refusal to be broken, a quiet declaration that the age of fear and domination was ending.
For the first time, Poseidon stepped back, not out of strategy, but out of uncertainty. The world shifted subtly, but unmistakably, as the tides of power began to flow toward the son and not the father.

The climax arrived in a moment of breathtaking intensity. They stood locked in a final, desperate struggle, their tridents intertwined in a deadly embrace. Tyvellmian saw a flicker of recognition in Poseidon's eyes, a moment of clarity amidst the raging chaos. It was a fleeting moment, but it was enough. Tyvellmian channeled all his remaining strength, his love for Galena, his unwavering hope into a final, decisive blow.

a

Time seemed to shudder around them, the battle field falling into a deafening stillness as the two gods strained against each other. The storm overhead froze in place, droplets of rain hanging like crystal beads in the suspended air. Tyvellmian could feel the raw ancient might of his father trying to crush him, to bend him beneath the weight of an age that should have long passed.

But he also felt something deeper, the fading heartbeat of the sea, crying out for renewal, for mercy. It was not hatred that guided Tyvellmian's hand, but love. Not only for Galena, but for the world still struggling to be free from the ancient chains of fear.

With a final cry out, Tyvellmian twisted his trident, not to destroy, but to cleanse.

Oceanic energy, pure and radiant , burst forth from him in a brilliant surge, wrapping around Poseidon's weapon and crawling up his arms like living ribbons of light and tide. The chaotic corruption screamed in protest, recoiling from the purity of Tyvellmian's will.

In that moment, father and son were bound together, not by hatred, but by an unspoken sorrow for all that had been lost and a fragile hope for what could still be saved. The energy surged, creating a blinding flash of light that momentarily eclipsed the world. When the light

a

subsided, Poseidon stood weakened, the chaotic energies that had consumed him receding. His form shimmered, the shadows slowly dissipating, revealing the familiar features of his father, though bearing the marks of a brutal battle. The rage in his eyes had been replaced by exhaustion, a deep, profound weariness. The vortex behind him was reduced to a simmering eddy, its power greatly diminished.

Tyvellmian stood, battered but victorious, not through a destructive triumph, but a hard-won, empathetic victory. He had not defeated his father, but he had saved him—and possibly the world, from the encroaching abyss of chaos. The battle was over, but the true reckoning had just begun. The path to healing, to reconciliation, would be long and arduous, but he knew, as he looked at his weakened, yet finally human-seeming father, that the fight for hope had been, at least for now, won.

A Fathers Regret.

The salty air hung heavy with the aftermath of their battle, the scent of ozone and brine sharp in Tyvellmian's nostrils. Poseidon stood before him, a diminished figure, the godlike aura

a

replaced by a weary vulnerability. The tempest in his eyes had subsided, leaving behind a stillness that was almost more terrifying than the previous rage. His skin, once a vibrant azure, now bore the dull, ashen hue of a man long spent, his body etched with the scars of their conflict, both physical and spiritual. The trident, once a weapon of chaotic destruction, lay broken at his feet, its three prongs snapped like brittle twigs.

Tyvellmian lowered his own trident, the weight of it suddenly immense in his hands. He felt no triumph, only a profound sorrow. He had broken what could not be broken. He had won the battle, but at what cost? He had faced his father, not as an enemy to be vanquished, but as a man to be saved. He had seen the flicker of humanity within the god, the desperate clinging to power masked by the insatiable hunger of the chaos that had possessed him.

Poseidon's gaze fell upon the shattered weapon, his voice a low rasp, barely a whisper. "I… I failed," he breathed, the words heavy with regret, each syllable carrying the weight of millennia of rule, of power, of a god's despair. His voice cracked, the sound as fragile as a seashell crumbling to dust. The god of the sea,

a

the ruler of the tides, was broken.

Tyvellmian approached cautiously, his heart heavy with a mixture of empathy and unresolved anger. He had faced monstrous creatures, beings of pure chaos, but nothing had prepared him for the sight of his father, reduced to this state of profound defeat.
He had known his father's temper, his ruthlessness, his unyielding pride, but this… this was something else entirely. This was the raw, exposed vulnerability of a god stripped bare of his power.

He knelt beside Poseidon, his hand hovering hesitantly above his father's arm. The touch was hesitant, unsure. He had known only the harsh discipline of a god, the unwavering demand for obedience. This act of compassion felt foreign, yet strangely necessary. He had learned compassion from Galena, from the unexpected kindness he had found in the face of devastation. It was a lesson he now needed to extend to the man who had fathered him.

Poseidon flinched at first, a remnant of the chaotic energy still flickering beneath his skin. But he didn't pull away. He let Tyvellmian's hand rest upon his arm, a silent acceptance of his son's compassion.

a

“It wasn't your fault, Father,” Tyvellmian said softly, his voice laced with the pain of understanding. "The Ancient Ones… they twisted you, corrupted your power. They fed on your fear, your despair.”

Poseidon let out a long, shuddering sigh, the sound of a storm finally calming. "Fear? Despair? Those are but weak words to describe the abyss that consumed me. I saw humanity turning away, rejecting the old ways, the ancient gods. My power… it was waning. I felt it slipping through my fingers, the tides of faith receding before my very eyes. I panicked. I grasped for control, for a way to maintain what I had lost."

His voice trembled. "I saw the storm brewing, the chaos unleashed by the Ancient Ones. I believed I could control it, bend it to my will. I was a fool. A blind, arrogant fool. I tried to hold back the inevitable, and in doing so, I unleashed a horror upon the world.” He looked up at his son, his eyes filled with a profound sadness. “I tried to save us all, in my own way. But I destroyed everything I sought to protect.”

a

The weight of his confession hung heavy in the air, the silence punctuated only by the rhythmic crashing of waves. Tyvellmian understood. He had seen the glimpses of his father's fear, the desperation in his eyes during their battle. He had felt the pull of the chaos himself, the seductive lure of unchecked power. It wasn't simply malice; it was a desperate attempt to cling to relevance, to maintain authority in a world that was rapidly changing.

"I understand, Father," Tyvellmian said, his voice filled with empathy. "But there's another way. A way that doesn't involve destroying everything in your path. A way that embraces change, that adapts, that finds strength not in domination, but in understanding."

Poseidon looked away, staring at the broken trident at his feet. "There are no more tides to command, no more storms to conjure. My reign… it is over."

"Your reign is not over, Father," Tyvellmian corrected gently. "Your role has changed. It's not about wielding power over others, but about guiding them, helping them navigate the changing tides of faith, of belief. You can still

a

lead, but in a different way. A way that reflects compassion, not cruelty."

A faint smile touched Poseidon's lips, a glimmer of hope piercing the darkness that had enveloped him. "Compassion…" he whispered, the word tasting strange on his tongue, an unfamiliar concept for a god accustomed to wielding power through fear and force.

The reconciliation wasn't a sudden burst of forgiveness, but a slow, painstaking process. It would take time to heal the wounds of their conflict, to mend the fractured bond between father and son. But as Tyvellmian looked at his father, at the exhaustion etched into his features, at the profound sorrow in his eyes, he felt a sense of peace. He had not only defeated his father's corrupting influence, but he had also begun to mend the broken relationship that had fueled it.

The waves continued to crash against the rocks, a constant reminder of the power of nature, of the cyclical nature of change. Poseidon, once the untouchable god of the sea, now stood humbled, diminished, yet paradoxically more human than Tyvellmian had ever seen him before. The battle was over, but the real work was just beginning. The path to healing, to reconciliation, to a future where power and

a

compassion could coexist, was a long and uncertain one, but Tyvellmian was ready to walk it, hand-in-hand with a father who had finally begun to understand the true meaning of his power. The world awaited them, not as a battlefield to be conquered, but as a realm to be nurtured, to be guided, to be healed. The tide had turned, and the true reckoning had only just begun, not in destruction, but in the difficult, and ultimately hopeful

,

work of rebuilding.

a

Chapter XVI

Redemption for all…

The weight of the unspoken hung heavy between them, a silence more profound than any storm. The broken trident, a symbol of Poseidon's shattered power, lay gleaming faintly in the twilight. Tyvellmian rose, extending a hand to his father. Poseidon, his face etched with a weariness that transcended millennia, hesitantly took it. The touch was fragile, a tentative bridge across a chasm of years of strained relationship and unspoken resentments.

The journey back to the palace was silent, the once-terrifying presence of the sea god now reduced to a quiet contemplation. The storm that had ravaged the seas had calmed, leaving behind a stillness that reflected the inner turmoil both father and son were grappling with. Tyvellmian, despite his victory, felt no elation, only a profound sense of responsibility. He had defeated the chaos that had consumed his father, but the true battle had only just begun: the battle for reconciliation.

a

Upon their arrival, the palace, usually a vibrant hub of activity, felt strangely subdued. The echoes of the recent tempest still lingered, a palpable sense of unease permeating the air. Tyvellmian's siblings, Athene, Triton, and Nereus, stood waiting, their faces a mixture of suspicion, resentment, and grudging respect. They had witnessed the battle, the fall of their father, and the unexpected mercy shown by their brother.

"He has been… altered," Athene, spoke first, her voice tight with controlled emotion. Her eyes, usually sparkling with an icy authority, held a flicker of uncertainty. She had always been the most ruthless, the most fiercely loyal to Poseidon’s unwavering rule. But even her resolve seemed shaken. "The chaos… it has left its mark. But so has Tyvellmian’s defiance."

Triton, ever the boisterous warrior, remained silent, his gaze shifting between Tyvellmian and their father. The usually fierce glint in his eyes was replaced by a contemplative stillness. He had been the most physically powerful, the one who relished the use of force. Yet, witnessing Tyvellmian's unexpected compassion, he seemed to question his own methods. For the first time in ages. Triton felt the certainty of his old ways begin to crack.

a

The thunder of battle, the pursuit of dominance, they had been his creed, the foundation of his very being. Yet there stood Tyvellmian, wounded but unyielding, Not winning by sheer strength but by heart, by a refusal to succumb to the endless cycle of destruction. Triton’s grip tightened on his trident, not out of rage, but from the weight of revelation in Tyvellmian’s act of mercy. He saw a reflection he had long ignored, a glimmer of something he had once known but buried beneath layers of pride. His thoughts drifted unbidden to Arconia, his daughter born of a fleeting love with a mortal woman, a bound he had always treated with uneasy detachment. Arconia, with her mortal heart and godly blood, had often been a source of conflict within him. He had pushed her towards strength, towards hardness, believing that was the only way to survive the harsh worlds of gods and men. Yet now, he wondered if he had been wrong, if the very mortality he had sought to harden out of her was her greatest gift.

A surge of unexpected tenderness welled in Triton’s chest, tightening his throat. Perhaps strength was not measured solely by the force of one’s blows, but by the courage to choose a different path. Perhaps Arconia’s stubborn compassion, which he had once scorned as weakness, was in truth the same strength he now

a

witnessed reshaping the fate of gods and mortals alike.

Triton lowered his trident slightly, a silent grudging acknowledgment, not just to Tyvellmian, but to Arconia as well. The tides were shifting and for the first time, Triton found himself willing , perhaps even eager, to change with them.

Nereus, the second youngest, the most enigmatic of the siblings, offered Tyvellmian, a slight nod. He possessed a keen intellect, a sharp understanding of the currents of power. His silence, however, spoke volumes. He understood the shift in the balance of power, the subtle change in Tyvellmian, and the potential for a future beyond the reign of unchecked power.

Poseidon, seeing his children, seemed to gather a shred of his former strength. His voice, though still weak, held a newfound authority, a resolve born not of dominance, but of acceptance.

"My children," he began, his voice surprisingly calm, "you witnessed the battle. You saw the chaos consume me. You also saw my son break free from its influence and instead offer me not

a

destruction, but salvation. Tyvellmian showed me what true strength truly is: a strength not found in wielding power but in showing compassion."

His words hung in the air, silencing his offspring. The revelation hung heavy, transforming the atmosphere of the palace. This was not merely a change in their father; it was a seismic shift in their understanding of their power and their purpose.

Tyvellmian stepped forward, his eyes meeting each of his siblings' in turn. He spoke not of power or dominance, but of the fragility of their existence, the importance of unity, and the need for a new era of understanding. He spoke of Galena, and the profound impact her life had had on him, and how his encounter with her had challenged everything he had known. He detailed the devastation of the storm and how, despite his initial anger, he'd learned that the human race deserved a chance at survival.

He spoke of the Ancient Ones, their manipulative power over them, and of the need to break free from their corrupting influence, to find strength not through destruction, but through empathy and understanding. He spoke of finding peace in the face of overwhelming

a

power. He spoke not of conquering, but of collaboration.

The ensuing discussion was long and arduous, marked by lingering suspicions and unresolved resentments. But a common theme emerged from the discourse: the shared acknowledgment of their father's past mistakes and the collective desire to rebuild their fractured family and forge a new path. They debated strategy, the future of their interactions with humanity, and the means by which they might combat the continuing threat of the Ancient Ones. The old ways were now being challenged not only from without, but from within, prompting introspection and a reevaluation of their roles in a world on the cusp of significant change.

Days turned into weeks, and a transformation washed over the palace. The air of tension gradually gave way to a collaborative atmosphere. Tyvellmian, once seen as an outcast, became a bridge, fostering dialogue, and encouraging understanding between his siblings and his now-reformed father. He didn't erase their past conflicts, but he helped them grapple with the underlying reasons that fueled them. They found common ground in their shared desire for atonement, for the chance to start anew, with a new set of

a

principles to guide their actions.

The reconciliation was not immediate. There were still moments of conflict, of friction, of ingrained habits that were difficult to break. But underlying all disagreements was a shared, unspoken commitment to a new way of being, a way that prioritized unity, understanding, and redemption. It was a path that would require constant vigilance and effort, but they were finally committed to walking it together.

Poseidon, stripped of his tyrannical authority, found a new purpose in guiding his children, not through force, but through counsel and mentorship. His understanding of the human condition had deepened significantly, and he found solace in supporting their new, compassionate approach. He learned to appreciate the subtle power that flowed from collaboration rather than domination.

The siblings, in turn, found strength in their newfound unity. They discovered the benefits of mutual respect and cooperation, a marked departure from their previous competitive dynamic. The focus shifted from vying for their father's approval and wielding their own personal power to working collaboratively to heal the rifts within their family and respond to

a

the challenges presented by the changing world.

Tyvellmian’s compassion didn’t just redeem him; it transformed his family. The reckoning that had begun with a devastating storm and a brutal battle concluded not with destruction, but with the slow, arduous process of healing and redemption. The path forward remained uncertain, but it was a path they would now walk together, united not by power, but by a shared commitment to a better future. The tides had changed, not only in the oceans, but within their hearts as well. Their journey was far from over, but for the first time, they faced the future not as divided factions, but as a family bound by a newfound empathy and understanding.
The reckoning was complete, and the true work of rebuilding had finally begun.

Reconciliation begins...

The initial silence following Tyvellmian's declaration hung heavy in the air, thick with unspoken accusations and years of simmering resentment. Athene, ever the pragmatist, was the first to break it. "You speak of compassion, brother," she said, her voice laced with a

a

skepticism that belied her words. "But compassion has no place in the war we wage against the Ancient Ones. Mercy is weakness, and weakness invites destruction."

Tyvellmian met her gaze, his own eyes unwavering. "The strength of the ocean lies not in its relentless waves, but in its ability to nourish life," he countered, his voice calm yet resolute. "The Ancient Ones thrive on chaos; they feed on our fear and our division. To fight them with their own weapons is to play into their hands." He paused, letting his words settle. "We must find a different path, a path of unity, of understanding."

Triton, his hands calloused from centuries of wielding his trident, scoffed. "Unity? We are gods, not mortals. We wield power, and power is not meant to be shared, but commanded." His voice was rough, edged with the ingrained belief that dominance was the only language the world understood. But even as he spoke, a flicker of doubt crossed his features. The storm, the near-destruction of their father, had shaken his own sense of invincibility.

Nereus, the quiet observer, remained silent for a long moment, his gaze scanning the faces of his siblings. He finally spoke, his voice a low

a

murmur that carried an unexpected weight. "The tide is turning," he said, his eyes fixed on Tyvellmian. "The old ways are failing us. The Ancient Ones have played upon our strengths, our weaknesses, our pride. But perhaps... perhaps Tyvellmian has found a way to break their hold."

The weight of Nereus's words settled upon them like the impending twilight. Athene and Triton, for all their inherent power, were forced to acknowledge the undeniable truth in his words. The battle with the Ancient Ones had not only nearly destroyed their father, it had exposed the inherent flaws in their strategies, the weakness in their reliance on raw power alone.

Poseidon, his face etched with the lines of his many years, watched his children with a mixture of hope and apprehension. The battle had stripped away the arrogance that had shrouded him for millennia, leaving behind a raw vulnerability that both frightened and empowered him. He had witnessed the truth in his son's words, the devastating consequences of unchecked power.

"My children," Poseidon began, his voice surprisingly soft, "I have spent eons ruling

a

through fear and intimidation. I have wielded my trident as a weapon, not a guide. I have demanded obedience, not understanding. And because of this, I have been near destroyed by forces that I never saw coming. Tyvellmian has shown me a different way." He gestured towards Tyvellmian. "He has shown me the strength in empathy, the power of compassion, the resilience that comes from unity."

The ensuing discussion was not a simple reconciliation. It was a brutal, honest excavation of old wounds, of years of rivalry and resentment. Athene confessed to her own fears, the insecurity that drove her to seek power and dominance. Triton admitted to the thrill he'd found in violence, the satisfaction of conquest. Even Nereus, the calmest of them all, revealed the subtle ways in which he had manipulated events to further his own agenda.

The weight of those confessions hung heavy in the air, but it was a weight shared. As they spoke, the unspoken resentments began to dissipate, replaced by a slow, tentative understanding.
They acknowledged their father's flaws, not as excuses, but as lessons.

a

They recognized the manipulative tactics of the Ancient Ones, the insidious ways in which they had exploited their internal conflicts to weaken them.

Tyvellmian, throughout the process, remained a steadfast guide. He didn't demand forgiveness, but offered understanding. He recounted his encounter with Elara, the unwavering compassion he felt towards her and the survivors of the capsized liner. He spoke of her courage in the face of overwhelming odds, her resilience, and the way her strength had resonated deep within him. He described not only her physical courage, but her inner fortitude, her capacity for hope in the face of unimaginable despair.

He spoke of the profound transformation that her existence had ignited within him, a shift from the vengeful son of Poseidon to a being capable of unexpected mercy. He described the internal struggle, the battle between his inherited rage and his newfound capacity for empathy. This vulnerability, this honest account of his internal turmoil, fostered a sense of trust among his siblings, a shared recognition of their own internal struggles and the need to confront their past demons.

a

As the days bled into weeks, a tangible shift occurred within the palace. The atmosphere, once thick with suspicion and hostility, became infused with a sense of shared purpose. They spent hours discussing strategies for confronting the Ancient Ones, not through brute force alone, but through a combination of strategic planning, careful manipulation, and an understanding of the Ancient Ones' own weaknesses and vulnerabilities.

They delved into ancient texts, forgotten prophecies, and long-lost lore, searching for clues to their enemies' plans and their own forgotten history. They unearthed secrets about their father's own past, understanding that his tyrannical reign stemmed from his own fears and insecurities. They learned to utilize each other's strengths, recognizing the complementary nature of their powers. Athene's strategic mind, Triton's raw power, Nereus's intellect, and Tyvellmian's unique blend of empathy and strength formed a formidable alliance, far stronger than the sum of their individual capabilities.

The reconciliation wasn't a sudden event, but a gradual process, a slow dismantling of centuries of ingrained behaviors and prejudices. There were moments of frustration,

a

of relapse into old patterns, but the commitment to a new path remained strong. Poseidon, stripped of his tyrannical authority, discovered a different kind of power – the power of guidance, mentorship, and unwavering support. He found solace in his newfound role as a counselor, a teacher, a guiding light.

Tyvellmian, once the outcast, became the unifier, the bridge between his father and siblings. He didn't erase the past, but helped them to understand it, to learn from it. He taught them the importance of listening, of empathy, of finding common ground despite their differences. They learned to trust each other, to rely on each other, to support each other, even when disagreements persisted. The old rivalries remained, but they were now tempered by a mutual respect, a shared understanding of their individual strengths and weaknesses.

The reckoning had concluded not with destruction, but with the arduous birth of a new era – an era of understanding, cooperation, and healing. The path ahead was uncertain, fraught with challenges and unforeseen difficulties, but for the first time, they faced it as a united front, bound not by the chains of power but by the bonds of family, forgiveness, and a shared

commitment to a brighter future. The tides had indeed changed, transforming not only the ocean, but the very fabric of their being.

A New Beginning...

The sun, a pale disc in the early morning sky, cast long shadows across the sprawling palace gardens. A gentle breeze rustled through the leaves of ancient olive trees, their branches heavy with the weight of centuries. Gone was the oppressive atmosphere of suspicion and hostility that had permeated the palace for so long. In its place was a quietude, a sense of peace that settled over the grounds like a gentle mist. Even the sea, usually a restless giant, seemed to mirror the newfound serenity, its waves lapping softly against the shore.

Tyvellmian, strolling through the gardens with his niece, Arconia, felt the weight of his past lift from his shoulders. The reconciliation with his siblings had been a transformative experience, a catharsis that had cleansed the bitterness from their hearts. Arconia, sensing his contentment, smiled. She had witnessed firsthand the turmoil that had plagued her uncle, the conflict between his inherited rage and his burgeoning compassion. She had seen the transformation wrought by his encounter

a

with Galena, the subtle shifts in his demeanor, the lessening of the grim determination that had etched itself upon his features. Now, a softer light shone in his eyes, a reflection of the peace that had settled over their family.

"It's different, isn't it, Uncle?" Arconia said, her voice barely a whisper, as if afraid to disturb the tranquility of the moment.

Tyvellmian nodded, a gentle smile playing on his lips. "It is. The air feels lighter, the burden... less heavy." He paused, looking out at the shimmering expanse of the sea. "For centuries, we have fought amongst ourselves, consumed by our own ambitions and insecurities. We allowed the Ancient Ones to manipulate us, to sow discord among us."

"But now," Arconia added, her voice gaining strength, "we stand united. We have learned from our mistakes."

They continued their stroll, the silence between them comfortable and companionable, filled with unspoken understanding. They passed by Triton, who was practicing his trident skills with a controlled ferocity, a stark contrast to his previous uncontrolled rage.

a

He paused his practice, a hint of a smile gracing his lips as he saw them.

"Practicing my aim," Triton said, his voice surprisingly mellow. "Trying to be a little more... precise."

Tyvellmian chuckled. "Precision is always better than brute force," he replied, acknowledging the subtle shift in his brother's attitude.

Athene, seated under the shade of a sprawling fig tree, was engrossed in a scroll, studying ancient prophecies. She looked up, her expression betraying a hint of weariness but also a newfound serenity. "I've discovered something fascinating," she announced, her voice devoid of its usual sharp edge. "A prophecy about a hidden weakness within the Ancient Ones – a weakness we can exploit."

Nereus approached them, his usual quiet demeanor replaced by a hint of eagerness. "I've been studying the linguistic patterns of the ancient texts," he said, his voice low and measured. "There's a key, a hidden phrase that could unravel their plans."

The four of them gathered, their faces illuminated by the soft morning light, discussing their strategies, their voices a harmonious blend of shared knowledge and collaborative effort. Gone were the days of heated arguments, of accusations and resentments. In their place was a shared purpose, a united front against their common enemy.

Over the next few weeks, a sense of order and purpose permeated the palace. The once-tense atmosphere transformed into one of collaboration and mutual support. Poseidon, having witnessed his children's reconciliation, seemed rejuvenated. He no longer ruled through fear and intimidation, but through guidance and understanding. He spent his days mentoring his children, sharing his vast knowledge and experience, helping them hone their powers and develop their strategic thinking.

Tyvellmian, despite his newfound role as a peacemaker, continued to search for Galena, his heart yearning for her presence. He often found himself drawn to the coastline, staring out at the vast expanse of the ocean, hoping to catch a glimpse of her, a flicker of her vibrant spirit amid the crashing waves. He knew his feelings were complicated; a mixture of profound gratitude and a deep-seated longing

for connection in a world that had grown increasingly complicated. His encounter with her had awakened something within him, a compassion that had been dormant for centuries, a capacity for empathy that had challenged his very identity.

He would recount his experiences to his siblings, sharing his growing understanding of the human spirit, its capacity for both remarkable resilience and devastating vulnerability. He spoke of Galena 's courage, her determination, her indomitable spirit in the face of such overwhelming tragedy. Her strength resonated deeply with him and profoundly shaped his perspective. He found that sharing these experiences forged a deeper connection with his family, solidifying the newly established bond of unity.

Their preparations for confronting the Ancient Ones intensified. They delved deeper into ancient texts, uncovering forgotten strategies and long-lost lore. They studied the patterns of the Ancient Ones' attacks, identifying their vulnerabilities and weaknesses. They utilized their unique strengths, creating a formidable team capable of facing any challenge. Athene, with her strategic mind, devised cunning plans to outwit their enemies. Triton, wielding his

a

trident with renewed precision, provided unparalleled force. Nereus, with his profound understanding of ancient languages and prophecies, deciphered cryptic messages and provided vital insights. And Tyvellmian, with his unique empathy and understanding of the human spirit, served as the bridge between the divine and the mortal realms.

The newfound unity wasn't solely about strategic planning; it was also about healing past wounds. They spent countless hours in open discussions, sharing their vulnerabilities, acknowledging their past mistakes, and learning from each other. The old rivalries still simmered beneath the surface, but they were now tempered by a mutual respect, a deep-seated understanding of their individual strengths and weaknesses.

One evening, as the sun dipped below the horizon, painting the sky in hues of orange and purple, Tyvellmian sat with his siblings, the quiet murmur of their conversation a testament to the peace that had finally settled upon their family.
Poseidon, observing them from a distance, felt a profound sense of satisfaction. He had witnessed the transformation not only of his children, but of himself. He had shed his

a

tyrannical skin, revealing a wiser, more compassionate being.

The reckoning had brought them to the brink of destruction, but from the ashes of their conflict, a new beginning had emerged—a beginning that was not only about defeating their enemies, but about forging a stronger, more harmonious family bond. The future remained uncertain, fraught with challenges, but they faced it together, a united front, bound not by the chains of power but by the unbreakable ties of family, understanding, and shared purpose. The tide had indeed turned, transforming not just the ocean, but their very souls. The peace was fragile, a delicate bloom in the aftermath of a devastating storm, but it was a peace worth fighting for, a peace they were determined to protect. And as the stars emerged, twinkling like diamonds scattered across a velvet cloth, a sense of hope filled the night, a hope for a new dawn, a new beginning, a new era.

In the Aftermath of War...

The world, once ravaged by the wrath of the Ancient Ones, was slowly, tentatively, healing. The scars remained – the fissures in the earth, the ghostly outlines of buildings reduced to rubble, the lingering taste of salt and ash in the

a

air – but a fragile green was pushing through the cracked pavement, a defiant testament to life's tenacity. The ocean, once a tempestuous beast, had calmed, its waves now lapping gently against the shores, a soothing rhythm replacing the destructive fury. The air, once thick with the oppressive weight of magical energy, felt lighter, cleaner, as if the very atmosphere had exhaled a sigh of relief.

Cities, once shrouded in darkness and fear, were slowly awakening. The sounds of hammers and chisels echoed through the streets, a symphony of reconstruction, a testament to human resilience. People, once huddled in fear, emerged from their shelters, their faces etched with the weariness of survival, but their eyes gleaming with a tentative hope.

The stories of the Tidal Man, of Tyvellmian's unexpected compassion, were whispered from mouth to mouth, becoming a beacon of hope in the wreckage. He wasn't just a god; he was a symbol of mercy in a world that had known only destruction.

a

The rebuilding efforts were immense. Governments, once fractured and weakened by distrust and fears, worked together, their differences overshadowed by the shared urgency of survival. International collaborations, once stifled by political tensions, thrived, driven by a common purpose – to rebuild the shattered world.
The shared trauma brought about a newfound unity, a collective resolve that transcended national borders and ideological divisions. Scientists, engineers, and architects collaborated, pooling their resources and knowledge, driven by a shared commitment to innovation and progress.

Innovative technologies, developed during the war, were rapidly deployed, facilitating rapid reconstruction and providing solutions to the environmental challenges left in the wake of the divine conflict. The focus shifted from military might to sustainable development, a recognition that true strength lay not in destruction but in resilience and collaboration.

Tyvellmian, having witnessed the devastation firsthand, felt the weight of responsibility upon his shoulders. His role as peacemaker extended beyond his family; it encompassed the entire world. He used his influence to encourage

a

cooperation and understanding, fostering a climate of mutual respect and trust between nations. He worked tirelessly alongside human leaders, leveraging his unique position to bridge the gap between the divine and the mortal realms, facilitating the creation of international accords that ensured mutual cooperation and equitable resource distribution.

He established a network of support for those displaced by the war, providing shelter, food, and medical care. He leveraged his abilities to heal the land, accelerating the recovery of ravaged ecosystems, ensuring that nature's ability to recover would surpass the devastation wrought by the Ancient Ones' fury. The speed of his healing was astounding; fields once barren and scarred now flourished, with life returning at an almost miraculous pace. Forests that had been consumed by fire quickly regenerated, their growth exceeding even the most optimistic projections. The very land seemed grateful for his intervention, offering rapid signs of renewal.

His relationship with Galena, the woman he'd rescued from the capsized liner, remained a source of profound inspiration. He had found her, weak but alive, in the aftermath of the storm. She had become his anchor in the chaos, a reminder of the compassion

a

that had sparked his transformation. Their connection transcended the boundaries of their worlds; she saw past his godhood, recognizing the human heart that beat beneath. Their bond was a testament to the resilience of love amidst the ruins of war. They worked side-by-side in the reconstruction efforts, her sharp intellect and organizational skills complementing his divine power.

Galena became his advisor, helping him navigate the complexities of the post-war world, guiding him through the intricate web of human politics and social dynamics. She was instrumental in shaping his approach to his new role, urging him to avoid the pitfalls of authoritarian rule, encouraging him instead to embrace democratic principles and prioritize human rights. Her counsel, rooted in her understanding of human nature, proved invaluable in shaping his actions and ensuring the longevity of the newly established peace. Her presence constantly reminded him of the importance of his compassion, the strength he found in his connection with humanity, and the power of empathy in a world desperately in need of healing.

However, even amidst this period of rebuilding, the threat of the Ancient Ones lingered. Though defeated, their influence

a

hadn’t entirely vanished. Whispers of their resurgence circulated, fueling anxieties and unease. The siblings remained vigilant, constantly monitoring for any signs of renewed activity. They understood that their victory was not a final end but a temporary respite, a necessary pause in a much larger conflict. The search for a way to truly obliterate the Ancient Ones' influence continued. Amphitrite delved into ancient texts, seeking vulnerabilities in their mystical power structure. Nereus meticulously studied the linguistics of ancient prophecies, seeking the key to understanding their potential for revival. Triton enhanced his training, ready for any potential confrontation.

Tyvellmian, despite his growing empathy for humanity, remained steadfast in his commitment to protecting his world. He knew that his powers were necessary, that his role as a guardian extended beyond his family to encompass the mortal world. He knew that the peace they had achieved was a fragile thing, that it required constant vigilance and unwavering commitment to maintain. He trained relentlessly, honing his abilities, preparing himself for any future threat, while simultaneously working to foster peace and cooperation between his world and the human world. He understood that the strength of his

a

world lay in the cooperation of the gods and humans.

The task before them was monumental. The world needed not just to be rebuilt, but also reimagined, transformed into a better version of itself, a world where peace and cooperation reigned supreme, a world free from the destructive forces that had threatened to consume it. The scars of war would remain, a reminder of the destruction, but they also served as a testament to human resilience, a symbol of the strength of the human spirit, a beacon of hope for a new dawn. The sun, rising each morning, cast a warmer glow on the world, a promise of a brighter future, a future where the sounds of rebuilding replaced the echoes of war, and the whisper of hope filled the hearts of all. The new world order was fragile, a delicate balance between divine power and human resilience, but it was a new world, nonetheless, a world where the possibilities, however uncertain, shone brightly in the eyes of those who were committed to building it. The world had changed, and with it, the very essence of the gods themselves.

a

Changing the World...

The air, once thick with the scent of salt and ash, now carried the gentler fragrance of blooming jasmine and newly tilled earth. The rhythmic crash of waves against the shore, once a terrifying symphony of destruction, now provided a soothing lullaby to the rebuilt coastal towns. The transformation wasn't merely physical; it was a shift in the very fabric of reality, a subtle but profound alteration in the relationship between gods and mortals. The lines that once separated them, clearly defined by fear and reverence, were now blurred, softened by a shared experience of devastation and a collective yearning for peace.

Tyvellmian, once a symbol of divine wrath, now embodied a new kind of power – a power rooted not in dominance, but in compassion. His act of mercy, his defiance of his father's will, had irrevocably altered the perception of the gods among humanity. No longer were they seen as distant, uncaring deities; instead, they were perceived as beings capable of empathy, of compassion, of flawed humanity.
This shift was as revolutionary as the physical reconstruction of the world, creating a seismic change in the social and political landscape.

a

The governments of the world, previously fractured by political rivalries and mistrust, now collaborated on an unprecedented scale. The shared trauma had forged a bond of shared purpose, erasing the lines that had divided them. International alliances, once forged in fear of conflict, were now cemented by the need for mutual support and cooperation. The rebuilding efforts, fueled by this newly found unity, were astounding in their scale and efficiency. Scientists, engineers, and architects from across the globe pooled their knowledge and resources, sharing innovations and technologies developed during the crisis. The focus shifted away from the production of weapons to the creation of sustainable solutions for a world still reeling from environmental devastation.

The relationship between Tyvellmian and Galena became a powerful symbol of this new order. Their bond, born in the midst of chaos and destruction, was a testament to the resilience of hope and the power of human connection.

Galena, a mortal woman, had seen past Tyvellmian's godhood, perceiving the vulnerable human heart beneath his divine exterior. She had become his closest advisor, guiding him through the complexities of

a

human politics and societal dynamics, her counsel proving indispensable in shaping his approach to governance. He listened to her with an attentiveness that surprised even himself, his decisions increasingly influenced by her understanding of human needs and desires. Their partnership was a visible embodiment of the changing dynamic between gods and mortals, a living testament to the possibility of cooperation and mutual respect.

This changed relationship, however, did not come without its challenges. Some humans, fearful of the unchecked power of the gods, formed resistance groups, advocating for limitations on divine intervention. They voiced concerns about potential abuses of power, emphasizing the importance of maintaining a balance of power between the two worlds. Others, deeply religious, insisted on maintaining traditional beliefs and practices, resistant to the changing roles of the deities in their lives. The new order was a delicate balance, constantly challenged by those clinging to the old ways or fearful of the new. These challenges forced Tyvellmian and Galena to engage in complex negotiations and diplomatic efforts, their alliance acting as a vital bridge between diverging viewpoints. Galena 's mortal perspective proved invaluable

a

in navigating the intricacies of human emotion and political strategy. Her ability to empathize with both the concerns of the resistance and the traditionalist factions allowed them to find common ground.

Within the divine realm, the changes were equally dramatic. Poseidon, still seething with resentment towards his son's defiance, remained a threat, but his authority was weakened. His attempts to reassert control were met with resistance not only from Tyvellmian, but from his other siblings as well.
Athene, once a staunch supporter of her father’s dominance, began to question his methods, particularly after witnessing Tyvellmian's compassion and its impact on the mortal world. Nereus, ever pragmatic, recognized the advantages of cooperation with humanity, understanding that mutual benefit offered a more stable foundation for their power than continued conflict. Even Triton, initially unwavering in his loyalty to his father, found himself drawn to the potential of a world where gods and mortals coexisted peacefully. The family dynamic, long defined by rivalry and competition, was slowly evolving into a more collaborative partnership.

a

The siblings began to work together, pooling their resources and expertise to address the lingering challenges. They established a council, combining their divine powers to accelerate the healing of the planet, to stabilize the altered climate, and to protect against unforeseen natural disasters. They used their influence to foster scientific advancements, helping human researchers develop new technologies to tackle the environmental problems caused by the Ancient Ones' wrath. This collaborative effort represented a fundamental shift in the gods' perception of their own power, a transition from individual dominance to collective responsibility. The old rivalry, while not entirely gone, was now tempered by a shared commitment to the well-being of both the divine and mortal realms.

The change in the gods was evident in their interactions with humanity. Instead of imposing their will, they began to engage in meaningful dialogue, listening to the concerns and opinions of mortal leaders. They established open communication channels, facilitating the exchange of knowledge and resources, ensuring a fair and equitable distribution of resources between the two worlds. The relationship between the gods and humanity evolved from one of fear and

a

submission to one of cooperation and collaboration, transforming the very definition of worship and faith. The gods were no longer simply worshipped; they were engaged in a partnership built on mutual respect and shared goals.

However, the shadows of the past remained. The scars left by the Ancient Ones' wrath served as a stark reminder of the fragility of peace. The constant vigilance against the potential resurgence of these ancient forces demanded the ongoing cooperation between gods and mortals. The threat was not entirely eliminated; it had merely transformed, requiring a different kind of defense. The new world order was still fragile, a delicate balance between divine power and human resilience, a partnership built on shared trauma and a mutual desire for a better future. But it was a new world, a world where gods and mortals walked side by side, bound not by fear, but by hope and shared commitment to a common destiny. The dawn of this new era was not without its challenges; yet, the sun rose each morning, casting its warm light upon a world slowly healing, a world transformed by the impact of a god's compassion and the resilience of humanity. The future remained uncertain, yet, in the eyes of those committed to building this

a

new world, a brighter tomorrow shimmered with potential.

Humanity's Slow Acceptance...

The initial shockwaves of revelation had subsided, replaced by a tentative, yet palpable, acceptance. The existence of gods, once relegated to the realm of myth and legend, was now an undeniable reality woven into the fabric of daily life.

News broadcasts, once filled with reports of devastation and political turmoil, now featured discussions on interspecies diplomacy, the collaborative efforts in rebuilding infrastructure, and the groundbreaking research into harnessing renewable energy sources – projects spearheaded by the gods themselves.

The shift was not immediate; it was a gradual process of adaptation, a slow, cautious dance between disbelief and acceptance, fear and fascination. Lingering resentment had to be overcome slowly and delicately.

The world's religious institutions, initially thrown into disarray, underwent a profound transformation. Some crumbled under the

a

weight of their obsolete dogma, while others adapted, incorporating the new reality into their theological frameworks. The lines between faith and science blurred as scholars and theologians worked together, attempting to reconcile ancient texts with the tangible evidence of divine intervention. Temples and churches were re-purposed, becoming centers for interfaith dialogue and collaborative efforts in rebuilding communities. The concept of "worship" itself evolved; it was no longer a passive act of supplication but an active partnership, a shared commitment to building a better world.

Humanity's adaptation manifested in myriad ways. The arts flourished, with a surge of creativity inspired by the newly revealed reality. Musicians composed symphonies inspired by the celestial harmonies, painters captured the ethereal beauty of the gods, and writers crafted epic tales that blended ancient myths with modern sensibilities. The scientific community embraced the opportunity to collaborate with the gods, gaining access to knowledge and technologies far beyond human comprehension. New fields of study emerged, exploring the intersection of science and divinity, seeking to understand the fundamental laws of the universe and the

a

nature of divine power.

The political landscape, once a battleground of competing ideologies, saw a remarkable shift towards unity.
International collaborations flourished as nations recognized the shared threat they faced and the mutual benefits of cooperation. The gods, in turn, actively participated in global governance, using their influence to foster diplomacy and resolve conflicts. The United Nations, once a symbol of fractured global politics, transformed into a forum for dialogue between humans and gods, a platform for resolving disputes and coordinating joint efforts in addressing global challenges. The shared experience of near-annihilation forged a new sense of global unity, a powerful collective consciousness that transcended national boundaries.

However, this new world order was not without its tensions. The fear of unchecked divine power remained a persistent concern, leading to the establishment of independent monitoring bodies to ensure the responsible use of divine abilities. Strict protocols were established to prevent the exploitation of human populations, and agreements were forged to ensure fairness and transparency in the distribution of resources

a

and aid. These measures were not only to prevent abuses of power but also to nurture trust and mutual respect between the two worlds.

The relationship between Tyvellmian and Galena became a pivotal force in shaping this new reality. Their bond, forged in the crucible of catastrophe and strengthened by shared purpose, served as an inspiring example of interspecies understanding and collaboration. Galena, with her deep understanding of human nature and political dynamics, became Tyvellmian's most trusted advisor, guiding him through the complexities of navigating the human world. Her voice, grounded in empathy and common sense, often tempered his divine impulsiveness, bringing a measure of balance to his leadership.

Their partnership was not just a personal one; it was a symbol of the new era, a testament to the potential for peaceful coexistence between gods and mortals. They tirelessly worked to bridge the gap between differing viewpoints, mediating conflicts, and fostering cooperation. They became beacons of hope, inspiring trust and fostering a sense of shared destiny among both humans and gods. Their love story, whispered throughout the world, became a

a

powerful narrative, demonstrating the capacity for love to transcend even the most profound differences.

The narrative of the gods, too, underwent a transformation. No longer were they seen as distant, uncaring deities, but as complex individuals with their own flaws, ambitions, and motivations. Their actions, once shrouded in mystery and interpreted through the lens of religious dogma, were now subject to critical scrutiny and ethical evaluation. The public demanded accountability, demanding transparency and fairness in the exercise of divine power. This shift in perception compelled the gods to re-evaluate their roles and responsibilities, forcing them to adopt a more ethical and accountable approach to governance.

The transformation was not universally accepted. Resistance groups, fueled by lingering anxieties and fears, continued to advocate for greater limitations on divine power, calling for a more equitable distribution of resources and influence.

Their voices, initially marginalized, gained increasing prominence, shaping the ongoing dialogue and ensuring that the new order remained responsive to the needs and concerns

a

of the human population.

The story of humanity's acceptance of the gods was not one of immediate assimilation, but a complex, evolving narrative marked by moments of conflict and cooperation, fear and hope. It was a process of negotiation, adaptation, and continuous reassessment, a journey that demanded empathy, understanding, and a shared commitment to building a world where both gods and mortals could coexist in harmony. This new era, built on the foundations of shared trauma and a collective yearning for peace, was a testament to the resilience of the human spirit and the transformative power of hope. The path ahead remained uncertain, fraught with challenges, but the shared vision of a brighter future, a future where gods and mortals walked side by side, propelled them forward, a beacon illuminating a new dawn.

a

Chapter XVII

Tyvellmians New Role.

The weight of the world, or perhaps more accurately, the weight of *a* world, rested on Tyvellmian's shoulders. It wasn't the crushing burden of absolute power, but a far more subtle, insidious pressure – the weight of expectation. The expectation of a god, yes, but more importantly, the expectation of a *savior* . His act of mercy during the storm, the sparing of lives amidst the divine tempest, had transformed him from Poseidon's rebellious son into "Tidal Man," a symbol of hope for humanity.

His days were a whirlwind of meetings, negotiations, and diplomatic efforts. He found himself seated at tables once reserved for world leaders, his presence commanding respect, even awe. He wasn't merely a figurehead; he actively participated in rebuilding efforts, using his powers to accelerate the healing process. He channeled the earth's energy to mend fractured landscapes, stilled raging fires with a gesture, and coaxed life back into barren fields. The sheer scale of the devastation had been staggering, but his efforts, coupled with the aid

a

of other gods and the tireless work of humans, were slowly but surely mending the world.

Yet, the adoration felt hollow, a gilded cage of his own making. The cheers of the crowds faded into the echo chamber of his own doubts. The woman, Galena, haunted his thoughts. Her face, framed by wind-tossed hair as she'd clung to a piece of driftwood amidst the raging storm, was etched into his memory. He hadn't just saved her life; he'd glimpsed a soul that mirrored his own – a soul capable of both profound kindness and fierce resilience. Finding her, understanding her, became an urgent, almost obsessive, need. It wasn't simply a romantic pursuit; it was a quest for understanding, a way to ground himself in the human world he now found himself so intimately involved in.

His relationship with his niece, Arconia, had become a lifeline. She, too, had witnessed the storm's devastation, a stark contrast to the sheltered life she'd previously known. She understood his struggles, the internal conflict between his divine nature and the burgeoning humanity within him. Arconia didn't offer simplistic solutions or platitudes.
Instead, she provided a steady, unwavering presence, a grounding force in a world rapidly

a

shifting beneath his feet. She challenged his decisions, pushed him to confront his internal demons, and most importantly, reminded him of his own inherent goodness.

But the peace was fragile. The resentment of his siblings, fueled by Poseidon's bitterness, simmered just beneath the surface. They viewed his actions as a betrayal, a weakening of their father's authority. Their covert acts of sabotage were subtle yet pervasive – minor inconveniences that gradually escalated into acts of open defiance. They exploited human fears and insecurities, whispering doubts into the hearts of those who once championed him. The whispers started subtly, questioning his motives, his methods, his very right to rule. "Tidal Man," once a beacon of hope, now found himself battling not only natural disasters but a cunning, well-orchestrated campaign of disinformation.

Poseidon, his father, remained the most formidable obstacle. His anger was a tangible force, a tempest brewing within the depths of the ocean, threatening to unleash another wave of destruction. Tyvellmian had defied his father's authority, not through blatant rebellion, but through an act of unexpected compassion. This act, in Poseidon's eyes, was far worse than

a

any act of open defiance. It represented a weakening of theestablished order, a deviation from the ancient path that threatened to unravel the very fabric of their divine society.

Tyvellmian understood his father's anger, the centuries-old resentment simmering beneath a façade of stoic authority. He also understood the fear, the fear of losing control, of losing his place in a world rapidly changing around him. He had always been the rebellious one, the one who questioned the old ways, the one who defied expectations. But now, his rebellion was not one of defiance, but of compassion, a choice that set him on a path diametrically opposed to his father's unwavering belief in order and dominance.

He attempted to negotiate, to explain his actions, to bridge the gap between his father's rigid worldview and his own evolving sense of empathy. But Poseidon remained unmoved, his anger a cold, unyielding force. The very concept of compassion was alien to him, a weakness to be scorned and punished. He saw his son's actions not as acts of mercy, but as acts of treason, as a betrayal of their family, their lineage, their divine authority. The ocean, his domain, reflected his fury; storms brewed on the horizon, a constant reminder of the

a

power his father still wielded, a power he could easily unleash.

The search for Galena continued, a thread of hope in a world increasingly defined by suspicion and fear. He sought not only to find her but to understand the impact of his actions on the human world. He spent hours poring over news reports, scanning satellite images, desperately seeking any sign of her existence. He found himself drawn to areas most affected by the storm, haunted by the ghosts of the disaster and the lingering hope of finding the woman who had unwittingly steered his life onto a new and unpredictable path.

His new role demanded more than just divine intervention; it required political acumen, diplomatic skill, and a deep understanding of the human condition. He learned to navigate the complexities of human politics, mediating disputes between nations, working tirelessly to prevent further conflict. He learned to listen, to understand, to empathize with the anxieties and fears of a world grappling with the reality of divine intervention. He learned the value of compromise, the necessity of cooperation, and the profound impact of a single act of compassion.

He was no longer just Poseidon's son, the

a

rebellious god destined to inherit his father's power. He was Tyvellmian, the Tidal Man, a symbol of hope, a bridge between two worlds, a testament to the transformative power of compassion in a world desperately in need of healing. And the journey had just begun. The path ahead remained fraught with peril, a tempestuous sea navigated by fragile alliances and uncertain futures. But he was no longer alone. He had Galena 's memory, Arconia's unwavering support, and the faint but persistent hope that a world where gods and mortals could coexist in harmony was not merely a dream, but a possibility worth fighting for. The weight on his shoulders remained, but it was no longer a burden; it was a responsibility he was determined to carry with courage, grace, and unwavering compassion. The tide had turned, and with it, the course of history.

A Lasting Impact.

The rebuilding efforts stretched far beyond the immediate aftermath of the storm. Cities, once vibrant hubs of activity, now lay in ruins, their skeletal frameworks a testament to the raw power of Poseidon's wrath. Yet, amidst the devastation, a new spirit emerged – a spirit fueled by Tyvellmian's unexpected compassion and the collective resolve of humanity. He didn't just mend broken buildings; he mended broken spirits. His presence, initially met with awe and fear, slowly transformed into a source of comfort and inspiration. He held town hall meetings in the ruins, listening patiently to the stories of loss and resilience, offering not just physical healing but emotional solace. He used his powers to create temporary shelters, providing warmth and protection until more permanent structures could be built. He taught the survivors techniques to harness the earth's energy, empowering them to participate in the rebuilding process. He wasn't just a god; he was a collaborator, a partner in the arduous task of recovery.

The world's political landscape underwent a seismic shift. The catastrophe served as a brutal reminder of humanity's vulnerability, forcing nations to confront their differences and collaborate on a scale never before witnessed.

Tyvellmian, unexpectedly, became a central figure in this new world order, mediating disputes, fostering alliances, and advocating for policies that prioritized cooperation and sustainable development. His interventions weren't always smooth; he faced resistance from those who clung to old rivalries and power structures, from those who sought to

a

exploit the chaos for personal gain. Yet, his unwavering commitment to peace, fueled by his encounter with Elara and his growing understanding of human needs, proved to be a powerful force. He navigated delicate diplomatic situations with remarkable dexterity, his inherent empathy allowing him to connect with leaders on a deeper level, transcending political rhetoric and reaching the core of their shared human experience.

The economic ramifications of the storm were equally profound. Entire industries crumbled, leaving millions jobless and destitute. Tyvellmian, working with economists and humanitarian organizations, developed innovative programs to revitalize the economy, promoting sustainable practices and investing in renewable energy sources. He empowered communities to rebuild their livelihoods, using his abilities to accelerate agricultural production and facilitate technological innovation. He understood that true healing required not just physical rebuilding but economic empowerment, ensuring that the recovery process would be equitable and inclusive.

a

He became a symbol of hope not just for the victims of the storm but for the entire global community, a reminder that even in the face of unimaginable loss, a better future was possible.

His relationship with Arconia deepened during this period. She became an invaluable advisor, bridging the gap between Tyvellmian's divine perspective and the complex realities of the human world. She helped him navigate the political intricacies, decipher the nuances of human emotions, and understand the motivations of different stakeholders. Her sharp wit and unwavering loyalty provided a constant source of support and strength, reminding him that compassion wasn't a weakness but a source of immense power. Their bond transcended the typical relationship between an uncle and a niece, evolving into a true partnership, a testament to the enduring power of family in times of great change.

The search for Galena remained a driving force in Tyvellmian's life. He poured over countless satellite images, combed through news reports, and even employed cutting- edge technologies developed as a direct result of the post- storm technological boom – a boom he himself had inadvertently inspired. The media frenzy surrounding "Tidal Man" made his search even more challenging; rumors,

a

speculation, and misdirection clouded his efforts, creating a formidable obstacle course of misinformation and false leads. But his determination remained unshaken; Galena represented more than just a lost love; she embodied the human spirit that he was now so dedicated to protecting and uplifting.

However, the shadow of Poseidon loomed large. His wrath, though temporarily subdued, simmered beneath the surface, a constant threat. Poseidon's siblings, fueled by his resentment and their own ambitions, continued their covert campaign of sabotage, exploiting human vulnerabilities and spreading disinformation about Tyvellmian. They whispered tales of his supposed arrogance and betrayal, fanning the flames of doubt among those who had once been his most ardent supporters. They launched subtle attacks, manipulating the media and planting discord among nations, testing the resilience of the newly formed alliances. These actions created fissures in the fragile peace Tyvellmian had so painstakingly constructed, reminding him of the ongoing struggle for control between the old order and the burgeoning new one.

Yet, despite these obstacles, Tyvellmian persevered. His actions, though initially

a

motivated by an act of spontaneous compassion, had triggered a chain reaction of positive change. He had inadvertently inspired a global movement towards cooperation, sustainability, and empathy. He had shown humanity that even in the face of overwhelming devastation, hope and resilience could prevail. He had become a symbol of the transformative power of compassion – a power that transcended the boundaries of divinity and humanity, shaping a new world order based on empathy, collaboration, and the unwavering belief in a brighter future. The journey was far from over, but the path ahead, though still fraught with challenges, was illuminated by the light of a newfound hope, a hope sparked by a single act of kindness amidst a devastating storm. And the ripples of that act continued to expand, shaping the destiny of both gods and mortals alike, forever altering the course of history.

The salt spray kissed Galena 's face as she stood beside Tyvellmian, the wind whipping through her hair. They were perched on a cliff overlooking the rebuilt city, a phoenix rising from the ashes of Poseidon's wrath. Below, the vibrant tapestry of human life unfolded – a testament to their resilience, a testament to the

a

hope Tyvellmian had ignited.
He had found her, not through sophisticated technology or exhaustive searches, but through a simple, almost serendipitous encounter. She had been volunteering at a makeshift clinic, her face etched with the weariness of tireless work, yet her eyes still held that spark of unwavering hope he had glimpsed during their first meeting. The reunion hadn't been dramatic; it had been quiet, intimate, a recognition of shared experience and a silent understanding of their intertwined destinies.

Their love story wasn't a fairy tale. It wasn't devoid of challenges, of moments of doubt and uncertainty. Galena, a mortal woman, was constantly grappling with the immense weight of his divine nature. She wrestled with the implications of her relationship with a god, a being capable of unimaginable power. The fear of the unknown, the ever- present threat of Poseidon's wrath, and the constant media attention created a tempestuous backdrop to their burgeoning romance. Yet, their connection transcended these obstacles, rooted in a mutual respect and a deep understanding of each other's vulnerabilities. They found solace in shared silences, in quiet moments of connection that defied the tumultuous external world. They built their haven amidst the storm,

a

their love a beacon of hope amidst the lingering darkness.

Tyvellmian, too, was undergoing a profound transformation. His compassion, once a spontaneous act of mercy, had become an integral part of his being. He found himself drawn to the intricacies of the human world, fascinated by its complexities, its resilience, and its capacity for both great love and devastating cruelty. He began to appreciate the nuances of human emotions, the silent language of unspoken desires and fears. He no longer viewed humanity as merely subjects of his father's divine will, but as individuals with their own unique stories, struggles, and triumphs. His role as a god was no longer defined solely by his powers, but by his capacity for empathy and his unwavering commitment to fostering a better world.

Their new life together was a delicate dance between two worlds – the realm of gods and the realm of mortals. They chose to live in a secluded coastal village, far removed from the bustling cities and the relentless media scrutiny. They had built a modest home, a sanctuary of peace and quiet, where they could escape the pressures of their unique circumstances. The simplicity of their life allowed them to appreciate the small joys – the

a

warmth of the sun on their faces, the sound of the waves crashing against the shore, the laughter shared in quiet evenings. They found comfort in the ordinary, in the simple act of being together.

But their isolation wasn't complete. Tyvellmian's responsibilities to the world he had helped rebuild remained. He continued to act as a mediator, a silent guardian, intervening subtly, influencing events from the shadows. He worked closely with Arconia, who now occupied a pivotal role in the new global order. Arconia had become more than just a niece; she was his trusted advisor, his strategist, his voice of reason. She helped him navigate the complex political landscape, ensuring that his actions were informed, strategic, and beneficial to all of humanity, not just a select few. Their collaboration was seamless, their understanding profound, a testament to the strength of their familial bond.

Galena, in turn, discovered a new purpose. She became a voice for the voiceless, working tirelessly to advocate for those affected by the storm and those who were still struggling to rebuild their lives. She leveraged her unique position as Tyvellmian's partner, using her platform to raise awareness, to inspire action,

a

and to advocate for policies that fostered equality and sustainable development. Her empathy and unwavering dedication mirrored Tyvellmian's own, creating a unified force for positive change. They became a powerful duo, influencing the world not through divine power alone, but through the shared power of compassion and unwavering determination.

Poseidon's wrath still lingered, a constant threat hanging over their lives. His siblings, jealous of Tyvellmian's newfound influence and frustrated by their failed attempts to overthrow him, continued their machinations. They whispered rumors, spread disinformation, and planted seeds of discord among nations. They targeted Galena, attempting to exploit her vulnerabilities and undermine her influence.
However, their efforts were thwarted by the strength of their bond and the unwavering loyalty of those who had come to respect Tyvellmian's leadership.

The couple understood that their path wasn't easy. They were pioneers navigating uncharted territories, balancing the responsibilities of their unique positions with the desire for a simple, peaceful life. They knew that the threat of Poseidon and his siblings wouldn't simply

a

disappear. It was a constant undercurrent in their lives, a reminder of the turbulent forces still at play. Yet, they faced the future with newfound courage, their love serving as an anchor in the storm of uncertainty.

Their future wasn't preordained. It wasn't a fairytale ending neatly tied with a bow. It was a journey, an evolving story, a testament to the transformative power of love and compassion amidst the chaos of a changing world. It was a story about a god who learned to embrace his humanity and a mortal woman who discovered the strength within herself to stand beside a god, not as a subject but as an equal partner. It was a story about finding hope in the darkest of times, about forging a future built not on power and dominion, but on empathy and understanding. It was a story of a new beginning, born from the ashes of destruction and nurtured by the unwavering flame of love.

Their nights were filled with quiet conversations, their days with shared experiences. Tyvellmian, used to the grand scale of divine interventions, discovered the beauty of the mundane. He learned the rhythm of the tides, the language of the wind, the intricate dance of life unfolding around him. He shared his immense knowledge with Galena, helping her understand the celestial

a

mechanics, the interplay of forces that shaped their world. He shared his fears, his vulnerabilities, stripping away the veneer of godhood to reveal the man beneath. Galena, in turn, introduced him to the beauty of human connection, the power of laughter, the warmth of shared intimacy. She helped him understand the nuances of human desires, the subtle intricacies of mortal emotions. She challenged him to look beyond his divine perspective, to see the world through the lens of humanity.

Their relationship fostered growth, transforming them both. Tyvellmian, tempered by human experience, became a wiser, more compassionate being, his power tempered by empathy. Galena, strengthened by her relationship with a god, discovered an unwavering resilience, a courage she never knew she possessed. Together, they represented a new paradigm, a harmonious blend of divine and mortal, a symbol of hope for a world striving to find its way after a devastating catastrophe. Their love was more than just a romance; it was a testament to the transformative power of compassion, a beacon of hope in a world still reeling from the wrath of the gods. And as the sun set over the rebuilt city, casting a golden glow over their secluded home, they knew their journey was just

a

beginning. The future held uncertainty, but it also held the promise of a love that could withstand any storm.

Uncertainties Remain.

The rhythmic crashing of waves against the shore was a constant companion, a soothing counterpoint to the unsettling quiet that often settled over their secluded home. Tyvellmian and Galena, nestled in their haven, felt the weight of the world's unspoken questions pressing down on them.

The rebuilding was impressive, a testament to human resilience, yet a deep unease permeated the air. The gods had revealed themselves, their power undeniable, their wrath a vivid memory. But what came next?

That was the question that echoed in the silent spaces between their shared breaths, in the unspoken anxieties that occasionally flickered in their eyes.

Galena, her fingers tracing the intricate carvings on a smooth, sea-worn piece of driftwood, voiced the unspoken fear. "They're watching us, aren't they?" she whispered, her

a

voice barely audible above the ceaseless whisper of the ocean.
Tyvellmian, his gaze fixed on the horizon, nodded slowly. He knew she wasn't just speaking of Poseidon and his vengeful siblings. The world watched them, fascinated, fearful, uncertain. The media, insatiable in its hunger for sensationalism, continued to paint them as opposing forces: the divine savior and the mortal woman who captured his heart. This simplistic narrative ignored the complexities of their relationship, their shared struggles, and their commitment to a future they were still defining.

The delicate balance they had created was precarious. The rebuilding efforts, while successful, hadn't erased the deep scars left by Poseidon's wrath. Tensions simmered beneath the surface of the restored cities, a quiet anxiety that pulsed in the collective heartbeat of humanity. The once-blind faith in the gods, shattered by their capricious intervention, was replaced by a cautious respect, laced with suspicion and a yearning for understanding. Tyvellmian felt the weight of this expectation, the heavy burden of being a symbol of hope in a world that was still grappling with its newfound reality.

a

Arconia, ever the pragmatist, had assembled a council composed of scientists, theologians, and political leaders, seeking to forge a new relationship between humanity and the divine. The discussions were fraught with tension, ideological clashes, and personal agendas. Tyvellmian’s role was delicate; he couldn't impose his will, yet his guidance was needed. He walked a tightrope, advocating for understanding and cooperation while battling the insidious whispers of those who sought to exploit the situation for their own gain. The challenge lay not just in bridging the gap between two worlds, but in navigating the treacherous currents of human ambition and distrust.

Even their love story, once a beacon of hope, now carried a layer of uncertainty. Galena 's mortal life continued, ticking away in contrast to Tyvellmian’s eternal existence. The disparity in their lifespans cast a long shadow over their future. They had shared dreams, plans for a future they could barely glimpse, yet the specter of mortality loomed, an unspoken fear hanging between them. The quiet moments of intimacy, once a refuge from the chaos, were now sometimes tinged with a poignant awareness of time's relentless march.

a

Tyvellmian, accustomed to the timeless flow of the divine realm, now grappled with the ephemeral nature of human existence. He found himself lingering on the beauty of Galena 's laughter, the gentle curve of her smile, memorizing the details of her presence as if to etch them forever in his memory. He understood intellectually that he would endure, but the thought of a future without her was a cold, sharp pang that pierced through his immortality.

The uncertainties weren't confined to their personal lives. The political landscape remained volatile. Nations, grappling with the aftermath of the storm and the revelation of the gods, were forming shifting alliances, their loyalties fluid and their agendas often opaque. The whispers of war were carried on the wind, a constant threat that lurked in the shadows of peace. Tyvellmian and Arconia worked tirelessly, striving to prevent a conflict that could unravel the fragile peace they had so painstakingly built.

But even their efforts seemed to be met with resistance, with unforeseen challenges arising from every direction. There were those who saw Tyvellmian not as a savior, but as a threat, a potential tyrant wielding unimaginable

a

power. They whispered their doubts, spreading distrust and sowing seeds of dissent. Others clung to the old ways, longing for the simplicity of a world untouched by divine intervention, unable to accept this new reality. Their resistance added another layer of complexity to Tyvellmian's task, forcing him to navigate a treacherous path between the conflicting desires and anxieties of humanity.

The ocean, their constant companion, seemed to mirror the turbulent state of the world. Sometimes it was calm, reflecting the serene beauty of their secluded haven; other times, it raged with untamed power, mirroring the anxieties that gnawed at their hearts. The setting sun cast long shadows that danced and writhed across the land, creating an atmosphere of both tranquility and impending unease. The mysteries of the future lay hidden beneath the waves, beneath the surface of human interactions, waiting to be uncovered.

Poseidon's shadow remained a looming threat. Though he had retreated, his displeasure was evident in the subtle shifts in the ocean currents, the unexpected storms that periodically lashed against the coast. His siblings, thwarted in their attempts to capture Tyvellmian or undermine his influence, continued their machinations, whispering in the

a

shadows, using their influence to destabilize the peace. Their actions were subtle, their presence a constant undercurrent of uncertainty, adding to the foreboding atmosphere.

Galena, however, refused to succumb to despair. She understood the weight of their responsibility, the immensity of the challenges they faced. She stood beside Tyvellmian, not as a mere mortal clinging to a god, but as a partner, equal in their commitment to creating a better future. Her strength, her unwavering faith in Tyvellmian and in the potential of humanity, fueled his determination, providing a much- needed anchor in the storm of uncertainty.

Together, they continued their journey, their steps cautious but resolute. They knew the future held countless uncertainties, that the path ahead was fraught with challenges and unforeseen obstacles. Yet, their love, their shared commitment, and their unwavering faith in each other's strength gave them the courage to face whatever came next. The mysteries were unresolved, the shadows lingered, but in their hearts burned a quiet, unwavering flame of hope – a beacon in the lingering darkness of an uncertain future. Their story was far from over; it was only just beginning, a tale of love, redemption, and the enduring resilience of the human spirit in the face of unimaginable odds. The future remained unwritten, a canvas awaiting the strokes of their determination, a testament to a love that defied the very boundaries of their worlds.

A Lasting Bond.

The fire crackled merrily in the hearth, casting dancing shadows on the rough-hewn walls of their haven. Outside, the ocean roared its timeless song, a constant reminder of the power Tyvellmian wielded, a power that was both a blessing and a curse. Galena, curled up on a worn rug beside him, her head resting on his shoulder, traced the lines of his hand with a delicate finger. The contrast between his rough, calloused skin and the smoothness of hers was a constant source of fascination for both of them. He was a god, ancient and powerful, yet he found solace in the simple touch of a mortal woman.

He leaned his head against hers, inhaling the faint scent of sea salt and wildflowers that clung to her hair. The scent was uniquely hers, a fragrance that had become intimately woven into the fabric of his existence. He had lived for

a

millennia, witnessed the rise and fall of civilizations, felt the weight of eons pressing down upon him. Yet, the time spent with Galena felt different, precious, irreplaceable. It was a grounding force, a counterpoint to the turbulent sea of his immortal life.

"Do you ever wonder," Galena whispered, her voice barely audible above the crashing waves, "what would have happened if that storm had never happened?"

Tyvellmian's heart ached at the question. It was a question he had asked himself countless times. A question without a definitive answer, a path not taken, a reality that existed only in the realm of "what ifs." He imagined a life where he never intervened, where the luxury liner sank beneath the waves, taking those precious lives with it. A life where he remained a cold, distant god, untouched by the mortal world. The thought sent a chill through him, a profound sense of loss that transcended the simple absence of Galena in his life.

He'd lost something more fundamental than a love, he'd lost a part of himself.

a

"Sometimes," he admitted, his voice a low rumble against her hair, "I wonder if I made the right choice. If saving you, saving them…if it was worth the price."

The price had been steep. The wrath of his father, the machinations of his siblings, the constant scrutiny of the world, the weight of responsibility that pressed down upon his shoulders. He had endured trials that would have broken lesser beings. Yet, in the face of it all, he found strength in Galena 's presence. Her unwavering belief in him, her unshakeable faith in his capacity for good, provided an anchor in the stormy sea of his life. It was a faith that even his own family seemed to lack.

"You did the right thing," she murmured, her voice firm, unyielding. "You saved lives, Tyvellmian. You showed compassion, something the world desperately needed. And you found me." She smiled, a small, almost imperceptible movement, yet it warmed him from the inside out. It was a smile that transcended words, a smile that spoke volumes about the depth of their connection.

He tightened his embrace, drawing her closer. He knew that their love was unconventional, a

a

love that defied the laws of nature, the boundaries of their worlds. He was immortal, she was mortal. Their time together was finite, a precious gift that he would cherish until the very end. But he refused to succumb to the despair of knowing her lifespan would inevitably end. He would not let mortality steal their love.

Instead, he embraced every moment with her, every shared laugh, every whispered secret, every stolen kiss. He would fill their days with joy, despite the darkness that lurked in their future.

Their haven wasn't just a physical place; it was a sanctuary of shared emotions and experiences, a place where the harsh realities of the world outside faded into the background.

They spent countless hours sharing stories, exploring ancient myths and modern philosophy. Tyvellmian patiently unraveled the complexities of his world, the intricate tapestry of divine power and familial conflict. Galena, in turn, exposed him to the depth of human connection, the capacity for love and empathy, the enduring strength of the human spirit. Each shared moment cemented their bond, creating an unbreakable link that transcended their differences.

a

One evening, as they watched the stars emerge from the darkening sky, Galena turned to him, her eyes filled with an uncharacteristic melancholy. "I've been thinking about the future," she confessed, her voice laced with a quiet anxiety that mirrored his own. "About our future."

Tyvellmian knew what she was hinting at, the unspoken fear that hung between them, the stark reality of their contrasting lifespans. He knew the weight of her words; words laden with the unspoken truth of her mortality, a truth that had cast a shadow over their idyllic existence. He reached for her hand, interlacing his fingers with hers. He felt the gentle pulse of her heart against his own, a rhythm that represented the precious, ephemeral nature of her existence, a stark contrast to his immortal heartbeat. The realization, though not new, struck him with renewed force. Their love was a poignant symphony, a beautiful melody played against the ticking clock.

"We'll face it together," he promised, his voice steady, unwavering. "Whatever the future holds, we'll face it together."

His words were not just empty platitudes, but a

a

genuine pledge, a testament to the depth of his commitment. He would love her, cherish her, protect her, and embrace every moment with her, regardless of the inevitable ending. Their love would be a legacy that would outlive the mortal coil. He would live on, his memories of her a never-fading flame in the heart of eternity.

They continued their journey, their love a guiding star in the often-turbulent waters of their lives. The challenges persisted – the simmering political tension, the ever-present threat from Poseidon and his siblings, the ongoing uncertainty surrounding the relationship between gods and mortals. Yet, their bond remained steadfast. Their connection was a source of strength, inspiration, and hope. They were two souls, woven together by a love that transcended the boundaries of time, a love that echoed through the ages, a testament to the enduring power of human connection in a world grappling with the extraordinary. Their story, a testament to love defying the odds, a tale of a god and a mortal woman finding solace and meaning in each other's arms, was only beginning to unfold. The future remained unwritten, a canvas awaiting the strokes of their hearts, a beacon of love amidst the uncertainties.

a

Hope for the Future.

The sunrise painted the sky in hues of rose and gold, mirroring the warmth that had settled in Galena's heart. She watched Tyvellmian, his silhouette framed against the burgeoning light, as he practiced his control over the waves. Each controlled surge, each perfectly sculpted crest, was a testament to his power, yet it was the quiet gentleness in his movements that truly captivated her. He wasn't just a god; he was a man, a being capable of both immense destruction and exquisite grace. And that was precisely what she loved about him – the paradox, the inherent contradiction that made him so uniquely, breathtakingly himself.

He turned, catching her gaze, and a smile, both reassuring and tentative, graced his lips. The weight of the world rested on his shoulders, the burden of his heritage, the responsibility of his position, but in her presence, he seemed to shed it, if only for a moment. It was in these quiet moments, these stolen breaths of peace, that she found her own strength renewed.

Their days were a tapestry woven with threads of love, interspersed with the ever-present threat of conflict. The political landscape remained volatile. The human world, still

a

reeling from the devastation wrought by the Ancient Ones, struggled to adapt to the newfound reality of gods among them. Rumors swirled, conspiracy theories blossomed, and fear was a constant companion. Yet, within their haven, a bubble of serenity persisted, a testament to the enduring power of their love.

They sought out moments of respite, exploring hidden coves along the coast, sharing stories under the starlit sky.

Tyvellmian, in his newfound compassion, had begun reaching out to those affected by the storm, offering silent aid, subtle guidance. He channeled his power not for destruction but for healing, mending broken boats, calming troubled waters, and subtly guiding lost souls back to safety. These quiet acts of kindness, unseen by most, were his way of seeking redemption, of atoning for the harsh reality of his father's wrath and his siblings' schemes.

Galena, in turn, became his anchor, his grounding force in a world that often felt chaotic and overwhelming. She introduced him to the simple joys of human life – the beauty of a blooming flower, the warmth of a shared meal, the comfort of laughter. She taught him the value of patience, the importance of empathy, and the enduring

a

strength of the human spirit, a spirit that had survived countless calamities and would, without doubt, survive this one as well.

Their love was not without its trials. The specter of her mortality cast a long shadow, a constant reminder of the finite nature of their time together. Yet, instead of succumbing to despair, they chose to cherish every moment, every shared breath, every fleeting touch. They embraced the beauty of their ephemeral love, turning it into a testament to life's preciousness and the enduring power of human connection.

One evening, as they sat by the fire, Galena spoke of her dreams, her aspirations, her fears. She spoke of her desire to contribute to a world that was trying to heal, to rebuild itself after the devastating storms that had passed. She spoke of the hope that flickered in the hearts of the survivors, the resilience of the human spirit in the face of adversity.

Tyvellmian listened intently, his heart swelling with pride and admiration. He saw in her the reflection of his own evolving nature, a spirit that sought not just to survive, but to thrive, to build a better world from the ashes of the old. He realized that his compassion, his act of mercy in the midst of chaos, had not only

a

saved her life but had also sparked a transformation in himself, a shift in his perception of his role in the world. He was not merely Poseidon's son; he was Tyvellmian, a force for good, a beacon of hope in a world desperately in need of it.

"We can create something beautiful together," he said, his voice filled with a newfound conviction. "Something lasting. Something that will transcend even the boundaries of time."

He didn't refer specifically to their love, though it was implicit in his words. Instead, he spoke of a broader, more encompassing vision – a future where gods and mortals could coexist, where compassion and understanding could overcome prejudice and fear. He saw a world where his power, wielded with wisdom and empathy, could help rebuild, heal, and restore balance. This wasn't about escaping their reality; it was about shaping it.

He spoke of utilizing his abilities to help humanity adapt to the changed world, to harness the power of the tides for sustainable energy, to heal the scars left by the storms, to develop technologies that could withstand future catastrophes. He spoke of bridging the gap between the divine and the mortal, creating a world where both could flourish.

a

Galena, her eyes shining with inspiration, embraced his vision. She saw the potential for change, the opportunity to create a better future, a world where the legacy of their love would be more than a personal story; it would be a testament to the power of collaboration, of hope, and of the enduring strength of the human spirit. They would face the uncertainties together, building a future not based on fear or division but on understanding and unity.

The challenge ahead was immense, the obstacles insurmountable at times. Poseidon's wrath still loomed, the machinations of his siblings remained a constant threat. The delicate balance between gods and mortals was still precarious. Yet, within their hearts, a new sense of purpose bloomed, a shared vision that transcended their personal fears and anxieties. They were no longer merely seeking solace in each other's arms; they were forging a path toward a future they could shape, a future where love and hope could blossom amidst the storms. Their love story was not just a tale of a god and a mortal, but a beacon of hope, a symbol of resilience, a promise of a future where compassion could conquer even the most daunting challenges. The uncertain future no longer felt daunting; it felt like a canvas

a

waiting to be painted with the vibrant colors of their shared dreams and the unwavering strength of their love. It was a future they would build together, a legacy woven from the threads of their hearts, a testament to the enduring power of hope in a world yearning for change. And in that hope, they found not just a future, but a destiny.

a

Epilogue

A soft breeze tickled Galena 's face as she stood beside Tyvellmian, watching the sun dip below the horizon, painting the sky in fiery shades of orange and purple. The ocean, usually a tempestuous reflection of his father's anger, was calm tonight, a mirror to the peace that had finally settled in her heart. The aftermath of the storms had left their mark – scars on the land, a lingering sense of unease in the hearts of humanity – but a quiet resilience had begun to bloom, a testament to the indomitable spirit of humankind.

Tyvellmian’s hand rested lightly on hers, his fingers interlacing with hers, a silent promise of enduring support. He had learned much in these past months, not just about the complexities of his own divine power but also about the profound strength of human compassion. His initial anger at his father’s decree, the resentment toward his siblings’ schemes, had begun to recede, replaced by a determined focus on forging a better future. His act of mercy during the storm, the saving of Galena’s life, had become more than just a defining moment; it was the catalyst for a profound

a

transformation within him.

He was no longer solely the volatile, untamed son of Poseidon. He was Tyvellmian, a force for good, a beacon of hope in a world struggling to reconcile with the existence of gods among them. He had started small, using his abilities to heal the land, to help rebuild shattered communities, channeling the power of the tides to provide sustainable energy, a resource desperately needed by a world ravaged by the storms. These were not acts of grand, divine pronouncements but quiet, steady efforts, a quiet revolution born from compassion.

Galena, in turn, had become more than just the woman he had saved. She had become his inspiration, his partner in this quiet rebellion. She had used her skills – her knowledge of architecture, her understanding of human psychology – to guide the rebuilding efforts, ensuring that the new structures were not merely functional but beautiful, sustainable and resilient, mirroring the spirit of a humanity that refused to be broken. She had become a bridge between the divine and the mortal, a voice that understood both worlds and sought to find common ground.

a

Their love, initially a beacon of defiance against the chaotic forces arrayed against them, had now evolved into a shared mission. It was no longer simply a passionate romance but a partnership, a collaboration built on mutual respect, shared goals, and unwavering belief in the power of hope. They understood the precariousness of their situation. Poseidon's wrath still hung over them like a dark cloud; the machinations of his siblings were a constant, simmering threat. The world was still volatile, a fragile ecosystem teetering on the edge of chaos. But they had found solace not in escaping their reality, but in shaping it.

They spent their evenings not merely sharing quiet moments of intimacy but strategizing, planning, discussing ways to bridge the chasm between gods and mortals. They had begun to assemble a council, a diverse group of mortals and lesser deities who shared their vision of a world where cooperation and understanding, not fear and conflict, prevailed. This was a delicate undertaking, requiring careful negotiation, diplomacy, and unwavering patience. It meant confronting centuries-old prejudices, dismantling ingrained power structures, and navigating the treacherous currents of political intrigue.

But they were not alone. They had found allies,

a

unlikely friends among those who had initially feared the gods, those who had witnessed the devastating power of the Ancient Ones, and had seen in Tyvellmian's acts of mercy, a sign of hope, a promise of a better future. The survivors of the storm, many of whom had lost everything, had become their most steadfast supporters, their faith in Tyvellmian and Galena a testament to the resilience of the human spirit.

The journey ahead remained fraught with challenges. The road to reconciliation would be long and arduous, filled with setbacks and moments of doubt. There would be betrayals and disagreements, moments when the weight of responsibility threatened to crush them both. But they had learned to face adversity together, leaning on each other's strength, drawing comfort from their shared purpose. They were building not just a future for themselves but a legacy, a new world order built on compassion, understanding, and the enduring power of human resilience.

Their love had become the foundation upon which they built their dreams, the bedrock upon which they constructed a future free from the tyranny of fear. It was a love that transcended the boundaries of mortality, a connection that

a

defied the limitations of their respective worlds. It was a love that nourished their hope, fueled their determination, and gave them the strength to face the uncertainties that lay ahead. It was a love that would not only endure but become the catalyst for a world reborn.

One evening, as they sat on the cliffs overlooking the now- calm ocean, Galena turned to Tyvellmian, her eyes reflecting the starry expanse above. "Do you remember the night of the storm?" she asked, her voice soft, yet filled with a quiet strength.

He nodded, remembering the chaos, the fear, the overwhelming power of the waves. He remembered his own initial fear, the anger, the confusion that had plagued him.

And then, he recalled the sight of her, clinging to a piece of debris, the vulnerability in her eyes, the fragility of human existence amidst the wrath of the gods.

"I saved you that night," he said, his voice husky with emotion. "But you saved me too."

Galena smiled, a knowing smile that acknowledged the unspoken truth of their shared journey. "We saved each other," she replied. "And in doing so, we saved a world."

a

Their words hung in the night air, a simple statement laden with meaning, a testament to the profound transformation that had swept through their lives, the ripple effect of one act of compassion, one moment of shared humanity. The future remained uncertain, the path ahead shrouded in shadows, but they stood together, hand in hand, ready to face whatever challenges lay ahead, knowing that their love, their shared purpose, would guide them through the darkness and towards a brighter dawn. Their story wasn't just a love story; it was a testament to the resilience of hope, a beacon shining in a world desperately seeking light. It was the beginning of a new era, a new world born from the ashes of the old, a world built on the unshakeable foundation of their shared love and unwavering belief in the power of compassion. And as the stars twinkled above, they knew that their journey had only just begun. The uncertain future was no longer a source of fear, but a canvas upon which they would paint a masterpiece, a world worthy of their love, a world worthy of their shared hope.

The sea was calm now.
The wind had lost its bite, the waves lulled into submission by Tyvellmian's will. The stars blinked above him, scattered and ancient, each one older than language itself. Galena slept

a

beside the dwindling fire in the cove, her breathing steady. He watched her from the shore, alone in thought, the rhythm of the surf matching the turmoil stirring inside him.

He had made his choice—he had chosen humanity.

But the consequences of that choice were only beginning to stir.

A distant tremor rippled through the world's oceans, not from tectonic shifts or underwater quakes, but something deeper—older.

Tyvellmian turned his head slowly, his eyes narrowing at the horizon. The water no longer obeyed him fully. It hesitated. As if waiting… as if listening to someone else.

The *Keepers of the Deep* had warned him.

"You are no longer hidden. The currents have carried your defiance to shores far beyond. The Old Ones will know. And they will not yield."

The sky darkened—not from clouds, but from the fabric of reality thinning. Somewhere far off in the Himalayas, an ancient monastery collapsed in upon itself as *Indra*, storm-bringer and king of the Vedic gods, opened his eyes for the first time in a thousand years. Lightning danced between his fingertips as he whispered in Sanskrit, *"Another has dared take the mantle of oceans."*

In the scorching deserts of the Maghreb,

a

Anubis, keeper of the dead, stepped forth from the temple's crumbling mouth. Jackal eyes glowing, he surveyed the stars. His servants had awakened him not with prayer—but fear.

In the frozen tundras of Siberia, the *Shaman-Kings* of the Evenki people screamed and tore at their furs, possessed by a presence not felt since mammoth-bone altars ruled the north. *Num-Torum*, the ancient sky god, had stirred.

The *Oni lords of Japan, the Feathered Serpents of Mesoamerica, the Devas, the Loa, and the Primordial Spirits of Dreamtime—all turned their gaze* to Earth's oceans, to the man who now held sway over tides that once belonged to them, or to their rivals. The Age of Silence was broken.

Tyvellmian clutched the sand in his hands as if anchoring himself to the earth.

"It's beginning," he said aloud.

From behind him, Galena stirred. "What is?"

He looked at her, the woman who saw the god and still held onto the man. "The others. The ones older than Olympus. The ones who never agreed to slumber."

Galena sat up slowly, wariness in her eyes. "You mean… more gods?"

"Not just gods," he said. "Kingdoms. Pantheons. Beings that never forgot the dominion they once held over Earth. Some want to reclaim it. Others want to destroy it."

a

She stood and came beside him. “And they’re coming for you?”

“They’re coming for everything,” he said, “but they’ll start with me.”

The ocean shimmered. A pulse. A deep echo. A summons.

He felt it in his chest—an ancient drumbeat that wasn’t his, calling him to war.

Somewhere deep beneath the ruins of Atlantis—far below any depth ever plumbed by submarines or sonar arrays—the Pantheon of the Abyss gathered. Forgotten sea gods, cast out by Poseidon himself eons ago, whispered in guttural languages, preparing their return. In their midst, *Sedna* of the Inuit people, half-woman, half-seal, arched her head back and shrieked into the ocean. Her scream carried through tectonic plates, through whirlpools and molten trenches, until even whales fled in terror.

One by one, the *Oracles of Delphi*, long turned to stone, cracked open. Eyes glowed red. One choked out a final prophecy before disintegrating to ash:

“A war of realms…

A man who is no man…

The tide that drowns gods or redeems them.”

And then silence.

In the Pentagon, defense satellites lit up with

a

anomalies. Pulses of heat from volcanoes thought extinct. Storms forming in perfectly symmetrical patterns over the Equator. A meteorologist muttered, "The Earth's... heartbeat changed."

Tyvellmian returned to the city only briefly, just long enough to retrieve what little he'd left behind. The streets were tense. News reports whispered of strange events across the globe—caves lighting with ethereal fire, statues weeping blood, thunderstorms forming over deserts.

Galena followed him through the chaos. "You can't fight them all."

"I don't have to," he said. "But I *do* have to answer them."

"Alone?"

He looked to her—truly looked. "I won't ask you to come."

She stepped closer. "I already did."

Their lips met, not as an escape, but as a vow.

The *first challenge* came from the Pacific.

An island rose—an island that had not existed for ten thousand years. Atop it stood a massive figure, cloaked in obsidian and coral. *Kanaloa,* god of the deep, father of octopi and leviathans. His voice roared across the waves, shaking ships from Tokyo to Auckland.

"Tidal-Man! You wear the trident, but you

a

have not earned it.
The ocean chooses its sovereign not by birth… but by battle."
Tyvellmian stepped onto the shore, barefoot and bare-chested, the trident humming in his grip.
"I didn't ask to be king."
Kanaloa's massive hand crushed a boulder into sand. "Then why did the ocean bow to you?"
"I bowed first," Tyvellmian answered, raising the trident. "Now let's see if you know how to kneel."
Lightning cracked the sky.
The war of gods had begun.
And in the middle of it stood a man who had once drowned beneath the surface—and rose not as a savior, not as a tyrant, but something far more dangerous.
A choice.
A reckoning.
A tidal force.

a

Next for Tidal-Man; War of the Gods

a

Acknowledgments

First and foremost, I extend my deepest gratitude to my family and friends, whose unwavering support and endless patience fueled my creativity throughout this long and often challenging journey. Their belief in my work, even during moments of self-doubt, was invaluable.

I'd like to thank **Gene Lemmings** for coming up with **Tidal-man** and allowing me to create a rich character profile and detailed story for him.

A special thank you to my beta readers, whose insightful critiques and passionate feedback shaped the narrative and polished the prose. Your keen eyes and insightful comments made all the difference.

I am also deeply indebted to my editor, for their guidance, expertise, and unwavering dedication to bringing this story to life. Their sharp eye for detail and dedication to crafting compelling narratives elevated this work beyond what I could have achieved alone.

a

Finally, thank you to all the mythology enthusiasts and lovers of epic fantasy who inspired me to weave this tale.

a

Appendix

This appendix provides a brief overview of the mythological figures and concepts referenced in the novel. While I have taken creative liberties with the traditional lore, I have tried to remain respectful of its essence.

Further research into Greek mythology, specifically pertaining to Poseidon and the Olympian pantheon, is recommended for a richer understanding of the underlying themes and influences.

Detailed genealogies of the characters and a more extensive exploration of the Ancient Ones can be found on the website: www.TheMegaverseCtiy.com

a

Glossary

Ancient Ones: Pre-Olympian deities, older and more powerful than the known gods, whose influence lingers even in their diminished state.

Tyvellmian: Poseidon's youngest son, initially volatile, but transformed by compassion.

Arconia: Tyvellmian's niece and Triton's daughter, a significant figure in his personal and spiritual growth.

Galena: A human survivor of a devastating storm, whose life Tyvellmian saves, sparking his transformation and a profound love story.

Divine Punishment: The cataclysmic storms unleashed by the Ancient Ones, reflecting their displeasure at humanity's abandonment of the gods.

For a more comprehensive glossary of terms and their contextual meanings within the narrative, please refer to the online companion resource at www.themegaversecity.com

a

References

While this novel draw inspiration from Greek mythology, the specific events and characterizations are fictional. The following sources provided background information and served as points of inspiration:

The Odyssey by Homer

The Iliad by Homer

Hesiod's Theogony
Mythos by Stephen Fry

a

Author Biography

E.S. Bennett is an adult fantasy author with a passion for mythology and blending ancient lore with modern settings. Growing up surrounded by stories of gods and monsters, he developed a lifelong fascination with the power of narrative to explore complex themes of love, loss, and redemption.

Their writing is characterized by richly developed characters, emotionally resonant narratives, and a dedication to crafting worlds that feel both familiar and fantastical.

You can find more information about him and his writing at **www.TheMegaverseCity.com** and connect on Facebook, Stage 32, Instagram and Linkedin.

a

About the creator of Tidal-Man

Eugene Lemmings was born in Lexington, North Carolina. He grew up and lived his entire life in the surrounding area. His many endeavors included raising beef cows and free range chickens. He is and avid outdoor man, which gives him plenty of time to think and utilize his imagination.

Even at a very young age, Greek mythology intrigued him, the rich tapestry of stories of gods, goddesses, heroes and monsters that offered insights into Greek worldview. He also read many different comic books of the time, a world filled with gods, super heroes and villains.

As an adult with children of his own, he was reminded how To be young all over again…and learn to look at the world With a little sense of wonder once more.

The idea of Tidal-man came from his love of the sea and spending much time in his boat adrift. Letting the waves gently rock him to tranquility so that his mind could wander.

He still has an appreciation for mythology and the stories they have inspired.

Mr. Lemmings still lives in Lexington, North Carolina with his wife and children, not far from his birthplace home. He can be reached through www.TheMegaverseCity.com

www.ingramcontent.com/pod-product-compliance
Lightning Source LLC
Chambersburg PA
CBHW070822020826
48982CB00014B/371

* 9 7 9 8 2 1 8 9 9 8 2 2 6 *